SATURD
ALL RIGHT
FOR FIGHTING

Clay's progress was irritatingly slow as the crowd pushed en masse up the street. As he drew closer to the commotion ahead, a hand caught the material of his vest and pulled.

Clay whirled, knocking locals back on either side. A dozen young men carrying distinctive long-knives shoved and slashed at people trying to flee down the narrow street. Then one of the boys stopped, eyes rolling, to scream insanely and slash himself with his own knife across his arms. Slavering, he struck out and cut down a woman pressed by the wall.

Distracted, Clay only caught the movement of a knife slashing toward him an instant before the blade reached him . . .

A LANDSCAPE OF DARKNESS

JOHN BLAIR

A Del Rey Book

BALLANTINE BOOKS · NEW YORK

A Del Rey Book
Published by Ballantine Books

Library of Congress Catalog Card Number: 90-92428

ISBN 0-345-36517-8

Manufactured in the United States of America

First Edition: July 1990

Cover Art by Neal McPheeters

To Sandy, R.D.,
and especially Linda.

The darkness of night, like pain, is dumb,
the darkness of dawn, like peace, is silent.

RABINDRANATH TAGORE, *Fireflies*

CHAPTER ONE

Tind squatted against the slate wall of the hut and hummed tunelessly to himself, his hands open on his bare knees.

The room was small and smelled of sweat and urine, but Tind was content. He felt serene, tranquil in the certainty of his purpose, rested, and eager. He hummed a mantra to himself and sang a silent hymn of praise to his ancestors and to *Hachiman*, who possessed his soul and who spoke even now in his mind of blood and battle. Tind's life now was to serve *Hachiman*, the Peacemaker, the god of battle. And all that the Peacemaker asked of him was death.

Nine others waited with him in the close, rank quarters of the room, each pressed against the rough stones of the walls, each watching with his whole attention the warped boards of the single doorway. Tind could smell the stink of their fear and excitement.

He didn't look, but he knew they were all young. Few were long past the *gembuku* manhood ceremony, and none knew of battle beyond sparring with their own brethren in the training villages. Tind had fought in the Great War, before he had become *yamabushi*. He had fought then and he had lived, though only a very few of the emperor's warriors had survived—and then there were no battles for more years than he could count, only the long tedium of waiting.

Tind felt his age in the faint stiffness in his knees and hands; he knew that gray peppered the sparse hair on his chest and made his thin beard the color of dirty snow. But Tind had the advantage of learned discipline and of having killed men before. Many men.

And soon, very soon, he would once again have battle.

By the faded quality of the light that streamed through the cracks in the walls and ceiling, he knew that he would not have much longer to wait. He had been fasting for two days in the tiny hut with the others, praying to his god and to his ancestors, and now he felt himself purged and pure, ready for the contest.

Earlier a priest had brought weapons and presented them to each of the ten. Tind had chosen with care, then had worked his steel on a flat stone he had managed to pry loose from the hut's wall until the blade was bright from tip to tang and the edge would shave hair.

The sharpness he was able to give the steel disturbed him for a time. Only Terran metal would take such an edge. The poorer alloys of Ithavoll's steels were too soft to take and hold an edge so keen.

He decided after some thought that the fact that the blade was Terran was of no real consequence. Good steel was good steel; its origins were unimportant, tainted though they might be. He admired the dim light's reflection on the new edge. It was good, he thought.

When the time came, the ten stood, one by one, and went through the door into the night, Tind last.

They were led a few yards beyond the hut to a narrow stairwell cut into the raw stone, down which the group walked in single file until they came out onto the flat packed-dirt floor of the royal arena. His lips moved almost unconsciously with the phrase that named this place of death, a name he had heard with awe and fear since childhood: "The Blood-Pit of Rokujo-ga-hara." Once it had been a place for simple public executions, and the men who had died there had been petty criminals and enemies of the state. Now, at the infrequent whim of the emperor, *yamabushi*—the mountain warriors—fought and died there for the glory of *Hachiman*.

In the center of the floor a bonfire cut against the darkening sky, and the ten stood in a semicircle around it, close enough that Tind could feel the heat of the flames scorch his thin beard.

He took the long-knife from his belt and felt the keen edge, then slipped the blade along the back of his hand, drawing a fine welt of blood. The others followed his example.

He brought the small, fresh wound to his lips and sucked until his mouth was full of the salty warmth, then he spit suddenly into the heart of the flames, his own heart's blood sizzling into steam, rising with the blood of the others to the gods. He could hear voices rising also, the crowd around the rim of the great pit sharing in the ritual. Inside his head *Hachiman* roared as well, a great flame that burned with pain and joy, promising glory.

Tind shouted a battle cry, the warm blood running down from his mouth into the hair on his chest, parried a thrust at his midsection from the man to his right, and drove the full half-meter length of the long-knife through the man's torso. Then he pulled the blade quickly free and dodged back to the stone wall from which the staircase led, its iron gate now shut and bolted.

There was a great roar from the onlookers. Tind raised his blade slightly in acknowledgment and looked warily around. Four had survived the first few moments. Each had pressed back against a wall of the arena.

One, a man Tind had singled out in his mind as the most capable of the nine, was bleeding badly from a wound near the base of his neck. He was trying to stem the blood flooding from the cut with his off hand, but he was already beginning to sway in the weakness of blood loss.

The gods are gracious, Tind thought.

He discounted the man instantly as an opponent and shut him from his mind. The other two were intact and considering him as carefully as Tind considered them.

One was large and heavily muscled—too much so, Tind decided. It slowed him. Power was secondary to speed when one fought with a blade.

The other was smaller and much quicker. He held his blade low, the tip slightly up, to drive under the ribs or into the throat.

Both were worthy, but Tind felt a rush of confidence—singly, he could kill either.

He waited. The first to move would expose himself as well as exposing the opponent he chose; the third could approach either with the advantage of distraction.

He did not have to wait long. The big man, confident in his advantage over the smaller man and, Tind thought, discounting

Tind for his age, rushed the little man, his blade held low in his off hand.

Tind could see after the first step what he intended; with his strong hand he would parry any thrust the small man might make, hoping to find a grip on the man's wrist or arm, then with his superior strength he would twist the man's weapon aside and thrust his own blade home.

By the second step Tind knew he had failed. He was too obvious, too clumsy.

The little man didn't thrust at all. He simply twisted from the bigger man's grasping hand and came under with his knife, stabbing into the ribs. It was over in a second, and the big man rolled away, choking on the blood flowing into the lung the knife's blade had pierced.

The little man followed, kneeling down and reaching into the big man's hair to pull his head back, quickly slitting his throat.

Before he could stand again, Tind was on him.

But the little man, knowing Tind would not be far away, rolled suddenly over the body of his defeated opponent, coming to his feet with the bulky corpse between himself and Tind.

Tind did not hesitate, taking the body in a stride, using the momentum to power his forearm past the little man's outthrust blade, opening his chest to Tind's own thrust. Tind's blade found bone, not flesh, though, and skittered across the man's ribs, opening a long but shallow gouge. For a fraction of an instant Tind stared into his opponent's brown, almond-shaped eyes. Then the little man pushed back and leapt away, swinging his blade in low as he did so, coming only a centimeter from disemboweling Tind.

They stood for a long moment, breathing hard, watching each other.

The man's eyes were narrow, Mongoloid. There was much Chinese in him, marking him as coming from the lowest caste, lower by several steps than Tind's own. Still, he was a good warrior, a good infighter. Tind regretted for an instant that he would have to kill the little man. But there was nothing for it.

He feinted suddenly high to his weak side, then dropped the blade low and thrust for the small man's midsection. It would probably have worked—the little man had followed the feint, leaving himself open low to Tind's knife—but Tind's knee betrayed him, folding under as he thrust forward. Tind stumbled, reaching desperately for balance, flinching under the blade he knew would follow him down.

The blow never came.

Tind rolled away, amazed, and scrambled to his feet to see the little man stabbing down at the one whom Tind had ignored as already dead. The wounded warrior was grappling with his last strength around the little man's knees, hacking weakly with his long-knife.

The little man stabbed again, and the dying man dropped away, but Tind was already behind him. He reached quickly around and lifted the small man's chin with the back of his off hand, exposing the throat, and brought his blade across the protruding esophagus, cutting deeply through windpipe and artery. Then he released the little man to drop away, drowning in his own fountaining blood.

Tind swayed for a moment over the body, cursing the age that made him weak, then straightened. There was one thing more he must do. His god demanded a trophy. *Hachiman* burned in his head like the stars.

He bent slowly over the still-shuddering corpse of the little man and wrapped his fingers in the thick young man's hair, then brought his long-knife around to the wound he had made in the throat and sawed through tendon and bone until the head was free.

Then he held the gory prize high and turned, offering it to the screaming mass of onlookers, the blood running thick and hot down his arm.

He had won. The night, the onus was his; he would not fail it. Inside his mind, *Hachiman*, satiated, grew quiet.

He shook the head for the crowd and gloried in his solitude, the night burning black above him.

CHAPTER TWO

When he stepped into the postal station, he immediately felt the itching sensation between his shoulder blades that he knew from long experience signaled something amiss.

He became suddenly conscious of a taxi that had appeared unbidden and had stopped conveniently behind his red convertible, blocking it in.

He walked on to his postbox without visibly registering any alarm. He opened the box with a show of unconcern and shuffled through the stack of mail, discarding the business circulars and pleasure-palace fliers in the bin the postal service had thoughtfully provided for that purpose.

Behind him the taxi's passenger stepped from the car and posted himself not inconspicuously beside the postal station's one door.

Most of the remaining mail was innocuous enough. A faxed letter from his grandmother, season soccer tickets he had ordered while still off-planet, credit vouchers for dividends on planetary stocks he had been given for past services on a half dozen different planets.

One piece was not so mundane or expected. It was a radio cable, postmarked Luna a month before. The envelope was marked URGENT URGENT URGENT and bore the conspicuous seal of the Combined Forces.

He stiffened.

Things began to fall into place. The uncomfortable misgivings of moments before jelled into the certainty of trouble.

He glanced over his shoulder and noted that two others, wearing the type of narrow-lapeled business suits that had once again just gone out of style, had appeared to join the taxi's passenger at the door. They made no pretense of not watching him.

He hesitated, then slit open the sealed cable with a fingernail.

It was a brief message, from the office of the commanding general, LUNCOM TAC, Combined Forces, Camp Ocala, Luna. It said simply enough, under a veneer of officialese, that he had been reinstated in the armed forces of Terra with a lieutenant's commission and that he was to report to the camp duty officer at Camp Ocala, Earth's moon, on a date that was already two weeks past.

His first impulse was to ignore the summons and bolt; he could make for one of the lesser-explored Territory Worlds and simply set up business anew. Getting off-planet would be the only difficult aspect, and he had a half dozen passports under various names sealed in the lining of his flight bag back in his hotel room.

If he could make it back to his hotel room.

He had no love for the Combined Forces. Armies—actual combat units—he could understand. Political strong-arm groups of the kind the Terran Combined Forces had become were given to acting from idealism—and idealism, unlike pure avarice, for the most part, had no qualms about method.

A good merc would do what he was paid for and leave the huts standing. Politicos would burn the whole damned place down just in case more wrong-thinkers might breed there. They were no more particular in their dealings with individuals, particularly individuals like himself, with a marked reputation for strong-headed apolitical leanings. That kind he was better shut of.

It didn't appear, however, that they were going to give him the chance.

Waiting for an attack was always bad tactics. Invariably it was better to take the battle to the enemy—best defense and all that.

He stopped ignoring the three at the door and waved them an airy salute. They didn't react but continued only to watch him through three pairs of dark aviator sunglasses as he stepped toward the door.

Okay, let's play, then, he thought.

As he came to the door, he kicked the clear plastic panel hard without warning, throwing the door open and spilling two of the three dark suits backward onto the hard resin-plastic of the parking lot. The third had been standing on the open side of the door.

Without slowing, he threw the mail he still carried into the man's face, then punched him hard with two knuckles in the solar plexus as he raised his hands to protect himself. As the man doubled over, he swept his feet from under him with the side of his foot, then kicked one of the other two, who had begun to rise, in the chin.

He grinned to himself, feeling the flush of battle exhilaration. Thickheaded strong-arm types were good, healthy close-in combat practice partners, and he didn't have to feel any qualms about breaking a few bones.

Then he sprinted for the taxi. He jerked open the door and climbed in, slamming it behind him against the third man, who had come up just on his heels as he reached the car. He slapped the door lock on and turned to the programming panel.

He noticed instantly that the taxi's controls were caged, locked away behind a stretched-steel grating, and discovered an instant later that the doors would not unlock when he punched the release button.

Without warning, the taxi jolted into motion of its own volition, and he knew he'd been had.

The third man waved, grinning crookedly, as the taxi pulled out into the traffic stream.

He grimaced and slammed the steel grating with an open palm.

Damn.

He shrugged to himself and settled in as comfortably as possible as the taxi's windows opaqued, shutting out the world. Someone, he pledged silently, is going to suffer for this, and he was going to enjoy doling it out. John Sebastian Clay was not a man who was easily used for purposes not his own.

With a certain amount of bashing and prying, he determined quickly that the steel cage around the car's programming controls was impervious to his machinations. And the doors were locked tightly by the car's guidance computer, which could be convinced to open them only by the controls hidden out of reach behind the grating. Neat, he thought.

The taxi was better than a jail cell. Even if he somehow managed to outwit the trouble his friends had gone to to keep him inside the car, it was moving fast enough that leaving it would be suicidal.

After beating on the cage a bit and finding it not only futile but not even very effective for relieving his frustration, John Clay simply settled back as comfortably as possible into the wide seat and dozed. The car, automatically considerate, dimmed the interior lights.

When he came fully awake again, it was dark and raining, and the car was still moving, its tires making a quiet sizzling sound on the wet pavement.

He sat up and squinted out into a darkness so nearly complete that it took him several moments to decide that the car's windows had indeed cleared while he was asleep. He could see the vague shapes of trees and fields on either side of the road, dark and blurred, passing by at well over two hundred klicks an hour.

After staring into the blackness for a time, he came to the conclusion that he wasn't about to figure out what part of the country the car was traveling through on the scant clues he could garner from the landscape rushing by.

He had a gift for orienting himself that he supposed he had inherited from the parts of his very mixed ancestry that were American Indian, but there were simply too many variables. He was lost.

He took stock. He had little doubt that the men who had grabbed him were operatives of one of the many covert branches of the Combined Forces; the people in control were not used to being denied, and they were never loath to take steps to ensure that they got whatever it was they wanted.

He also had absolutely no idea why it was they wanted him, especially as ten years before they couldn't get shut of him fast enough.

His one previous hitch in the Combined Forces had resulted directly in several deaths, including that of his direct superior officer. It had also resulted in his dishonorable discharge, though he was cleared later of the murder charge for reasons the Forces had chosen to keep to themselves.

John Clay suspected that they had been motivated by the fact that at the time the officer had been killed, he and Clay and five others had been in a place that by interplanetary treaty they were not allowed to be, trying to kill a man who was, also by that same treaty, supposedly immune.

The officer had felt it his duty to assassinate not only the heir to the throne of a planet the United Democracies wanted leaderless long enough to step in and take control but also his two wives and two of his sons.

When Clay had found him, he had still had the piano-wire garrote wrapped around the thin neck of one of the boys. That had been enough.

John Clay had executed him without hesitation, before the bastard could turn, emptying his rifle's clip in one long blast. When the rifle was empty, he fired the six shots in his service revolver into the major's body.

Only three of the six-man squad had survived long enough to get off-planet. That had been ten years before, when John Clay had been twenty. The situation placed before the Combined Forces High Command was potentially volatile and unequivocally embarrassing. They quietly handed him a dishonorable discharge and suggested strongly that he take up some mundane, low-profile profession off-planet.

But the Combined Forces had taught him well in a trade at which he seemed especially adept. In the interim he had worked as a mercenary and bounty hunter, had been wounded four times, and had made a not inconsiderable fortune fighting minor wars on a dozen different planets.

His particular forte was search and destroy in difficult terrain, with little or no field support and a minimum of mess. It was a specialization that had kept him much in demand in the rough climates and terrains of the assorted worlds at the edge of the United Democracies' holdings.

Those were planets given to frequent coups d'etat and various sorts of social unrest, but they were also very reluctant to become noisy about it lest the U.D. and its all too eager Combined

Forces should see a reasonable excuse to step in and quickly and violently assert their own brand of peace.

Now the U.D. and its Combined Forces wanted him back, had already given him the assigned rank of first lieutenant, and had told him, not in so many words, that he had no choice in the matter.

It was enough, though, that they hadn't waited for him to answer; he had decided already that he wasn't in a cooperative mood.

The fellows outside the postal station had caught him without his pistol or most of the assorted weapons he usually kept about his person. He'd left them, reluctantly enough, in his hotel room, as most buildings in the megalopolis that was Miami had sensitive electronic sentries at their entrances to keep out the unpleasant sorts who went around armed, and he'd had business in the city.

But they hadn't left him defenseless—they couldn't do that short of disabling him. He had learned much during and since his short initial tenure in the Forces in the way of infighting techniques, and they were soon going to discover just how much he had learned.

And despite appearances, they hadn't left him totally disarmed.

He leaned back against the door of the car and kicked the steel cage that protected the programming console with the heel of his boot, then again, harder.

It made no impression on the stretched steel of the cage, but after the second blow the heel of the custom-made black leather boot wrenched loose, spilling a handful of thin, fletched hard plastic darts onto the car's floor. The darts were an effective weapon; they could easily be thrown several meters, and they were tipped with a drug that paralyzed for three or four hours.

Clay gathered the darts from the floor and jammed the heel back onto his boot. Then he sat back to wait.

The car drove on through the night for another four hours, Clay estimated, before it slowed and turned suddenly off the smooth plastic paving of the main road and onto a considerably rougher surface that Clay guessed was an ill-maintained old-type tar-and-pebble road.

He grimaced. That meant that he was a long way from the

postal station in Miami where he'd been picked up; he doubted there was an honest-to-god tarmac road left anywhere in the state of Florida. The resin-plastic roads were standard issue in any large city, and Florida was nothing anymore except city, from the Everglades north to what was left of the Okefenokee swamp.

More likely, he thought, Mississippi, or maybe Arkansas; it was impossible to tell until he'd had a chance to look around in the light of day. Wherever it was, the road would indicate that it was remote enough to be largely unpopulated. Agricultural land, no doubt—growing food was the only use other than housing that was still vital enough to command a great deal of acreage. And even then only certain gravity-sensitive crops were still grown on Terra; most agriculture and heavy industry orbited the planet in huge self-contained bio-spheres.

People, billions of tons of thriving, crowded humanity, were now Terra's primary crop.

Clay allowed himself a moment of anger for the monetary loss the side trip was causing him. He'd left a client who had expected him several hours before waiting at the Cocoa Beach Shuttleport, and the client was just nervous enough about the thought of hiring Clay's services that he had doubtless boarded the shuttle up to the passenger liner alone and headed home to Compson's Planet hours earlier.

He pulled his boarding pass out of a jacket pocket and tossed it into the car's waste receptacle, only slightly perturbed that the twenty-thousand-NATO-dollar ticket was now nothing more than waste paper.

He fully intended to extract its full value—with interest—from whoever was waiting at the end of the line for the car to deliver him.

A few minutes later the car slowed again, turned off the tarmac, and stopped. The green arrival light blinked steadily on the car's dash, and the doors on either side opened suddenly with a pneumatic puff of air.

CHAPTER
THREE

He waited, tensed, on the edge of the seat, a dart ready in either hand, but nothing happened. After a few moments he stepped carefully from the car to the muddy dirt road and looked around.

There was nothing but a few trees and a fence, behind which a vast field of some sort of grain stretched away into the thick darkness. A breeze blew restlessly through the tops of the trees, and the low rush of the leaves seemed strange and quiet after the hours he'd spent in the speeding car.

Hell's Bells! he thought. Not even a reception committee of the brainless types from the postal station on which to take out his frustrations.

He relaxed, shook himself, and stretched his cramped muscles.

A light showed faintly down the dirt road, and after a moment's survey of the endless dark in either direction down the tarmac road, he started off toward it, the mud sucking heavily at his boots.

About a kilometer down the road he came to a huge dark barn, and behind it a frame house, of the sort Clay could remember seeing on the old faded calendars in his grandmother's flat when he was small. He couldn't tell in the dark, but he was sure the barn was red, the little house whitewashed and sporting a chimney.

The front of the house was dark, but there was a light on the side that faced down the road he had just walked up. Clay went boldly up to the door that stood beside the lighted window.

He knocked without hesitation.

He had little doubt that whoever was in the farmhouse expected him, and he was certainly in no mood for discretion. Anger, Clay reflected absently, sometimes made one dangerously direct.

But then, he really was no longer angry, just eager for answers—and, he admitted, eager to cause somebody a little discomfort.

A burly, thick-shouldered man whom Clay immediately recognized as the familiar dark-suited brand of hired muscle opened the door, and Clay grinned cheerfully up at him from the stoop and drove the dart that he held in his left hand into the man's thigh muscle.

The man jerked away, reached for the dart, felt his strength giving way, and tried to reach inside his coat.

Clay watched as his eyes rolled up and, after a long half second, his hand dropped, letting a large handgun clatter down the steps as his knees suddenly gave way. Clay supported him for an instant as he toppled forward, then let the limp form fall heavily into the grass beside the stoop.

He then strode quickly up the steps and into what appeared to be a kitchen.

Off to one side, opposite an antique glass-fronted cabinet, three men sat at a small table; one, dressed in coveralls and a shirt, was sitting. The other two wore narrow-lapeled business suits and were standing, right hands tucked inside their jackets.

All watched Clay.

Clay stared for a moment at the business suits, his wrists cocked to flip out the darts he held in either hand. But both, as if on signal, took their hands from their coats and held them, palms out, away from their sides.

The one with the coveralls, an older, heavyset man with the beginnings of a beard grizzling his cheeks, gestured to the others to take their seats at the table. He pointed to a chair and indicated it was for Clay.

"Sit.

"That—" He indicated the door. "—was unnecessary. But then, I don't suppose you knew that."

"I knew it. I'm just a little irritable." Clay took the offered chair. "He'll wake up in a few hours with a headache. I should have broken his goddamned neck. What the duece is this about?''

The older man held up his hand.

"Introductions first, Lieutenant. I'm Howard S. Rankin. Colonel, Combined Forces, semiretired. I'm the fellow who arranged to have that wire sent that you've taken so long to answer.''

Clay didn't see any reason to mention the fact that he had never intended to answer it at all, at least not in any direct fashion. He ignored the man's hand. The man shrugged and withdrew it.

"So why was I shanghaied? If you wanted my services, they're available, for a fee.''

Rankin waved the question aside. "We'll get to that. Oh, I know about your lack of affection for the Services. But one thing at a time. We've much to talk about. As I suppose you've guessed by now, these two gentlemen are agents with G-three. I'm afraid it'd be pretty hard to convince them not to shoot you, should you get too out of hand.''

Clay nodded. "They look like military intelligence. The heavy brow and the bad taste in clothes. I suppose the fellow I put to sleep belongs to them.''

"Uh huh, afraid so. Listen, son, why don't you relax. One of you fellows, get Lieutenant Clay a cup of coffee. Do you care for bourbon, Lieutenant?''

Clay considered, nodded yes. It seemed safe enough, and he could use the stimulant it offered; there seemed no reason why they would want to drug or poison him, at least not at that point. They obviously wanted him aware and reasonable. One of the business suits rose from the table and took a bottle of dark amber liquor from the antique cabinet, then went into the kitchen proper.

Clay took the cup he brought back and tasted it. The coffee was strong, and the bourbon burned pleasantly.

"Directness is a virtue, John, one it is my policy to practice whenever possible. We need your help, your expertise and experience.''

Clay noted that he had dropped the "lieutenant" and understood that Rankin had used it in the first place simply to remind him of his status as One Who Must Take Orders. He sipped the coffee.

"I gathered as much."

Rankin raised an eyebrow. "Do you know why?"

Clay shrugged. "No. Though I expect you will tell me. I suspect you need a mercenary, one who is reasonably experienced, perhaps one who can't be easily tied in to the Forces. Or, better yet, one who would have good damned reason to have nothing at all to do with the C.F. No other good reason to bring me here, I would think. I've already been dishonorably discharged. And I also suspect that, were anyone to look, that field commission you've given me wouldn't show up on any Combined Forces service records."

Rankin grinned. "Yes. You're right. John, we simply want to use you and your abilities for something we can't do openly, and we want to pay you for it. I've heard your name mentioned by men who know soldiers. You're good. The present governments of three different planets have given you their highest military citations. Those are the ones I know of. Hell, those folks that ran the planetary government on Comfort had never given their top honors to an off-worlder before you. That alone is an impressive recommendation."

"Revolutionary governments are pretty free with the medals," Clay said mildly. "They aren't quite so free with the pay. What about you? At this point it would seem you know one hell of a lot about me, but I don't know a damned thing about you. Your name, for instance. I don't believe I've heard it mentioned."

"You might know more about me than you think. Rankin's not the name I was born with. I was a Spaceborne Ranger in the Earth/Luna conflict; since, I've helped with assorted hard-to-deal-with projects on behalf of the Combined Forces. In a way, I'm in much the same field as you. Covert operations. Quick in, quick out, taking care of difficult situations with a minimum of mess and bother. We're simply business rivals, of a sort."

Clay decided suddenly and unreasonably that he liked Rankin, even though he didn't like some aspects of his tactics.

"Somehow, Colonel, I kind of doubt it. I never cared much for bureaucracies, or for the Combined Forces, for that matter. Or bureaucrats. Or officers. You seem to incorporate all of the above."

One of the business suits shifted in his chair, and Clay let his hand drop by his side where he could flick one of the darts into the man's belly under the table. Rankin saw his shoulder drop and held up a hand.

"Careful. No reason for rash moves. Not yet, anyway." He gestured toward a doorway that Clay assumed led to the living room of the farmhouse. "Why don't you fellows shift into the other room. Give us a little privacy. He got here from the car on his own; I don't think he's going to bolt on us. Are you, John?"

Clay shrugged noncommittally.

"Well, all the same. I can handle things, I think."

The business suits stood and shuffled into the next room. After a moment Clay heard a click and the buzz of a three-D coming on and then the low sussurus of an empty channel. He glanced at Rankin.

"Making a report to his higher-ups—I'm not the only one involved in this project. I expect the noise from the vid is just in case the place is bugged or you're listening in somehow. They are not given to trust."

"If I agree to do whatever it is that you want me for, will I have to work with the likes of those?" Clay jerked a thumb toward the living room.

Rankin shook his head. "They're muscle, nothing more, nothing less. This little project will require a much finer touch than that sort is capable of. I don't care much for having them in my home, but one does what one has to. Their bosses didn't think I could get you to sit still long enough to listen on my own."

Clay looked around at the small kitchen and its ancient appliances. He was startled to see a huge device that he recognized as an old compressor-type refrigerator. It seemed to be running and in use.

Curiouser and curiouser. For a bird colonel in the Combined Forces, the old fellow certainly seemed to live the rustic life.

"This place is yours? And where the hell is it? Where are we?"

"Oklahoma. Not far from Fort Sill. It's an artillery base—lots of open spaces. They test missiles and the like out here.

Occasionally they launch a shuttle when it's inconvenient to use one of the regular lines.''

Clay was surprised. The car had been moving faster, then, and for a longer time than he had thought. He reflected sourly that certain of his ancestors—the Cherokee Indian ones, not the Sioux Indian, Oriental, and white Anglo-Saxon Protestant that made up the rest of his rather mixed ancestry—had also been taken by force from the eastern states to Oklahoma a couple of hundred years before on the "trail of tears." Most of them had never come back.

"Oklahoma? And why? I hope you and your friends realize that you've caused me one hell of a lot of trouble with this business."

Rankin nodded. "Your friend from Compson's Planet. Well, I'll admit I can't do much to make up for bad customer relations—"

"No problem," Clay interrupted. "There are plenty of wars around." He was a little surprised—and a little shaken—that Rankin knew about his customer. He'd have to be more careful in his arrangements in the future. Someone had been a little sloppy.

"True enough. I can, however, make sure the Combined Forces pays you enough for this so that you can take one hell of a long sabbatical."

"You still haven't said why. Or what."

"Fair enough. Settle in, it's a long story." He cleared his throat and continued. "One of the outer planets has a parliamentary monarchy, of sorts, that the United Democracies wants toppled for reasons we won't go into. That's not our job; the intelligence boys are working on that particular piece of business. Meanwhile, it would be helpful if the current monarch were not allowed to completely consolidate the planet. That *is* our job."

Rankin had been leaning forward across the table, studying Clay's face as he spoke. He stood and walked to the cabinet that held the decanter of bourbon, poured a shot into a tumbler, and added a splash of water at the kitchen tap. Clay sipped his coffee.

Rankin took a swallow of his drink and sighed.

"It's hard to get really good bourbon anymore; something they've done to the corn with all that genetic fooling around, I'd guess, or the fact they can't get real charcoal much anymore to filter it through, now that they give you prison for cutting a tree. Doesn't bring back the misspent days of youth like it used to."

"Okay," Clay said impatiently, "how do we keep him from 'consolidating the planet'? If I decide to go along with what you've got in mind, of course."

Rankin looked down into his drink. "Perhaps I'd better tell you now that if you learn any more, it'll be too much for us to allow you to have any choice about going along with what I have in mind. I need an answer now."

"All right." Clay pursed his lips and looked deeply into his own cup. "I'll throw in with you, but for no more than a month, and for no less than, let's say, a million new-issue NATO dollars."

Rankin whistled. "You think highly of yourself."

"If you didn't agree, I don't suppose you would have asked me to the party."

"True . . ." He hesitated. "I think I can get you a half million. If you're willing to take off-world currency, I can probably set you up on the planet of your choice with the local equivalent of a million."

Clay shook his head. "No, I'll take the half. Why not? Besides, I like Terra. More things worth spending your money on." He gestured generally at the farmhouse. "I know what agricultural land is worth. You've got much more than that invested here."

"Yes. The Combined Forces pays well. They figure it keeps you grateful and quiet." He grinned widely.

"All right. What else should I know?"

"Well, we'll be dealing with something we've never seen before. Something possibly alien."

Clay raised an eyebrow. "Alien? No one's ever found an alien. Hell, no one can even prove they exist. They've found some stuff on the outer planets that some idiots have *claimed* were artifacts, but—"

"I know, I know," Rankin broke in, waving a hand. "Hell, I think it's bullshit, too. But that's what the experts say. Something—we don't know what—really is down there, and it's raising a lot of hell. I don't know if it's alien or if these folks have just gotten lucky and stumbled onto something, an artifact, a

magic wand, some new branch of physics—though that doesn't
seem likely given the overall level of technology and research
on this particular ball of dirt—or what have you. But suddenly
and without us knowing how, the fellow who runs the greater
part of this particular planet has gotten his hand onto something
powerful. Something different from anything we've ever had to
deal with before. Take a look.''

He reached under the table, and Clay stiffened instinctively
for a moment, then relaxed as the tabletop beneath his cup flickered and became suddenly transparent, then resolved into a
holographic relief map of a planetary surface. His cup was half-
engulfed by a mountain that would be, if the planet were the
size of Earth, a good sixty miles high and more than a thousand
wide.

He drew in a sharp breath. He knew the planet. He'd lost
good friends there, in the mountains and valleys represented on
the table-top projector by ripples and mounds of coherent light.

''Ithavoll.''

Rankin nodded slowly. He pointed at the image of the huge
mountain.

''Settled by the Sino-Japanese bloc ninety-odd years ago. The
planet has two primary land masses, each roughly a quarter of
the planet's surface. The southern continent is dominated by one
great mountain that is largely uninhabitable, though a certain
amount of it is arable steppes and valleys. The inhabitants of
this region are independent types, generally nomadic, and have
raised hell with the current emperor's census takers and tax
assessors. It tends to give the rest of his subjects ideas. The
emperor has tried three times that we know of to consolidate
this part of his world—and damned violently—and the last time
he had a limited success. We want to try to keep him from
completely succeeding.''

Rankin pointed to a red dot on the continent's coast near
where the mountain trailed away in steppes to the north.

''There is only one real city on this part of the planet, Kurama. Years ago it was taken by Shotoku, the emperor I spoke
of, with conventional forces on the third attempt after one hell
of a long and expensive battle. But then it was retaken a month
later by a mob army of enraged tribesmen. This time Shotoku
has not been so subtle. Something—again, we don't know

what—has leveled three-quarters of Kurama. The buildings are gone, the people have disappeared without a trace. Whatever it was that destroyed the city was as neat as a scalpel. Turned most of it to dust, and what it left was untouched—except for what was on the border of the holocaust. Some buildings were only half gone, and where whatever it was took away that half, the brick was crazed through with tiny fissures and cracks. Some of 'em are still falling down as we speak. It wasn't atomics. And it was *surgical*. From the air you can follow the line through the city. There's shattered brick and concrete for a quarter meter on the surviving side but no other appreciable damage. There were people who stood a meter in on the safe side and saw a flash, and then their friends, not so lucky on the affected side of the line, were simply *gone*. Along with the rest of the city, turned into powder. We think somehow something neutralized the atomic bond in the very substance of the matter that composed the place, and presto, it all just fell apart. Absolute and utter destruction. It's like nothing I've ever seen, and believe me, I've seen a great deal. Like the hand of God had reached down and snatched it away."

Rankin shook his head in awe at the idea. "And it happened again, at least three times that we know of. One smaller village was wiped out, another nearly so. Whatever Shotoku has, he still seems to be a little clumsy at using it. His third 'shot' missed a rebel weapons dump by at least a klick and took out a chunk of mountainside and about a hundred men, women, and children with it. But it seems that Shotoku, using this weapon, power, whatever it is, is intent on turning the scattered tribes into dust one at a time before they can consolidate themselves again into any sort of force."

Clay nodded. "I don't know about this weapon, but I know about Shotoku and his wars. I was there. I helped the rebels retake Kurama."

"I know. That's one of the reasons I insisted they get hold of you for this. You've fought there before. You know what to expect from these folks." He looked hard for a moment at Clay and said evenly, "And, if it were necessary, you could pass for a native."

Clay knew he was right. The Chinese in his ancestry was fairly minute—a great-grandfather had arrived on the west coast

of America after the third cultural revolution had made it unwise
for academics to stay in his native Shanghai and had married an
Anglo girl fresh out of UCLA law, Clay understood. Still, his
features had just enough of the Oriental cast to make him blend
in fairly easily, and his American Indian heritage gave him the
right skin tone.

The new natives of Ithavoll were a mix made mostly of the
two races that had settled the planet, Japanese and Chinese. The
Japanese had found a convenient work force in the Chinese, and
for a token fee, China had been more than willing to allow a
percentage of its population burden to be relocated. Now, on
Ithavoll, only the upper caste had any real semblance of racial
purity; most were a compound of Japanese, Chinese, Mongol,
Korean, Polynesian, and a not inconsiderable amount of western
genes introduced over the years.

Clay had found his own appearance to be an asset on his last
tour of the planet. Now he discovered that he was, for the first
time he could remember, somewhat irritated by the physical
evidence of his ancestry.

"Perhaps. What exactly are we to do?"

"I imagine you already know this, but I'll go through it anyhow, just to fill in holes; a lot's changed in the last few years.
The planet is Ithavoll; the present monarch calls himself Shotoku. The northern continent, while more developed than the
southern, is still almost entirely forested. The part we'll be
working in comes damned near jungle. Ithavoll applied several
years ago for territory status in the United Democracies. Before
it can be granted, of course, a complete census and a fairly
thorough planetary survey have to be completed. U.D. teams
have been working on it on and off for the last ten years or so;
it's time-consuming work, mostly because the land mass is so
considerable and the population is spread out in innumerable
little villages scattered throughout that jungle I was talking about,
mostly on the northern continent.

"We will go in near here—" He pointed out a spot on the
map, "—as a U.D. census and survey team. A spy satellite we
managed to keep in orbit for a few hours before Shotoku's people shot it down witnessed part of one of the 'burns' that are
taking out Shotoku's enemies. It recorded activity near here, a
power surge that crossed the entire spectrum of known energies,

from visible light on up, and occurring at the exact same moment as a village disappeared. But what the satellite gave us isn't enough. Shotoku has somehow created some impressive mayhem, but what he's done isn't blatant enough—or even explainable enough—to warrant overt action on the part of the U.D. or the Combined Forces. So whatever action is to be taken has to be covert. Our job is to find whatever it is Shotoku has hidden out there in the jungle and destroy it.''

"Simple as that?''

"Simple as that. We just have to do a little walking, tramp through a little jungle.''

He drew a small circle with his finger on the map. Clay guessed conservatively that it encompassed roughly two hundred square kilometers.

"And all the minds the Democracies has in its think tanks can't tell you what the hell this thing we're supposed to destroy is. Seems improbable,'' Clay said.

Rankin spread his hands. "Wish I could tell you more. But that's it. Objective unknown, but dangerous is the best I can get out of 'em.''

"Who else is coming along?'' The suits in the next room still worried him. That sort of clumsiness could be fatal to everyone involved.

"Two other operatives. Good people, both ex-Combined Forces officers now in the private sector; both are demolition experts, damned fine soldiers, and both have visited the planet at one time or another in their careers. And me. I'll be leading the team.''

Clay raised his cup up from the translucent mountain's interior and sipped at the coffee that had grown cold while they spoke.

"Have you ever been there?''

Rankin nodded. "I was there that third time at Kurama, too. On the other side. The planet's government was in favor with the U.D. then.'' He seemed to be waiting for a reaction on Clay's part, but none was forthcoming.

Fortunes of war, Clay thought. You can't always pick your side. Sometimes it is given to you.

"When do we start?''

"In the morning. Meanwhile, you ought to get some sleep.''

He stood and gestured at the door through which the business suits had left. "There are bedrooms through there. Those fellows are in the first two. You can take the third down the hall, next to the john. I'll be up a bit longer; I've some work to do."

Clay emptied his cup and stood. Rankin held out his hand, and Clay took it.

"Sleep well."

"I usually do," Clay said. He turned and walked through the now-empty living room, leaving Rankin in the kitchen. He passed by the first two closed doors and entered the room at the end of the narrow hall. Without turning on the light, he undressed quietly, turned back the quilt on the brass double bed, and slipped between cool sheets.

He lay for a long time thinking, watching the darkness that pooled in the rafters in the high ceiling over the bed. Despite the abrupt fashion in which he had fallen into it, he told himself, what Rankin had offered him was simply another job.

When it was over, he would be just another civilian again, free to take or leave his own assignments.

It was enough for now to think that that was in fact the case.

Finally, he slept.

CHAPTER FOUR

The morning was bright and fresh, sunlight streaming through an open window into the room. Clay woke to the almost unfamiliar smell of hot coffee and frying bacon. He rarely ate breakfast, and when he did, it was generally little more than soya-coffee lightened with something that had never been near a cow. And synthetics did not smell the way the cooking-food odor from the kitchen smelled.

When he came into the room, Rankin was standing over the ancient stove, manipulating a spatula and a skillet. There was no sign of the two business suits—the doors to the rooms Rankin had identified as theirs had been open when Clay had walked by, and the rooms had been empty.

Clay glanced at the pan as Rankin flipped an egg. "Real eggs?"

"Yup. And bacon. Advantage of living on your own farm. If you grow it, you can afford it. One of the reasons I bought this place—I was sick of soya-garbage. Everywhere else you've got to have the connections of a senator to get this kind of stuff. So little arable land left on poor ol' Terra, the government's a little reluctant to let much soil be devoted to anything but super-high-yield grains. And soybeans. Always soybeans. Animals take up too much space."

Rankin shoveled the eggs onto a plate and handed it to Clay. "Eat."

Clay tasted the food and made an appreciative noise. "Not bad."

"Damned good, you mean."

Clay nodded agreement. "Where's our friends?"

"Outside, waiting for us. They're going to fly you out to Fort Sill." He lifted a forkfull of egg and gestured generally to take in the business suits outside. "I had to let them stay here, but I sure don't have to feed 'em."

When they finished, Rankin led him outside behind the barn he had noticed the night before. In a small open field just inside the fence that held in the much larger fields of hybrid grain was a commuter helicopter. The two C.F. intelligence agents were waiting inside the cockpit.

As they approached the copter, the agent who was piloting the vehicle started the blade jets. As Clay climbed aboard, Rankin tapped his shoulder for his attention and held up two fingers, shouting to be heard above the whining roar of the copter's jets.

"Two days! I'll see you again in two days!"

At Fort Sill, Clay spent most of the first day in an infirmary being poked and prodded and immunized despite his protests that he'd already had every vaccine against alien bugs known to man. C.F. nurses were known throughout the universe as being for the most part exceptionally homely and energetically brutal, and he saw nothing new to dispel the rumor.

He spent almost the entirety of the next day with the armorer assigned to Rankin's project, arguing over equipment.

The man was a veteran of the Earth/Luna wars, graying, heavyset though not particularly fat, and a strong advocate of the very expensive fighting suits that had just begun to make an appearance in the small outer-world wars in which Clay had been fighting.

Clay was impressed with what the suits could do—they were of a reasonably lightweight fabric that was not only both bullet-proof and resistant to low-wattage lasers but adjusted itself automatically to the coloration of the surrounding terrain. One such suit could be a healthy advantage in hostile territory. To see and not be seen was almost as important as being shot and surviving it, and the suit would help with both. It was the foolish—and soon dead—merc who depended on firepower alone to get him through. If an insertion was made, and the team was in, accomplished its mission, and was gone without ever having fired a shot, the survival rate went way up.

As General George Patton had said more than a hundred years before, "No one ever won a war by dying for his country. You win a war by making the other poor bastard die for his." Damned good reasoning, Clay thought, whether one was fighting for country or for profit.

He was tempted, but he disliked the feeling of invulnerability wearing one of the suits gave him—overconfidence had killed more men in the battles Clay had fought than had simple bad luck. It was old and reliable wisdom that the idea that one was unkillable tended to breed heroes, and as the general had known, a dead hero was of no use to anyone, especially himself.

As good as the suits were, there was still much they couldn't stop, and all told Clay preferred to depend on his own abilities to keep himself whole. He would stay alive longer that way.

As a concession Clay did have the armorer furnish him with a vest of the same material. It would be enough, he thought, to provide some protection without promoting recklessness, and it was much more comfortable and much easier to get out of if the need arose—in the event, say, he fell into a sufficiently deep body of water—than the fighting suits were.

The armorer, Clay quickly discovered, was a man who believed in preparation. When Clay turned down the light-duty laser pressed on him, he shook his head wearily.

"Son, are you a student of American history?" He cradled one of the lasers in his arms while he opened a side plate with a screwdriver.

Clay shrugged. He was to an extent, but he had discovered early that answering the man's questions about what he did and didn't know about things, especially weapons and military history, only tended to get him into arguments. It was safer to be noncommittal.

The armorer didn't look up but took Clay's silence as an answer. "Well, a couple or three hundred years ago, a cavalry officer by the name of Custer—"

"I've heard of him. Horse cavalry," Clay said, and regretted it.

The armorer raised an eyebrow. "Yeah? Well, I suppose you know why he got himself killed, then?"

Clay shrugged again. "Some of my ancestors relieved him of his hair."

"What?"

"Indians."

"Of course Indians. But why else?"

"I suppose it had something to do with tactics. Or lack of resources. Or intelligence."

"All three, to the extent that through a lack of intelligence about the strength of his enemy and a certain amount of tactical ignorance, he refused to bring along a resource that sure as I stand here would have saved his ass, and his command, too."

Clay waited a moment, then prompted, "Which was?"

The armorer snapped shut the side plate with a flourish. "His equivalent of these lovelies, the Gatling gun. It was a kind of heavy machine gun with several revolving barrels. Fired large-caliber cased rounds using a rather primitive propellant made of sulfur, charcoal, and potassium nitrate—black powder. Very effective for its time. He had access to two of 'em and decided they'd slow him down too much, and he left them behind. Bad mistake."

"Did he have to carry them in on his back?"

He raised his eyebrows. "Of course not. Damned things must have weighed forty kilos apiece."

"And how much does one of those lasers weigh, with battery pack?"

The armorer grunted. "Okay, I get your point. Still, nothing's going to clear a path like one of these. Better safe than sorry."

Clay shook his head. "No. I'll stick to projectile weapons. I doubt I'll be shooting at anything but people, and a ten-millimeter caseless round will kill just as surely. And without all the mess and flash."

It was the armorer's turn to shrug. "Your funeral."

Clay grinned. "Probably. Now, can you come up with a good Israeli ten-millimeter assault rifle?"

And it was done. The man hadn't been unreasonable, just stubborn. He still managed to foist upon Clay equipment Clay thought unnecessary, but as the man pointed out many times, it was easier to dump something he didn't need than come up with something he needed and hadn't thought to take.

It was actually, Clay decided, one hell of a luxurious feeling to be able to equip the way he pleased, damn the cost; too many times in wars in which he had been hired help, budgets had been too strict for any sort of truly modern battle gear, much less the state of the art he had access to now that he once again belonged to the Combined Forces. He had fought once in a colony war with rifles that had been imported with the first colonists and were literally and shockingly surplus from the Terran Second World War.

And we won, he mused. He didn't discuss it with the armorer, of course, but he did know something of the events at Little Big Horn in the old American West, and it was his opinion that it wasn't so much the lack of the Gatling guns that had killed Custer and his men as pure arrogant stupidity. Whether you were fighting with arrows or rifles or gigawatt lasers, if you weren't on the ball, you died—and if you were, more often than not, eventually you won.

He spent the first night on the base in the room in the bachelor officer's quarters he'd been given, catching up on current Terran news, making it patently obvious to anyone who might be interested that he was going along with the program without a fuss.

He was aware the entire time that he was on the base that he was being watched closely, but he didn't test the surveillance. He felt fairly confident that he could have eluded his guards without much trouble, but the rewards didn't seem worth the effort. Now that he had committed himself to the Combined Forces, leaving would be construed, at least by a military court, as desertion, and probably, he thought, they could arrange quite easily to make it desertion during an action, which would get him a hangman's noose. He didn't believe it would ever get that far, but it would preclude his ever returning to Earth, and he had more than just a fondness for old Terra, as scarred as she had become.

On the evening of the second day he was taken by car—this time with a human driver—to the shuttle that would take the team up to the ship. The base had no formal shuttle-launching facilities, only a small six-passenger shuttle that was taken aloft by old-style liquid-fuel boosters. As the car pulled up to the pad, Clay was thinking that launching schedules for every spaceport on the continent west of the Mississippi were probably being shuffled around to make a window for them. *Very* inconspicuous.

The car pulled to a stop beside the launch tower, and Clay stepped out. He was alone for a moment on the field of concrete that surrounded the tower, then a swarm of technicians and assorted launch personnel in the midnight-blue uniforms of the Combined Forces surrounded him and hustled him toward the waiting shuttle.

A female corporal took the pack with his personal gear from him and scurried off to load it into the cargo hold of the little ship. Clay watched her rear with interest as she hurried away, thinking that the cut of Combined Forces uniforms had improved since his discharge.

He reached inside his flight jacket as if to rub a sore muscle and touched the reassuring weight of the C.F.-issue nine-millimeter automatic he had lifted from the room of a captain in the bachelor officer's quarters. The man had been conveniently involved a few doors down with a female artillery lieutenant.

Clay smiled to himself. A coed army certainly had its advantages.

He joined a hard-looking pair of guards in the cramped lift, and it jerked into motion, pulling them slowly up the length of the ship. He glanced at his companions, noting the heavy megawatt laser carbines both cradled across their forearms, the battery packs strapped onto their backs. Clay gave them both a big grin.

"Smile, boys. This is easy duty." Neither did. Clay shrugged.

The lift eased to a stop beside the main hatchway, and one of the two held open the heavy mesh door while Clay climbed out and onto the access boom.

Rankin met him at the hatch.

"The others are already inside and strapped down. Double time on in, and let's get this bloody show on the road."

"Aye, aye," Clay said. He ducked his head and climbed into the crew compartment.

"He's here," Rankin announced. Clay nodded to the two other members of the team, both of whom were sitting—or, rather, reclining—in launch couches, facing up toward the sky-pointing nose of the ship. The nearest nodded back curtly. He was slightly surprised that the other was a woman, though he knew certain Don Juan types who might refuse her the title. She was small and slim to the point of being shapeless, and what he could see of her in her flight suit indicated that she was muscular and rather masculine. Her hair, cut in a very short military flattop, contributed to the effect.

His couch was next to hers, behind Rankin, who was piloting the craft. She offered her hand as he approached, and he shook it, pleased to find that her grip was firm but light and that her voice when she introduced herself was soft and completely feminine.

"I'm Greene, Lieutenant. The fellow in the copilot's couch is Fitzgerald."

Clay glanced forward. Fitzgerald swiveled and offered his hand.

"Glad to meet you."

"Yes," Clay replied, "same."

Clay settled into his couch and arranged the straps with the ease of much practice. When he was secured, he worked the couch's controls, and its motors eased it around to orient it forward so that his weight was on his back, facing up into the shuttle's nose like the others.

Rankin began his preflight preparations, adjusting controls and mumbling in arcane figures with the ground control team. Fitzgerald and Greene spoke to one another as they waited, and Clay recognized in the conversation the easy familiarity of comrades who had served together. He was, then, the only odd man out—which was not good if there came a point in time when a need for a snap decision as to who among them was most easily sacrificed came about. He stored the information in the back of his mind. When and if that time came, he would at least be aware of his status.

In the few words they exchanged, Clay felt something about Fitzgerald that bothered him, though not enough to keep him from qualified liking for the man. Fitzgerald had a quick smile and a speaking voice that was, if anything, softer than that of Greene. He struck Clay as capable, and Clay trusted him immediately.

Rankin finished his conversation with the ground crew and settled back, letting the launch computers take over.

"Thirty seconds," Fitzgerald shouted over the building roar of the shuttle's engines.

Clay cleared his mind and tried to relax, waiting, strapped down in the reclined seat, for the sudden weight of the rockets' thrust to press him into the chair's cushioning. When it came, suddenly and without the calming subsonic tone over the loudspeakers that he had half expected—commercial flights took a few more pains to make the launches bearable—he concentrated on breathing through the acceleration, drawing air in slowly, letting it out through his nose.

He began to feel very fatigued, the muscles in his neck and shoulders especially beginning to ache from the pressure, and it suddenly came to him then what it was about Fitzgerald that bothered him.

The man was tired. Now that he realized the cause of his unease, he remembered and understood the subtle clues he had noticed, almost subliminally: the way Fitzgerald held himself, the look in his eyes when they shook hands.

The man was simply fatigued, not physically but in a way that Clay had seen many times before in veteran mercenaries who had fought too many battles, a fatigue of the soul, the tiredness that came from having seen and done too much that was better forgotten.

Clay took a deep breath and let it out, the acceleration pressing the air from his lungs, feeling the presence of his own fatigue growing cogent and heavy, sitting on his mind like a dark cloud.

After what seemed a very long time the pressure let up, and he relaxed, dozing until the shuttle docked with the station where they would board the ship to Ithavoll.

The trip was long but uneventful. Rankin had managed passage for the team and its gear on an independent ion-longship, which blasted out of the system and dropped into the black emptiness of the nearest collapsar, appearing simultaneously near another system some hundreds of light-years from Sol. It took three jumps to reach the singularity that was closest to Ithavoll's sun, then several more days at sublight speeds to arrive at the planet itself.

They shuttled down to the planet's surface in one of the ship's cargo haulers—civilian transportation was the standard for survey teams, as military craft of any kind were generally forbidden by the less-than-trusting governments of the outworlds. Even the United Democracies embassy consulates were forced to hire private ion-ships for their business.

Much of the equipment they were to carry was bulky and was only ill concealed among the more innocuous survey equipment they were to take. Clay spent much of the day before planetfall in the hold with Greene, arranging the equipment packs so that they would appear as innocent as possible.

Clay's own equipment was not that difficult to conceal; the Israeli assault rifle broke down easily into discrete components, all of which fit neatly into the hollow innards of a machine he guessed was originally designed to analyze vegetable matter. A few other gadgets, some of which he planned to hide on his person at planetfall; his own kit was, on the surface, as unimpeachable as that of any true U.D. Survey technician.

Rankin and Fitzgerald had also chosen light, fairly small armament, and both were conventional projectile weapons. Greene's kit, however, posed a much greater problem. Her choice had been one of the light-duty lasers that the poker-faced guards at the shuttle pad had carried, and while the rifle components could be concealed to an extent, the distinctive bulk of the battery pack posed something of a problem.

Clay finally decided that whatever customs officials they might run up against would be likely to believe the pack was something a survey team might legitimately carry; if not, the chances were very high that they would be amenable to a bribe. Either way, there was no concealing the battery pack from any purposeful search, so he settled for simply wrapping it in opaque sheet plastic and placing a legitimate piece of equipment on top of it in the overseas bag in which Greene had carried it aboard.

Clay pulled together the hasp at the top of the bag and locked it, then arranged it under his own equipment pack. He stood and beat the dust from his hands on his fatigue pants.

"Why the hell did you order up this cannon? If we get into rough country, you'll end up ditching it and using your teeth and nails to keep the heathen from burying you."

Greene shrugged, then pried loose a tiedown from a stack of sacked grain and hefted one of the hundred-kilo sacks chest high, then over her head. She tossed it up, caught it, and set it down again.

"Because *I* can handle it."

Clay grinned. "I can see that."

She grinned back. "Much more than a pretty face, soldier. I can burn the hair off a flea's butt at a hundred meters with that torch. Hell of a lot quieter than those popguns, too, silenced or not."

Clay nodded. There was only a certain amount of a large-caliber rifle's report that a silencer could cancel out without affecting muzzle velocity to the point where the weapon lost effectiveness at any range. The Israeli ten-millimeter he carried, even silenced, roared like a shuttle engine.

"To each his own brand of mayhem."

"Amen, soldier."

She retrieved her fatigue shirt, and he admired the ripple of muscle across her shoulders and under her T-shirt as she pulled the outer shirt on.

"See you at oh eight hundred, Lieutenant."

Clay nodded and watched her duck into the hatch and out of the hold. When she was gone, he settled back onto the sack of grain she had pulled loose from the stack lashed to the deck nearby.

The shipment of grain was small compared to the rest of the contents of the hold, which for the most part seemed to be industrial machinery and luxury goods. The grain wasn't food-stuff but high-yield seed grain that was being imported in the hope of feeding the hundreds of thousands of Ithavoll's people who lived in a state of near starvation on the northern continent.

Like most of the lesser-developed colonial worlds, Ithavoll imported much more than it exported and owed billions in NATO dollars to various creditors, mostly Terran. It was the primary reason for both the surface geniality of the planet's emperor—as a member of the United Democracies, he stood to gain immunity for many of those debts—and the underlying resentment of its general population toward Terrans and the United Democracies. Their poverty, they were told, was a direct result of the usury of the Terran creditors.

But then, the average freeholder or farmer wasn't privy to the expenditures of his emperor for missiles and the machinery that filled the longship's hold. Ignorance made for pliability. A directed rage against an economic enemy that was largely unseen kept the attention of the people off their own leader and on the straw man of the Terran corporations.

Clay quickly checked over the equipment one last time, then found his handgun where he had stashed it among the grain sacks and pulled the shoulder holster on, covering it with his shirt and then a short jacket. The chances were good that at that point in the game Rankin and company would care less that he was carrying a personal arm that wasn't torn down and hidden away. But he didn't care to take the chance that Rankin would object.

He didn't intend to embark on Ithavoll without a weapon. He knew that particular planet much too well.

Then he followed Greene out the hatchway and returned to his cabin.

The shuttle broke through the cloud cover and began its descent toward a short runway just outside the northern continent's largest city, a sprawling, dirty metropolis named Honshu. Clay watched the city grow through the pilot's window as the shuttle made its approach and thought dryly that as cities went, it wasn't much.

There were few buildings he could see that were over a half dozen stories, and most of the city proper was composed of low, stolid concrete buildings punctuated intermittently by tall smokestacks—Clay remembered having read somewhere that Honshu was the center of the planet's infant textiles industry. Most of what he could see from the shuttle, then, was doubtless sweatshops and weaving plants.

All in all, the impression was more of a burgeoning industrial-revolution-type squalor and complexity than of an unexplored outer world.

But as the shuttle turned for its final approach to the space-port, he could see through the haze of the atmosphere the dull-hued green of endless forest beginning a few kilometers beyond the city, the concrete and plastic giving way in a sudden demarcation from gray to a lush olive and blue.

"Not very pretty," a voice said over his shoulder. He turned to see Greene standing there, squinting at the murk beyond the Plexiglas.

"No, not here. There are places on the southern continent, though . . . well, they're a hell of a lot more pleasant to look on." He pointed out the field of blue-green in the near distance. "I'm more concerned with what the countryside out there's going to act like, though. That's some damned untame terrain."

She shrugged. "Whatever it's like, I've seen worse."

"Yes? Where, for instance?"

She thought for a moment. "Iga-to. The atmosphere is only borderline breathable there and smells like bat piss—full of ammonia. They're trying to terraform it, but if the choice was mine, I'd say bag it up and move on to some place more pleasant. And cooler. Daytime temp there averaged about sixty centigrade. We were fighting an indigenous life-form that looked like a surrealist's dream with fangs. I had eleven in my squad, and even with pretty good armament, we only had six left, including walking wounded, when we were relieved. Nasty place, that." She shuddered.

"Better buckle in." The pilot pointed back to the cargo section of the craft with a thumb.

Clay nodded, and they joined Rankin and Fitzgerald in the

rear of the shuttle, where several removable acceleration couches had been bolted to the deck. Rankin grinned and flashed a thumbs-up.

"Now the fun begins."

Clay dropped into the reclined seat and buckled the straps. A few moments later the shuttle's tires touched the runway's plastic with a squeal, and they settled with a bump onto the surface of the planet Ithavoll.

Clay realized as the shuttle rolled to a stop that he had, strangely enough, been holding his breath and that every muscle in his body was tight with tension. He frowned to himself and concentrated on relaxing.

As a rule, he was very loose at the beginning of a mission. Action never terrorized him so much as it made him feel alive, invigorated.

But something—the planet itself, maybe—had him sweating like a recruit on his first drop.

He closed his eyes and waited for the tone that would signal that he could unstrap and leave the suddenly too close innards of the landing craft.

CHAPTER FIVE

Clay was relieved to discover that customs searches at the Port of Honshu were cursory and unenthusiastic. The handful of raggedly uniformed customs officers who halfheartedly opened and closed their gear bags had seen hundreds of Terran U.D. survey, census, and cartography personnel pass through the shuttleport, and they saw more or less what they expected to see in the equipment satchels.

Too, Rankin's pushy manner made them eager to move the team through with minimal fuss. Clay noted that and remarked silently to himself how dangerous the ingrained habit of condescension to the appearance of authority could become. Men too used to not questioning authority quickly became indiscriminate about the source of that authority. More than one leader had fallen because his men had obeyed the most forceful voice.

Their passports were handed back after being given only a cursory check—though because of his face Clay was given more than one hard glance—and he allowed himself to relax to a degree.

The passports were forgeries, and under close and knowledgeable scrutiny they could be spotted easily enough. This was intentional. The C.F. could well have given them perfectly legitimate passports under any assumed set of identities they chose.

The fake passports were a security precaution. If they were caught, the fact that they carried forged papers would give weight to the United Democracies' protests of innocence in the matter. And it was one additional piece in a lengthy trail of bad paper they were leaving behind them to demonstrate to later investigators that they were in no way connected to the Combined Forces or the United Democracies once the mission objective had been completed.

To an investigator who didn't know any better, it would seem as if the U.D. Survey Corps had been infiltrated from the outside by someone with only reasonable access to intelligence and documentation.

The air in the shuttleport was hot, humid and thick with strange odors, swarming with insects attracted to the foodstuffs, and animals that were penned near the terminal's loading docks, ready to be exported off-planet.

Other than textiles, Ithavoll's only real exports were exotic fruits and vegetables and preserved meats intended for the worlds closer to Terra and for Terra herself, where space to nurture animals or grow low-yield luxury foods was severely limited.

There was also a peculiar smell to the air that he remembered from his last tour on the planet, an odor that, as before, made him feel as if he badly needed to sneeze. He'd get used to it, he knew, but it was damned annoying in the meantime. He rubbed his itching nose vigorously with the back of his hand and noticed Greene doing the same thing. She grinned, catching his eye.

"Pollen. Thank God for antihistamines."

He nodded, smiling back.

Once through the shabby terminal, Rankin hustled the team toward a battered and rusty ground-effect bus. Clay looked doubtfully at the machine as they approached the concrete pad on which it squatted. He had used less than optimal transportation often enough in the past, and he wasn't about to be picky now, but the vehicle that was to take them to the U.D. survey post outside the city was old and abused enough to appear positively dangerous.

Which didn't bother him as much as did the thought that if that was still what they were to find in Ithavoll's largest and most modern city, there had not been very much change for the better on the planet since he had left the first time. And that meant there would be no modern transportation whatsoever in the wilderness.

As they reached the open door of the bus, Rankin pulled at Clay's sleeve and drew him aside.

"After we start off, brace yourself for some fun." He glanced down and to the side, and Clay followed his eyes. As Greene mounted the bus's steps, having more trouble than was plausible getting her duffel into the bus, Fitzgerald reached under the bus's heavy skirt and placed something near the fan motors. Clay heard the click of a magnet taking hold and knew it was some sort of limpet charge.

Rankin smiled and motioned him aboard.

The bus already held a driver and, Clay noted without surprise as he climbed in, a uniformed Ithavollan soldier. The soldier sat comfortably in one of the front seats, watching them with minimal interest as they boarded, an old but efficient-looking carbine cradled in his lap. Rankin gestured for everyone to stow his gear on the racks in the back of the bus and take a seat.

"They'll be taking us to the survey outpost. A free service, courtesy of the emperor of Ithavoll. Keeps off-worlders like us from wandering unchaperoned through this fair city and sticking their noses into places where they don't belong," Rankin said wryly. He smiled widely at the guard, who stared back without commenting. He understood the insinuation Rankin had made well enough. Terran Standard was a more or less universal language, and every child on every settled planet learned it, usually almost to the exclusion of any entirely ethnic language or idiom.

There were degrees of accent, though. A Terran from the United States of a couple of centuries back would have probably been surprised, Clay thought, to see a city of a million people who were to all appearances Chinese living in a Chinese culture but who spoke Terran Standard—only somewhat different from twentieth-century English—with an accent that sounded vaguely like a bad mixture of educated Cambridge public school and New Orleans ninth-ward Cajun. Their sentences were clear and somewhat clipped, but most of them, Clay noted, said something close to *ax* for *ask* and *der* for *there*.

The driver revved the bus's motors, and the machine rose from the pavement with a shudder and a groan, its turbines complaining with a loud whine about their age and lack of maintenance, and jerked into motion.

Clay's first impression of the city from the air proved close to the mark. The streets were narrow and rough, running between endless alternating rows of foul-smelling textile mills, grimy warehouses, and squalid row houses. Thin, dirty children played listlessly in the street, moving quietly aside as the bus wheezed by them; others sat in open doorways, solemnly watching the bus go by.

The scene was familiar enough. Wars, at least those requiring the services of the mercenary trade, were rarely carried out on wealthy worlds. The only difference here was the distinctive Oriental cast to the children's features. He saw few adults, and then only the very old. The others, he thought, were working, buried somewhere in the rumbling, windowless bowels of the mills.

The bus had been in motion for about ten minutes when the charge went off. The explosion was tiny and muffled, and for a split second Clay thought Fitzgerald had underestimated the ancient machine's resilience, but an instant later he heard the tortured grinding of metal as the damaged turbine destroyed itself.

The other three turbines whined in protest at the sudden additional load, and the bus, off balance, lurched to the right and grazed a building, knocking down a section of wall. Then the remaining turbines, overburdened, shut down, and the bus dropped onto the cobbled paving with a grinding, jarring thump and skidded to a stop.

"Damn!" Clay muttered between clenched teeth.

The bus's driver sat stock still with shock. The Ithavollan soldier scrambled to his feet from the deck where he had been thrown by the bus's haphazard landing and stood in confusion for a long moment, then crouched, staring out through the dirty windows, his carbine in his hands, looking for an enemy. Then, seeing none in evidence, he sat suddenly down again, dazed and confused.

Through the gap the bus had made in the wall of the building it had struck, Clay saw dozens of faces in the dim shadows, staring out over a maze of weaving machinery at the wrecked bus and its occupants.

Rankin pulled himself up from his seat with a grunt and marched to the front of the bus with the obvious intention of exiting. The soldier stood again and blocked the way, holding the rifle across his chest like a bar.

Rankin glowered down at the man and barked a command that Clay didn't catch. The man hesitated, then reached past the still stunned driver and touched a control to unseal the bus's door. It opened with a rusty squeal, and the soldier preceded Rankin out.

Rankin barked again, and the soldier scurried off, intent on his new mission.

Clay shouldered his duffel. Fitzgerald motioned him to put it down again.

"No need for that stuff. It'll be safe enough here, or this fellow's going to tell me why." He pointed to the bus driver. The man stared blankly at Fitzgerald for a moment, then nodded assent.

"Let's go, then."

Clay restowed his gear and followed him out.

"Fitzgerald, Greene, stay near the bus. Make sure things stay secure here. If the guard shows up, we went to find a private place to answer the call. More than two's going to be a crowd, I think. We don't want to spook anyone."

Rankin gestured for Clay to follow, and they set off down the street. He answered the question in Clay's glance at the building into which the Ithavollan soldier had disappeared. "I sent him to order us up new transportation, chop chop. The way things work around here, that should keep him on the line begging forgiveness from his superiors for quite a little while. We've got some information to garner from a local source before we hit the jungle. This is the only way we'll get the opportunity to make contact."

Clay nodded. "I understand."

He suppressed the irritation he felt at being left out of the scheme Fitzgerald and Rankin had carried out to cripple the bus. He didn't like surprises, and he sure as hell didn't like being left in the dark by his own comrades.

Still, he supposed they had no good reason to completely trust him yet, and as much as he liked Rankin, Rankin was still first and foremost a C.F. officer, and the C.F. lived by the rule of need-to-know.

Rankin started off down a side street, then turned into a series of narrow, twisting alleys. No need for wider streets, Clay guessed, because here everyone walked. Only the highest of the myriad officials in Shotoku's court and his closest cronies owned ground vehicles, and only the wealthiest of the planet's small bourgeois class, mostly black marketeers, could afford so much as bicycles.

The buildings rose up around them, close and windowless, block after block of cement and brick piles, identical and characterless.

After wending through a maze of the streets so narrow that in places he could almost touch the walls on either side simply by reaching out with either hand, they found themselves inside a square of towering row houses. Clay noted the curious faces staring out at them from a hundred glassless and screenless windows, those too old to work or too young.

The atmosphere of the place was squalid and thick with the smells of living, primarily, Clay thought, of sewage and cooking, though he was hard put to tell which was which. The buildings were ten stories each, and the primary route by which the tenants disposed of waste was through the small windows that pocked the buildings' flanks.

They entered a large common area between three of the buildings, and Rankin pushed open a sagging door and ducked through the low doorway into a dirty hallway. Clay followed and immediately was almost overwhelmed by the smell of rot and urine that filled the low-ceilinged tunnel. It was dim and unlighted and damp with mildew.

He followed Rankin through the hallway and into a tiny court-yard grown into a chest-high jungle of weeds and vines. Rankin pushed through, following a path marked by flat pieces of broken concrete.

"Where—" Clay began.

Rankin silenced him with a gesture. They came to another low door, and Rankin rapped softly against the rotting wood with a knuckle. After a few moments he rapped again. He had raised his hand for a third try when the door was dragged slowly open, the sagging frame fighting against being moved.

"What do you want?"

Clay saw a girl of perhaps thirteen in the shadow beyond the door. She peered out suspiciously, her face thin and drawn and smudged with ash and dirt.

"Zhaoming," Rankin said. He held his hands out in front of him, palm up, to show, Clay assumed, the innocence of his intentions.

"Not here." She started pushing the door closed in Rankin's face. Rankin pushed back.

"Where's Zhaoming?"

"Dead," the girl snapped, and shoved harder. Rankin wedged a boot in the door and pushed her back, throwing the door open. Beyond it Clay saw another short hall and then nothing but more shadow. Rankin strode through, the girl on his heels, cursing for all she was worth in what Clay guessed was a Chinese dialect, maybe Cantonese, mixed liberally with the worst brand of gutter Terran Standard.

He was a little surprised at her vehemence. She snatched up a length of wood from behind the door and swung at Rankin's back. With a speed that belied his age and size, Rankin spun and jerked it from her hands, then tossed it out the way they had come, into the jungle of weeds outside the door.

The girl stared at Rankin in silence for a long, shocked second, then screeched in rage and frustration and fled down the hall.

"A little high-strung," Clay commented.

"Indeed."

Rankin made his way down the hall, following the girl, and Clay trailed along a few steps behind. He touched the reassuring weight of handgun snugged in its holster under his arm and with a finger pushed the safety over to the FIRE position. He noticed that Rankin did the same.

The hall intersected another, and Rankin looked left, hesitated, then turned right. Clay caught up with him as he stopped before a bead curtain that closed off another low door. The strings of wooden beads still swung slightly, clicking eerily together in the damp silence of the empty hallway.

"Bingo."

Clay peered through the curtain but could see nothing.

Rankin nodded, and he drew his pistol and lifted aside the curtain with the barrel. There was a snap from the room beyond, and Clay flinched but held his fire. A lamp popped and hissed to life, and Clay saw the girl grimacing at them as they stood in the doorway.

She held a lamp high, over her head, and its wan light revealed a small, square room claustrophobically crowded with crates and boxes and piles of sacks. The air was thick with the smells of cooking and unwashed bodies. Stowage nets filled with goods of some unidentifiable sort hung from the ceiling, making it seem to press even lower. The walls were buried behind rugs and bolts of cheap fabric.

Something large shifted among the dirty blankets spread on the battered lounge chair over which the girl held the lamp.

"What do you want?" a voice asked, thin with age and infinitely weary.

Rankin was peering intently at the figure on the lounge. "Zhaoming?"

"Zhaoming? No. No, not Zhaoming. Shu. I am only Shu." The voice rose in pitch, and Clay could hear in it an undercurrent of stubborn strength. "I asked you, what do you want? I am old. I don't know anything, and I don't want to talk anymore."

"Where's Zhaoming?"

There was silence, then, "Not here. Gone."

"Where?" Rankin demanded impatiently.

"Gone, I said. Just gone." The voice rose to a high-pitched whine.

"Hell's Bells," Rankin snapped. He strode over to the girl and grabbed her wrist, forcing the lamp down close to the face hidden in the shadows and dirty pillows. In the weak yellow light Clay saw the weathered and bone-thin face of an ancient woman.

Rankin turned to the girl again.

"You. Where is Zhaoming?"

Clay could see his grip tighten on the girl's wrist, and tears sprung to her eyes. "Auntie Shu!" the girl yelped, struggling to pull away.

Clay took a step forward. Mission or no, Rankin was treading close to a line that Clay was not going to let him cross.

"The traders' market. Go to the market," the old woman croaked, struggling against the pile of stinking quilts that hid her.

"Market? What market?" Rankin demanded, letting go of the girl's wrist and pushing the old woman back down. The girl sobbed and backed quickly away but still held the lamp dutifully high.

"Go away," the old woman groaned.

Rankin stood over the lounge. "Damn it, where?"

The girl rushed forward. "I'll show you. Leave Auntie Shu alone and I'll show you, okay?" Clay could see she was shaking with fear, not for herself but for the old woman. Her cheeks were streaked with tears. He felt a twinge in his heart and hardened himself against it.

There were too many like her, too much tragedy in a very imperfect universe. If he let himself feel too much, it would probably make him hesitate when hesitation could cost him his life, and it could bring him entirely too close to a place he'd seen too many good soldiers go, into despair and madness.

"Fine, fine," Rankin said, suddenly jovial and polite. "Lead the way."

The girl snapped the lamp off, and they were suddenly enveloped in a tangible thick darkness. Clay turned, remembering the position of the curtained doorway, and stumbled across something large that barked him against both shins.

He heard the clatter of beads and realized that Rankin was out of the room. Then he felt a firm touch on his arm. He resisted for a second, almost slapping the hand away, then gave in and let it lead him forward.

After a moment he felt the beads brush against his face and part, and then he was in the hallway. The hand led him forward and out, and soon he saw the dim light at the bottom of the door, now closed, that gave into the overgrown courtyard. The door opened, and he saw Rankin's bulky form silhouetted in the daylight.

The girl tugged at his sleeve again, and he quickly followed her out.

CHAPTER SIX

"This way."

Auntie Shu's girl led the way across the unkempt courtyard, and Clay and Rankin fell in behind. For the first time Clay noticed how painfully thin she was, the bones of her emaciated shoulders and hips tenting out the coarse, worn fabric of her coolie tunic and pants.

"Where the hell are we going?" he asked quietly of Rankin's back.

"I don't know for sure," Rankin answered over his shoulder. "I think some sort of black market, some place where they trade restricted goods, stuff they don't want taxed. Illegal as hell and punishable by death here. That's how our man Zhaoming makes his living. Buying and selling—good, solid, not too honest capitalism. We're just two more customers so far as he's concerned."

"I hope he doesn't see us as just two more commodities to sell."

"He won't betray us. He doesn't dare," Rankin said darkly.

Clay shrugged and let the discussion drop.

As they came out onto the streets, the girl scurried ahead, not looking back to see if they followed. They kept up a good pace for fifteen or twenty minutes, weaving into and out of narrow back alleys where open sewers ran in shallow troughs. The stench was incredible, and the attendant flies hung in shifting clouds over the streams of effluent.

"Pleasant," Clay commented under his breath.

Rankin glanced back but said nothing. The thought was on both their minds that Rankin's boss—and my own, Clay reflected wryly—the United Democracies, was as responsible for the squalor in which these people lived as their emperor was. They had, after all, made it possible for Shotoku to keep his grip on most of the planet for as long as he had. The old Sino-Japanese confederation had held some sway at one time with the U.D., but that had been long ago and, for the most part, far away, back on Earth.

For almost as long as man had lived in Ithavoll, petty tyrants of many kinds had drained away what little wealth and hope it had ever had.

Shotoku was only the latest of a long line and probably by no means the worst. The people had little to keep them alive, but still they endured. To them, the burdens of their servitude were like their adopted planet's weather, constant and largely unchanging.

Ahead, the girl—Clay reminded himself to ask her her name when he had a chance—stopped at an opening between buildings that looked to be another one of the innumerable dank alleys they had already passed by and through. She called out in the same dialect Clay had heard her use earlier on Rankin. A low voice answered from within the alley in the same dialect. After a short exchange the girl walked back to where Clay and Rankin waited.

"They are afraid to let you come in. You have to give me your weapons or they will not let you enter."

Clay shook his head. "Not a chance. What's to stop us from just walking in?"

The girl looked surprisingly solemn. "They would kill you,

then flee. It would be very bad for everyone. The police would come and many people would be punished.''

"Fair enough," Rankin said, pulled out his handgun, ejected the clip, and cleared the chamber, then offered it to her butt first. She took it and tucked it away somewhere inside her tunic.

Clay hesitated. It rankled to simply turn over his primary weapon to the narrow-faced little girl.

He looked hard into her eyes, but they were guileless and innocent. The brown almond eyes stared back at him without blinking. He reached under his vest and pulled forth the handgun, cleared it, and handed it over. Like Rankin's, it disappeared into the dirty tunic.

"Okay. Walk slowly, follow me."

They did as they were told, and she led them into the recesses of the alley. The man to whom the girl had been speaking squatted against one wall, hands dangling over his knees. Clay noted the long, machetelike knife sheathed at his belt.

The man grinned and nodded as they passed. Easy meat, he's thinking, Clay thought, but perhaps not so easy as you might think, old boy.

Fifty meters in, the alley jagged suddenly to the right and opened into a wide avenue of booths. Vendors displayed wares, and customers shopped and haggled by the dozens. For all appearances it was nothing more or less than a bazaar, an open marketplace where buyers and sellers came and went without fear or furtiveness.

"Pretty wide open for a black market," Clay observed aloud.

Rankin nodded. "Not much pressure on them. They grease the wheel well here. The police and local magistrates take their cut, and everyone does good business. The guards at the entrances are purely precautionary—there's always a chance some minor official will get the word from above to crack down. I imagine in any case they'd all have more than enough warning to save their skins and their wares.''

The girl hung back. "The trader's is there." She pointed at the largest booth, a brightly painted wood and canvas affair set back against and into a wall a dozen meters into the street that held the bazaar.

Having delivered them, the girl turned and fled back the way they had come.

"The guns—" Clay began.

"I'm sure she'll have them when we come out," Rankin said mildly.

Clay watched her go, again wishing he had asked her her name. This world is filled with nameless people, he reflected. In a place such as this, people were simply what they were—a girl or a trader or an old woman. Except for Zhaoming. It would be good to finally meet someone on Ithavoll he could call by a name.

Rankin strode up to the booth, and Clay followed, regretting the empty holster under his vest.

"Keep a weather eye," Rankin muttered, then pushed aside another beaded curtain and stepped into the tented confines of the booth.

For the second time that day Clay entered a room filled to bursting with goods, mostly, he noted, the sorts of off-world items that would be considered high luxury on a colony world like Ithavoll, durable goods and clothing, plastics and synthetics. And it was nearly as dim as the room that had housed the old woman who had called herself Shu, a single lamp supplementing the thin bars of daylight that fell through the bead-curtained doorway.

There was no frail old woman there, though. Three men, all of an age that made them candidates for the sweatshops and factories, sat at their ease, cross-legged on the carpeted ground around a low table strewn with cards. Beyond them, so hidden in the dark recesses of the booth that Clay had to strain to make it out, was an altar of some sort, though it was like nothing Clay had ever seen.

Thin smoke rose from a brazier placed before small idols. One of the figures in particular, black, shapeless, and almost invisible in the darkness, caught Clay's eye. The figure was misshapen and strange but somehow compelling.

Clay felt an irrational longing to go up to it, to touch it and examine it, but repressed the urge. That would be bad manners at best, and he knew nothing could offend as readily as a lack of consideration for religious sanctities. As they entered, one of the card players, a thin, sallow man of perhaps thirty, stood and bowed slightly to Rankin. Rankin nodded in return.

"I would like to speak with a fellow named Zhaoming," Rankin said.

"He's not here," the thin man replied, smiling and bowing again.

"Goddamn it," Rankin said, bristling. "Get him out here or I'll wring your bloody neck."

One of the men still at the table stood with some difficulty and bowed to Rankin. He was, Clay noted, amazingly heavy for an Ithavollan. Until that moment he had yet to see one of the people of Honshu who weighed more than fifty kilos.

This man weighed at least twice that, the fat making him round and Buddha-like. He smiled broadly and bowed again, this time to Clay. The thinner man backed away and squatted again at the table.

"I am Zhaoming," the fat man announced.

"Ah, good." Rankin bowed slightly to the man. "I think we have some business together, friend."

Zhaoming bowed again, though whether in agreement with Rankin or not, Clay couldn't tell.

"Is there some place we can talk?"

"Of course, of course. Always happy to talk."

He said something quickly to the men at the table that Clay didn't catch, and they stood and disappeared through the bead curtain, bowing and smiling.

Zhaoming settled himself with a grunt in his place behind the table. Clay and Rankin followed suit, squatting down on the thick dusty carpets.

Rankin looked over his shoulder meaningfully. "Can we speak here without being overheard?"

"I could trust those men with my life." He spread his hands on the table before them as if to display their innocence for Clay and Rankin to see. "But of course I do not." He tapped the tabletop three times with a thumb ring. After a moment a hum filled the room.

"Privacy sonics," Rankin nodded appreciatively.

The fat man grinned and shrugged. "In some ways we are not so backward as we appear."

"I'm gratified that's the case."

"Gentlemen, what is it you want of me?"

"You've been contacted. You've also been paid. You know what I want."

Zhaoming shook his head as if in wonder. "Contacted? Paid? I don't even know who you are."

"I understand," Rankin said, his tone reasonable and even. He reached out across the table as if to shake the Oriental's hand. The fat man flinched back, but not quickly enough. Rankin seized one puffy wrist, squeezed, then dropped the hand.

Zhaoming stared blankly at Rankin, then down at his own hand. On the inside of his wrist, above where the veins lay buried in fat, a thin silver square of metal the size of a thumbnail was stuck to the brown skin.

Zhaoming reached as if to pluck off the inoffensive-looking square, and Rankin held up a warning hand.

"That's a small charge of a very powerful explosive. It will explode if you try to remove it, and I guarantee it will be enough to blow your hand clean off. I also guarantee I'll pin you down until you bleed to death."

Zhaoming, showing remarkable calm, Clay thought, carefully eased the afflicted hand back onto the table and looked to Rankin to go on.

"It's a tricky little gadget. Detonator is on the underside, against the skin. When I pressed it on, it armed, and if it's moved, it detonates. There might be someone other than myself on this planet who knows how to remove it intact, but I kind of doubt it. Besides a few off-world gadgets, I'm of the impression that Ithavoll is indeed pretty backward from what I've seen. Oh, and it's fused to go off all by itself regardless in five minutes or thereabouts. Messy. Damned noisy, too, I'd imagine."

The fat man's face grew tighter, and his imperturbable smile, already bent, vanished. "We can be reasonable. We can discuss—"

Rankin put out a warning hand again. "Not much time. I suggest you talk fast."

"I'll get it, I'll get it, please!" The fat man stood clumsily and rushed out through the bead curtain, his hand held out from him as if it were a snake.

Clay looked to Rankin, his doubt evident in his face.

"Don't worry, he won't bring back thugs. I'm betting he's

much fonder of his own well-being than he is even of his profits.''

Clay pursed his lips and looked down at his hands. "Do you mind telling me what the hell it is you want from that fat old man? And why you didn't just offer him more cash for it? That's pretty obviously all he wanted."

While he spoke, he moved toward the back of the trader's place of business, to where the altar stood. The ceiling was hung with thick curtaining, and he stooped to get close. He reached out to touch the figure he had felt drawn to earlier, then stopped.

Something about the small idol suddenly repelled him as strongly as it had attracted him only moments before. The twisted surface of the figure seemed almost to writhe nauseatingly of its own accord. The *thing* depicted by the figurine was as strange, as alien, he thought suddenly, as anything he had ever seen. Rankin broke his fascination by answering his question, and Clay forced his gaze away from the ugly little figure and turned back to Rankin.

Rankin looked soberly at Clay. "I would've, if I'd thought it'd get us what we need. Wouldn't have worked, though. His kind don't give in easily, not where money is involved. He would have turned over the goods eventually, but not until he'd bled us thoroughly and put us off for a good long while. We don't have that kind of time."

Clay didn't like the easy way Rankin said "his kind." He knew that sort of generalization was dangerous for both the maker and the individual who was thereby pigeonholed. Prejudice of any kind not only was morally untenable, it was generally dangerous as hell, as very few members of the now wide-flung human race fit neatly into categories.

Still, it was hard to deny Rankin's rationale in the trader Zhaoming's case. The man had given very little evidence of trustworthiness.

"What is it he's supposed to have for us?"

"Computer memory. A black box. Remember that spy satellite of ours they shot down? Zhaoming has its memory packet. Luckily for us, almost anything can be bought here if you know the right seller. Zhaoming was bright enough not to try to sell it to the local authorities. We hope—" Rankin paused to lean back and glance out through the beaded door, then down at his watch. "Zhaoming had better hurry. We hope that the satellite saw more than it sent back, maybe after it had been hit and before the atmosphere burned out its cameras. Maybe it got a little closer look at where it is we're headed."

"I see. What makes you think Zhaoming really has the thing?"

Rankin shrugged. "We'll find out soon enough."

As if on cue, the fat trader burst through the bead curtain. In his hand was an object that was quite literally a black box, about thirty centimeters a side and seamless. Rankin rose and took the box from the panting Oriental. He tapped an etched series of numbers on one side of the box.

"Bingo. This is it."

"Now you will take this?" Zhaoming held out his afflicted wrist.

Rankin grinned. "I don't know. I hear on this world the law says thieves are supposed to lose their hands. Leaving that thing where it is might just be my civic duty."

"Please," Zhaoming said, his voice rising.

Rankin took the trembling hand Zhaoming held out and with a fingertip tapped the silver square twice, waited, then tapped it again, once. He turned the wrist over and caught the device as it dropped away. Zhaoming scrambled back from him, rubbing his wrist and muttering vehemently in the same patois, using many of the same words Clay had heard earlier from the girl.

Rankin tucked the black box into the crook of his arm as if he were carrying a football. "I thank you for your cooperation. I'd also like to warn you against trying anything unpleasant, such as having some poor fellow come after us with one of those machetes. While you were out—" Clay could swear Rankin smirked, "—I hid a small electronic incendiary device in your showroom here. If I so choose, I can press a button on the detonator I have here in my pocket and your whole inventory will go up in flames."

Zhaoming glared at Rankin. "I should kill you anyway for what you've dared."

Rankin shrugged. "That's up to you. I hope there's nothing in this trash heap you value." He turned and ducked through the curtained door, and Clay followed, feeling exposed as they exited into the open street. He noted that most of the locals who had been milling about the black-market bazaar were now gone and that the few who remained about were of a particularly surly-looking variety.

"Quickly but with dignity," Rankin said, striding rapidly away the way they had come. Clay nodded, again regretting having given up his sidearm. He forced himself to relax, controlling his breathing and concentrating on readying himself mentally for combat.

If they were jumped, their assailants would still be in for a nasty surprise, handgun or no handgun. But he would have been much happier with that reassuring weight in the empty shoulder holster under his vest.

They moved quickly up the alley, passing the guard at the entrance without the man showing any interest in their going. He simply squatted as he had when they had entered, his back against the wall and a long-knife hanging from his belt.

"Good enough," Clay muttered, scanning the street outside the alley for the girl who had taken the pistols. The street was deserted, only the eternal rumbling of the factory sweatshops disturbing the stillness.

"Hell's bells," Rankin said quietly.

"What now?" Clay asked.

Clay was oddly gratified that Rankin seemed a little dumbfounded. "The little urchin wouldn't have dared . . ."

There was a movement a dozen meters down the narrow street, and Clay tensed, then relaxed. The girl edged out from a doorway, the pistols held by the barrel in either hand. Rankin advanced on her and took the handguns roughly from her grasp, then tossed Clay his. Clay caught it, checked the action and reloaded it, then slipped it back into its holster.

"This, too," Rankin said, and tossed him the black box. "I need both hands."

"I'll take you back to Auntie Shu's," the girl piped.

"No need." Rankin reloaded his weapon, slapping the clip home and working the action to bring a round to the chamber. "We can find our own way."

The girl looked distressed. "Auntie Shu said—"

Rankin cut her off. "It's all right. We can get back by ourselves. You go on, tell her you saw us leave."

The girl hesitated. "Scat," Rankin said, and slapped her on

her thin rump. She dodged away and glared back at him from a safe distance.

"Hadn't we better be moving?" Clay asked impatiently.

"In good time." Rankin turned back to the alley. "Give it a minute." Clay noted that the girl didn't leave but only moved away to the vantage point of a sill that ran along the bottom of a nearby wall. She squatted there and waited.

Rankin stood watching the alley's entrance. After a long moment a head peeked out around the corner. Quick as a thought, Rankin raised his pistol and snapped off a shot, knocking out a chip from the crumbling brick a good half meter above the head. It withdrew in haste.

"Just to give them something to think about." He holstered his weapon with a flourish. "Let's get back to the bus."

The girl, Clay noticed, was following them as they made their way through the twisting streets. She kept far back, slipping from doorway to doorway, around corners and behind the frequent piles of rusted machinery worn out in the factories and discarded into the street.

Clay jerked his head in her direction as she scampered across the street from an abandoned air-truck to a closer doorway. "Why's the little one sticking with us?"

Rankin glanced back. " 'Auntie Shu' is Zhaoming's wife, or one of them, anyway. He married her for her capital, and she needed someone to keep some ambitious sort from simply taking it all away from her—she's the real 'trader.' The business he runs was hers. No doubt she told the girl to keep track of us and see where we go. They probably planned, and still plan, to try and kill us."

Rankin paused and glanced back over his shoulder. "They don't trust Terrans—we might report them to the authorities and demand some action, especially if they had managed to break our little arrangement and keep the box or extort more cash. I don't think the little pest's any danger to us, but if it would make you more comfortable, you could knock her around a bit and send her home."

Clay shook his head. "Not my style."

"I didn't think it was. Just thought I'd mention the option."

The girl persisted even as they drew closer to the one street in the city's twisting maze of nearly identical streets where the crippled bus and the rest of the team waited. Clay had put her at the edge of his consciousness, devoting the greatest part of his attention to keeping himself oriented and aware of movement ahead, behind, and above that he had not already identified and dropped as an immediate concern.

As they neared the bus, the streets became more populous. Crowds of chattering locals began to trickle and then pour from the surrounding buildings, threading around the detrius from the factories that crowded all but the center portion of the streets.

"Change of shift," Rankin commented. "Fresh fodder for the machines."

They were less than half a klick from the bus when Clay suddenly became aware of a commotion in the crowd that had closed in behind them.

His first thought was that Zhaoming and company had found them, but he quickly dismissed that possibility. The trader lived by stealth; any move he would make would be quiet and hidden. Clay's second thought was for the girl. He heard a thin scream, and the crowd surged.

As Clay turned, Rankin's hand fell on his shoulder, pulling him back.

"Move out, trooper."

Clay shook off the hand. "I'll be along."

He pulled away from Rankin and pushed into the surge of bodies.

"Goddammit, Lieutenant!" Rankin's angry voice was lost in the frenzied shouting of the crowd as it flowed into the gap between them.

Clay's progress was irritatingly slow as the crowd, moving away from the disturbance ahead, pushed strongly en masse up the street. As he drew closer to the commotion, a hand caught the material of his vest and pulled him back in the direction from which he had come.

He whirled, knocking locals back on either side. Almond-shaped eyes stared back at him, wide with fear.

He caught the hand that held him and swung hard with his free hand, then checked himself and brought the blow up short.

The girl stared back at him defiantly. He kept his grip on her wrist and pulled her up close.

"What the hell is going on?" he shouted at her above the panicky chattering of the surging mob.

"*Gembuku!*" she shouted back. Clay could hear the terror in her voice.

"*Gembuku?*" The word struck a chord in Clay's memory. He had heard it before, he was certain, perhaps the last time he had been on Ithavoll . . .

Before he could dredge the word's meaning up from his suddenly stubborn memory, the cause of the crowd's panic overtook them. A dozen young men carrying the distinctive long-knives Clay had seen the bazaar guard wearing earlier shoved and slashed at the people trying to flee down the narrow, debris-strewn street, their faces a frenzy of rage.

All of the youths were bleeding heavily from wounds on their arms and faces, and Clay wondered for an instant how the un-armed and rabbit-meek factory workers who fought only to flee could have caused such damage.

Then he saw one of the boys stop, eyes rolling, to scream insanely and slash himself with his own knife across his fore-arms. Slavering like a rabid dog, the boy then struck out with the heavy-bladed knife and cut down a woman who had pressed herself against the dubious protection of a head-high rusted hulk of machinery.

Distracted, Clay caught the movement of a knife slashing out toward him only an instant before the blade reached him. The blow struck him below the ribs hard enough to take away his breath but was turned aside by the bulletproof material of his vest.

The blade's tip snagged for an instant on a fastener, and Clay grasped the wrist holding the knife with one hand and struck sharply downward with the metal edge of the black box he held in the other, cleanly breaking the arm at the elbow. The youth howled more in rage than in pain and pressed the attack with his remaining arm, clawing at Clay's eyes. Clay knocked the hand aside and jabbed the boy hard in the esophagus with two stiffened fingers.

The boy's knees gave, and he slowly collapsed, choking, his larynx crushed.

Clay stared into his eyes as he fell; they were filled with a scathing hatred and, he realized with a shock, with something else, something alien and terrifying.

For an instant Clay felt something flow from the dying boy like electricity passing from the boy's mad gaze into his own mind. He felt a presence touch him deeply like a finger reaching to his soul.

For an instant something *possessed* him—there was no other word for it—and he felt an all-consuming rage and blood lust fill his mind like a fever. Then it withdrew as quickly as it had come and was gone, leaving Clay standing alone, shaking.

After a long, helpless moment he recovered himself enough to draw his handgun and crouch low to face any new threat, but the pack of youths was gone, scattering into the mazelike side streets. The street emptied quickly, those who could walk, the whole and the wounded, scurrying away from the scene of the carnage.

Six or more bodies lay within sight, dead or nearly dead. The woman Clay had seen struck down lay slumped against the machine she had tried to hide against.

A meter away he saw Auntie Shu's girl lying in a growing puddle of her own blood, her throat cut almost from ear to ear. He stared dumbly at the thin, wretched body for a long moment, unable to react.

Then a hand touched his arm. He whirled, bringing the pistol to bear. Rankin backed away a step, the barrel of Clay's weapon an inch from his chest.

"Whoa, son. It's over; they're gone."

Clay held the pistol on Rankin a moment longer, then let his hand drop down to his side.

"What in God's name was that?" he asked, forcing his voice to stay level.

"I don't know. Street thugs, some kind of gang."

Clay shook his head. "No. They were crazed, or drugged, or something. That boy's eyes. I felt . . ." He couldn't go on; there were no words for what he had experienced when he had looked into the dead boy's eyes.

Rankin looked at him strangely. "Back to the bus before the authorities arrive."

Clay nodded slowly. "Yes. Let's get the hell out of here. *Now.*"

Rankin started away, but Clay hung back. He stood for a moment over the girl's still body, then stooped and closed the dead, staring eyes. Then he stood and followed Rankin down the deserted street.

CHAPTER
SEVEN

A new bus—as aged, battered, and tired as the first—had arrived to replace the one damaged by Fitzgerald's sabotage.

The first bus, mortally wounded, still sat at an angle against the wall that had stopped its last grinding charge. It would, Clay imagined, soon become just another of the myriad rusted piles of junk that littered the city's streets. Greene and Fitzgerald lounged comfortably in the vehicle's tattered seats.

The Ithavollan soldier had returned, and he looked both angry and relieved to see Clay and Rankin returning. As they approached, he leapt down from the bus, his rifle held out before him in obvious threat. He started to speak, but Rankin silenced him with a gesture.

"Is the crate in working order?" he barked, his voice hard with impatience.

Fear of the authority in Rankin's voice made the man swallow his irritation. He faltered, looking with suspicion at the black box Clay still carried. He stepped from foot to foot with indecision and frustration.

Then he grimaced and without a word climbed back aboard the bus, where he vented his spleen by shouting in a mixture of Terran Standard and the now-familiar local patois at the driver, who sat regally unperturbed in his seat, ignoring the tirade.

Finally the guard allowed him to start the bus's turbines and set the rusting machine into motion.

For twenty minutes they crawled through block after block of the same bleak rows of ghettolike housing interspersed with the faceless brick bulk of factories and textile mills.

Not long after the bus was under way, the Ithavollan guard grew tired of hovering suspiciously near Rankin and Clay and reclaimed his seat near the driver; soon they were arguing amicably together about something that Clay couldn't quite follow.

When Clay was confident the guard was fully engrossed in the conversation, he shifted from his seat and moved close beside Rankin.

Rankin leaned close and whispered, "You have a question, soldier?"

"What is *gembuku*?"

Rankin's eyebrows rose in surprise. "Where did you hear that?"

"From the girl. Before she was killed. It was what she called the boys with the knives."

Rankin shook his head. "No. Not the boys. What they were doing, maybe. *Gembuku* is old Japanese. It means 'manhood ceremony' or something close to that. It meant basically what a boy must do to prove his worthiness, his dedication to his ancestors and the creed of the warrior, the *bushido*. But it never meant wanton slaughter of the sort we saw today, or at least it hasn't for four or five hundred years. The self-mutilation is a new twist—that's not Shinto or *bushido* or anything else from old Japanese custom. Something perhaps from some earlier Chinese cult . . ."

He stopped for a second, lost in thought, then continued. "Regardless, I'd guess that what we saw was an initiation rite of some sort. You said you thought maybe those thugs were drugged—"

"No. At least, I'm not sure. Something else, I think. I felt . . ." Again words failed him. "I felt *something*, a *power* inside that boy I killed. I can't explain it."

Clay heard an intake of breath behind him. "Killed? What the hell happened out there?"

Greene leaned in over Clay's shoulder. "Ask Rankin," he answered. "I'm not quite sure myself."

Rankin grunted. "Some locals on the rampage. Clay killed one who was doing his damnedest to kill him first. Clay thinks the boy was possessed."

Greene looked questioningly at Clay. He shrugged noncommittally.

"Well, let's see if we can at least get on site before we kill any more of the locals, *gembuku* or no. We've a mission to carry through. Drugs, spirits, whatever; what happened back there doesn't have anything to do with us or what we've come here for."

"No argument, Colonel. Probably just imagination working overtime."

Clay leaned back in his seat and closed his eyes, signaling, he hoped, that he had had enough of the conversation. He needed time to think, time to consider what had happened. As the bus moved through the blank, dirty heart of the city, for a fleeting second, he felt again the sensation he had felt looking into the boy's eyes, and for the first time in a very long time he felt a touch of fear.

He wasn't to get the time he hoped for.

A few minutes after Rankin had shifted to another seat, he felt a presence move into the place Rankin had occupied beside him. He opened his eyes and saw Greene's thin face hovering near.

"You okay?" Clay heard genuine concern in her voice.

Clay smiled wanly. "Fine. Takes more than a scuffle with the natives to rattle me."

"I don't doubt that. Still, you looked a little . . . *perturbed* by what happened."

"Perhaps I am. Then again, maybe I'm just getting to be too damned old."

Greene returned his smile. "Not so old. Maybe just a little war-weary." She sighed. "I'm feeling a bit that way myself these days."

"Maybe."

"What was it you told Rankin about a dead girl?"

Clay shook his head. "Nobody. A local kid, maybe fourteen, starved and streetwise, who got her throat cut for no good reason. Nothing important; happens every day in these backward cesspools." Clay was again surprised at the vehemence in his own voice. The girl had gotten to him at a level at which he thought he was no longer vulnerable.

Greene was obviously taken aback. "She meant something to you?"

"No." Clay took a deep breath, drawing on his inner calm. "No. Just a local. It's not something you get used to seeing, I guess."

Greene nodded agreement. "No, that's true enough. On Compson's Planet I saw a school—a hundred children, all ages—after the wolves—that's what the settlers called the local life-form we were there to protect them from—managed to get through a security field and into the classrooms. I almost quit the C.F. then, resigned my commission. That's a memory I'll never lose, no matter how much I might like to. You live with it. You go on."

"Yes, you live with it."

Throughout time that had been the soldier's burden, he thought to himself. Ghosts, guilt. When you stopped feeling, you stopped living, but those feelings damned well could make you miserable in the interim.

Greene stood, swaying slightly with the motion of the bus. She touched his shoulder. "Hang tough, trooper."

The city had no real suburbs; he had seen that from the air. Around the crowded industrial center stretched a wide band of shanty towns made up of open-sewered, thrown-together shacks where those less affluent than even the city workers lived.

At the edge of the band of shantytowns was the jungle. Clay grimly watched the abject faces of the people as the bus passed through the shantytown, faces set against a backdrop of a crazy quilt of plastic panels, packing crates, and grass thatch, the only materials those unfortunates had for shelter. The pungent stench of the open sewers blew in through the open windows of the bus, making his stomach heave.

Then the bus plunged into the cool overgrowth of the forest. The whine and rumble of the turbines grew loud, echoing back from the thick wall of olive-green and blue-gray on either side of the narrow roadway.

The balance of the trip was uneventful. The survey outpost was only about thirty kilometers from the city. It was nevertheless firmly in the thick heart of the wilderness that covered most of Ithavoll's broad northern continent. The bus drew to a halt and settled onto a concrete pad placed before the knot of small buildings around the central dome of the outpost complex.

"All out," Rankin rumbled.

They lifted the gear out and piled it onto servo-carts, which hummed off to wherever Rankin had arranged to have the equipment taken. Clay didn't ask. His pistol was a reassuring weight under his vest; he could let the assault rifle and the rest of his kit out of his sight for a time.

The driver smiled and nodded, and the bus lifted once more with a groan and rushed back toward the city.

There were few personnel around. It was a working day, Clay thought; they're out in the field. Still, the place gave the uncomfortable impression of desertion, the tall jungle trees looming in close to the buildings as if ready to reclaim the clearing.

The team wound as a group through the outbuildings and entered the central dome, passing through a door that gave out the distinctive *chuff* of an air seal as it closed. The itching in his nose, which he had already forgotten to notice, disappeared. Inside, the dome was brightly lighted and the air was wonderfully dry and cool. Clay could feel the sweat that had soaked through his fatigues grow chill and begin to dry.

"Nice," Greene commented, wiping her face dry with a sleeve.

The dome was largely empty, the far wall pierced with closed doors leading off to offices. In the center of the open space was the sort of Plexi tactical board used by battle commanders to plot troop movements. On it was a large-scale holographic topographical map of the northern continent, largely colored in blue, with small sections tinted green. Clay guessed the green sections were those which had already been surveyed and mapped in detail. Around the map board computers hummed, fed by a handful of personnel at data-entry keyboards.

A tall, gray-haired officer—Clay noted that he was a C.F. major—stood from a desk before the map board and held out a hand to Rankin, which Rankin took.

Clay was a little surprised that Rankin didn't come to attention and salute before approaching the desk. Rankin's ostensible rank was captain, and a handshake, whether in the field or on the parade ground, was no way to greet a superior officer.

Which meant the major knew Rankin's true status and probably knew the nature of their mission on Ithavoll. Clay felt a nervous crawling of the skin along his spine. There were too many people involved in this too closely, too many who obviously knew enough to blow what seemed to Clay to be an already shaky cover. Rankin might trust the C.F. and its officers, but Clay did not—far from it.

"Ben," Rankin addressed the major.

"Captain."

Rankin introduced the members of the team.

"Are we sound-clean here?" Fitzgerald asked.

The major nodded. "The dome is checked every morning." He shuffled through the stacks of paperwork on his desk. Finding what he wanted after a moment, he handed a thin sheaf of papers to Rankin.

"Your orders and authorizations. Now you see Qianzhi, the *shikken* in charge of overseeing our operations here. *Shikken* means something on the order of 'regent' or 'eminent consul.' He was given us by the locals to watch over our operation, to get local authorization."

The major pointed to a door in the center of the rear of the dome. He lowered his voice to a whisper. "He's a suspicious bastard but no great shakes. The emperor's people make us keep him around to check on what we do. He's not going to like the province you've been assigned to survey, though it's a good twenty klicks from the area your objective's supposed to be in. But he doesn't really have much choice about authorizing it. If he refused, it would be too obvious they're hiding something up there. By the way, good to see you again, Colonel," he added. "It's been a long time."

Rankin nodded solemnly. "Since Luna. Lost some good friends there. I'm glad to see you're still right in the thick of it."

The major smiled. "Thanks, Colonel. I'm sure Qian's waiting for you. One of his boys doubtless called ahead to say a new field team was on its way."

"Sure." Rankin tucked the papers into a pocket and started for the door.

"Captain!" The major called him back. "He'll want to see the whole team."

Rankin frowned. "Yes?"

"Humor him, if you don't mind. Like I said, he's a suspicious bastard. I think he thinks he can spot a spy just by looking at 'em. Oriental mentality—" He glanced at Clay. "They set a lot of store by signs, the look in a man's eyes, omens and the like."

Rankin grunted in irritation. "Whatever it takes, I suppose. File in, folks."

Clay, Greene, and Fitzgerald followed in single file to the Ithavollan official's door. Rankin tapped lightly, and the door panel slid back.

They entered. The office was large, and unlike the Spartan, utilitarian appointments in the dome behind them, it was decorated in soft earth tones from the walls to the painted screens behind the desk. There were no chairs in the room other than the one occupied by the man behind the desk. Rankin stood to in front of the desk, properly this time, and the rest of the team lined up behind him.

"Captain Ronald Wilson, Combined Forces Survey, sir. I was told we were to see you about clearances for work in the province to which we . . ."

"Yes," the man behind the desk interrupted. "Allow me to see your papers, please."

Rankin took the sheaf of papers from his pocket and placed them in the waiting hand. Clay watched the official scan the authorizations. He was, Clay could see, a small man. Clay guessed he was near middle age, though it was difficult to say with any real confidence. His face was unlined, narrow, and high-cheeked. Dignified. A perturbed look passed quickly over the man's face and then was gone again. He looked impassively up at Rankin, studying the stout Survey Corps captain who stood before him for a long moment.

"We had no indication that this province was to be surveyed so soon."

"I'm sorry, sir. The orders were given to me without my input. If you would care to take up the matter with my superiors . . ."

"No need," he said quickly.

Clay watched his face, caught the faintest hint of furtiveness in his eyes. He didn't like how close their survey area was to an area that C.F. survey personnel couldn't be allowed to snoop around in, Clay thought. He didn't like it one damned bit.

The official glanced beyond Rankin to the members of the team. Clay felt his eyes linger on him for a long moment, and he felt an inexplicable chill run up his spine. Then the man reached suddenly into a drawer of the desk, pulled forth a hand stamp, and quickly stamped the papers with a blue-inked design and held them out to Rankin. "Please restrict your activities to the areas indicated. You may go."

Rankin saluted and turned, and the team followed him from the office. The door panel slid shut behind them.

Rankin glanced back and smiled. "Now comes the hard part."

The major stood as they came out. "Well?" he asked, his voice low.

"We're on."

"Excellent! I'll arrange transport out to the site. After that, you're on your own."

"That's usually the case," Rankin said humorlessly.

The major's face fell a degree.

"No criticism intended, Ben. It's part of the job description. Where can we get some chow?"

The major showed them the mess hall and, after they had eaten, temporary quarters. The entire team bunked in the same room. They filed in, and Rankin closed the door behind them, then took a small, square device from his pocket and placed it on the deck in the center of the room. It suffused the small space with a momentary green glow that shifted to a bright and steady red.

Rankin retrieved the glowing square and walked around the room. At one point the steady red glow changed, flashing an alternating green and red. Rankin took a button-sized object from another pocket—Clay recognized it as a static generator—and placed it against a spot on one wall.

"We can talk."

Clay felt an inexplicable urge to hold up his hand for attention. There was something undefinably professorial about Rankin. He made Clay feel respectful, but not as one did toward a superior officer in the field. More as one might feel toward a knowledge-able history teacher.

"That was a strange little opera we just went through with that Qianzhi fellow. I would have thought any necessary author-izations with the locals would have been taken care of through channels by the C.F."

"Son, that *is* channels here. The political hierarchy of this place is so complex, even they're not certain half the time who is actually responsible for what. They're used to dealing face to face here. If the C.F. wants to send a team somewhere out in their wilderness, the team begs permission of the current lord-high-eminence *in person*. Memos and letters don't go down well here. As Ben said, they believe they can see a man's intentions in his face. From what I've been told, they consider that they're doing us one hell of an honor by allowing us to give their 'em-inent consul,' or whatever he's called, that office in the middle of our complex and anything else his dignified heart desires."

"I see."

Fitzgerald spoke. "The Oriental mentality is very ordered but also too often very slow to adapt. It wasn't until early in the twentieth century that the old country of Japan began to allow the influx of any outside influences. Old ways of doing things have value simply in their age. Much respect here for prece-dence. Even more for dignity, and change too often involves indignities." He glanced at Clay. "Excuse the easy generali-zation."

"No problem," Clay said calmly. He was trying very hard not to become touchy about the second looks and the kid-glove treatment he was getting from all quarters because of his ap-pearance. Race was something that by and large had become a nonissue on the civilized planets. It was something odd and new to be singled out because of the tone of his skin and the shape of his eyes.

"Just so," Rankin said, ignoring the exchange. "Hopefully, that will work in our favor. The 'eminent consul' will be forced to report the fact that we will be working in a sector adjacent to the one in which we believe they've hidden their new toy. There is a good possibility we can be in and through with the job before the information reaches someone with the authority to actually interfere with us. If we'd had 'channels' to work through, there would be a squad of troops out there right now, waiting to escort us through the motions. As it is, we ought to get a certain amount of time unmolested. We aren't actually *in* the area the surveillance satellite placed the weapon in. He won't be suspicious enough of us to put much pressure on his higher-ups; he's probably not really aware of just why that particular handful of sectors should be watched. He'll give us time—there's no dignity in hurry.''

"Should be a milk run, then.'' Greene said it as if it were a statement of fact, but Clay detected a tone of doubt in her voice.

"Any reason it shouldn't be?''

"No. At least nothing concrete. A strange feeling, that's all.'' She shrugged. "That official, Qianzhi—something about him makes me a bit nervous.''

Clay had felt it, too. He said nothing, though. No need to reinforce something as unsubstantial as the chill he had felt in that room with Qianzhi even if Greene shared the feeling. Bad for team morale.

"Got a present for you, Fitzgerald,'' Rankin announced, and nodded to Clay. Clay retrieved the black box from where he had stowed it in his duffel.

Fitzgerald nodded and took it from Clay. "The satellite memory. Good. I'll see what I can do with it.'' He took the box from Clay and set it on the table before him, then began rummaging through his equipment.

After a few minutes he indicated that he was ready. One side of the black box had been opened, and a spaghetti maze of wiring ran from it to the equipment Fitzgerald had set up beside it. Fitzgerald punched a lengthy numerical sequence into an attached keyboard, and after a long moment the screen set into the largest of the devices he was using flickered to life. Clay saw a picture that was confused and ill defined because of distance and the smallness of the screen, but Fitzgerald seemed to have no problem understanding what they were seeing.

"This is the last few seconds recorded before the satellite took the hit. It's in the middle of its pass over the northern continent. That—'' He touched the screen with a fingernail to indicate a tiny dot of light growing brighter in a corner. "—is what we're here for.''

As they watched, the dot of light grew, expanded to nearly

the size of Fitzgerald's nail, then held steady, seeming to throb slightly as it began to cross the screen as the satellite traveled over it. Suddenly the picture on the screen skewed, steadied, then went dark.

"That was the missile taking it down."

"My God, that thing must have been ten kilometers wide," Greene gasped.

"More, I'd say." Fitzgerald went back to the keyboard and made adjustments. "This will give us a lower-angle perspective so we can see a little more dimension. We got quite a bit more from the memory here than we did from the original transmission. The cameras stayed on for a couple of seconds after the impact had taken out the transmission antennae, and the computer can do a bit more with it."

The picture, enhanced by Fitzgerald's computer, twisted so that they were viewing the phenomenon slightly from the side. To Clay, it looked as if a white tornado of light were rising from the jungle. The swirl of light wasn't solid; rather, it was as if the light rose in thin tendrils, pierced by the black of the planet's night. Or almost as if it were a shifting double helix, like a classroom three-D of a strand of DNA projected in pure white light. Then the column of the tornado compacted and spread until it was a thick, pulsing disk. Then the picture skewed and went black.

"What in the hell was that?" Greene asked quietly.

"And how are we supposed to destroy it?" Clay added.

"I can't answer either of you in any definitive way—" Fitzgerald began.

"Doesn't matter what it is," Rankin interrupted, "and I've yet to see the weapon that couldn't be sabotaged with a little plastique."

"What if it isn't a weapon?" Clay pressed.

Rankin waved the question away impatiently. "Of course it's a weapon. A weapon, by definition, is something which is used to attack or defend. Those people on the southern continent would agree, I think, that this thing is a weapon."

"I mean, what if it isn't a *thing*? What if it's something you can't get a charge under?"

"Well, if that's so, then our mission will fail. Regardless, we won't know till we're out there." He turned his attention to

Fitzgerald. "Were you able to get a better idea of the location of that thing's source?"

Fitzgerald nodded. "To within five klicks, I think."

"Good. We start in the morning."

Behind the closed door of the office, Zhou Qianzhi pondered the interview he had conducted with the new Terran survey team. He was perfectly aware of the danger posed by the presence of a Combined Forces survey group in the province he had given them permission to survey.

The Terrans could not be allowed to find *Irin-ri*. The Hidden City must remain hidden. The Hidden One, the God of Peace, the God of War, *Hachiman*, must be allowed his secrecy or he would exact a great and painful retribution.

Qianzhi calmed himself, letting the irritation caused by this new problem flow from him, the tension like drift on a great smooth river. He controlled his breathing, folding his hands loosely over his knees.

The required course of action would be to set in motion the slow machinery that would result in an audience with the emperor and his orders to have the new survey team escorted while working near the province. There were many obvious dangers inherent to that path.

The movement to action would be necessarily slow, and the action itself would too likely be indecisive. Even with *Hachiman* to guide his hand, Shotoku was far from being one of the great warrior emperors who had ruled old Japan with unflinching mercilessness. Terror and bloodshed were necessary tools the present emperor was too loath to use as much as was sometimes needed.

Sensing the blasphemy in the thought, Qianzhi admitted silently to himself that the present emperor was something of a clumsy fool.

Shotoku would be loath to offend the Terran government and its police armies; the United Democracies and Ithavoll were, after all, allies. Yet that hesitancy could endanger plans that had been brought very close to completion through much expense and sacrifice.

And *Hachiman* would not tolerate delays or failure.

A decision was necessary, yet his mind was in turmoil.

He stood suddenly from the desk and pulled back one of the painted paper screens standing before a corner of the room.

On a small table in the corner stood three wooden figures, two of which had graced the personal temples of his father and his father's father before him, in Kyusho, on Terra.

One of the figures was made of a grayish, twisted metal; it was squat and, unlike the others, almost shapeless. Beside the figures stood a small gong and a brazier.

Qianzhi knelt before the small altar, gently placed a small lump of incense as an offering, both to *Hachiman* and for his own ancestors, into the brazier standing near, and lit it. He struck the small gong, closed his eyes, and let his mind clear, flowing into the low tone of the gong, his thoughts focusing, gathering to his center.

He meditated, concentrating on the sublime powers the figures represented. He concentrated on touching the omnipotent mind of *Hachiman*.

A sharp surge of pure pain thrust itself into his mind, illuminating his soul like a flash of lightning. His mind cringed away, and *Hachiman* entered, taking his place in Qianzhi's mind like an emperor taking his throne. Qianzhi quaked in pain and fear.

Hachiman spoke. The pain became the most sublime of ecstasies. Qianzhi writhed on the floor, reveling in his humiliation.

After a time he rose. The decision was made; his way was clear.

He gathered what he needed and left the office through his personal entrance. As his car lurched up and sped down the road toward the city, he reflected that the course he contemplated would eventually require his own suicide. Those of purer blood than his would demand a sacrifice, and he would be the obvious choice. The thought did not disturb his inner tranquillity. He folded his hands and waited.

CHAPTER EIGHT

The room was dim and chill, the only light dropping thinly through a small window at the top of the far wall. Though Clay was cold in his bare skin, he resisted the temptation to search around in the darkness for his fatigues or to find a candle or a torch. The brisk air cleared his head, pushing back the fatigue of first waking.

He took three quick deep breaths and stood from the pile of musty wool quilts that had been his bed, his legs weak and crampy, feeling the hard chill of the stone flooring stealing away the warmth through his bare feet. He pulled aside the blanket that covered the low doorway and looked out across the scrubby, burned-over pasture that separated the hut from the village.

It was about midmorning in the twenty-five-or-so-hour local day, he thought, judging from the quality of the daylight, though it was difficult to tell with any real certainty. Ithavoll's distant but relatively warm sun was simply a brighter patch in the general haze, glowing dimly through the constant thick cloud cover.

Rankin lounged in the weak sunlight outside, spread across a rough-woven blanket, a tall and improbably brown drink balanced on the bulge of his stomach. Rankin gestured to Clay with his near hand.

"Morning, Lieutenant."

"Ugly day," Clay said.

"I've seen worse . . . and better. Though not here. Weather's one of the few constants they've got going for them. Wretched but not unbearable. This part of the planet it's mostly pretty temperate."

Rankin rolled up from the blanket, catching his drink. He set the glass down and pointed out beyond the village, into the wilderness. "No roofs out there, though. And damned little of anything else. You'll learn to like it." He seemed to think about that for a moment. "Or you won't. Doesn't matter; you're here."

Clay nodded. "Altitude made it a bit cooler at Kurama. This isn't half-bad."

He took a deep breath and held it, then released it slowly, the anticipation waking him thoroughly from the last remnants of sleep. He was being paid good money to be here, but it was all the better that, for now at least, there was no real way to leave.

Self-reliance made one sharp—a man was naturally more dependable when he had no choice, no quick out. The survey copter had dropped them in the hinderlands late the previous afternoon and would pick them up in exactly one week, if all went well, outside the same village. That was the plan; there was no changing it.

The team had a radio, but it would doubtless be of little use if they ran into trouble. Terra, at least publicly, kept only a very token military presence on Ithavoll, and that only in the form of civilian security hired as consulate guards. So far as the consulate and the Terran ambassador were concerned, Rankin and his team were personae non grata—they were an official presence only so long as they remained a survey and census team.

If they were captured or killed while in possession of the explosives and other forbidden equipment among their gear, the Terran consulate on Ithavoll would profess a shocked ignorance, and the United Democracies would send an official representative to witness the executions and applaud the swift justice of it all. Through planning and a certain amount of luck, they'd had no real trouble so far. At least not, Clay thought wryly, with concealing the reality of their identity.

Clay sat in the withered grass outside the doorway and leaned back against the hut's mud-stuccoed front wall. "I'm almost afraid to ask where the others are."

Rankin settled back onto the blanket, using a pack that Clay knew held explosives to prop his bulk upright. He pointed with the drink at the village.

"I told them to be back in an hour."

Clay nodded and watched as Rankin took a long pull on his

drink. Fitzgerald and Greene, he understood, were "doing the town," bolstering their cover by playing up the part expected of them by the locals—to all appearances they were just C.F. survey personnel on duty in the native sector, making the best of the lack of supervision.

Rankin finished the dregs of his drink and picked a piece of withered fruit from the glass, which he examined for a moment, then tossed out into the pasture. Clay let his eyes follow the brown wedge until it hit, bouncing once and disappearing into the stubble of whatever crop had been grown and harvested there before they'd burned it over and set the cattle out to graze on the new growth.

"Where did you get that?" Clay pointed to Rankin's empty glass.

Rankin indicated the village again. "That's why I like it here so much. All the nature you can stand and a goodly liquor supply. The natives make it by the barrelfull from, so far as I can tell, rice and a nasty-looking native insect about as long and wide as your thumb, and it's the only thing they aren't stingy with. And all we have to do for the next six weeks is troop through the wilderness counting heads and making maps while making sure the natives haven't gotten restless and hidden strange naughty weapons and such out in the underbrush—and blowing them to kingdom come if they have. To all appearances a factfinding tour, nothing more, nothing less. Been doing it for years. There's even willing native women, I understand, if you don't mind taking the chance of getting your throat cut for a roll in the hay."

Rankin scratched his belly through his shirt. "Keeping up appearances. Terra, ever thorough." He peered at the glass, then tossed it after the fruit.

Clay raised an eyebrow. The liquor the natives were giving away so freely must be potent indeed. Rankin had been friendly enough in the week and a half since Clay had joined the assault team, but he'd been reserved, acting the part of the aloof but cordial senior officer. The new flamboyancy seemed out of character.

"I take it you like your work, carrying forth the C.F. cause into unsubdued lands. And not just because it pays well." Clay realized even as he asked it that the question was unabashedly barbed.

Well, take it as he will, he thought. He must be aware of what the Combined Forces have become.

Rankin looked thoughtfully at the weathered stone wall of the hut they had been given by the locals. It was set off from the others by a good hundred meters of fallow pasture, and Clay suspected it had been built either as some sort of quarantine hut or expressly for the purpose of housing Terrans. It was a rank little place, thick with the smell of stale sweat and the grease candles the locals used for lighting in the buildings that hadn't been equipped with electricity or the cold chemical light that the survey parties favored.

"I follow orders whether I like 'em or not. It's my job, I do it. Beats listening to my wife every night—or overeducated and underemployed civilians complaining on the vid about the inadequacy of the public dole. These folks don't like us much—" He gestured to take in the bulk of the village. "—but at least they don't talk you to death."

He had avoided the direct question, but Clay let it pass. If Rankin wanted the conversation innocuous, then Clay was willing to follow his lead. "You're married? You don't seem the sort."

"Nothing wrong with being married, son, so long as you remember vows aren't legally binding anymore. Intelligent people take the best it offers and don't worry too much about antiquities like fidelity and ownership. The rest of the population should stay shut of it; too many of them muck it up and color the institution in a bad way. Makes it unpleasant for the rest of us."

"I suppose that's where I stand, among the ignorant that are better off without it." Clay pushed himself up and stood with a groan. He was beginning to feel old.

"I'm as stiff as army coffee. I need a stretch." He moved to the side of the hut and ran through a series of calisthenic and aerobic exercises, feeling the muscles begin to warm and loosen, the blood pumping through his arms and legs slowly but surely invigorating him. When he was young, ten minutes a day had sufficed. Now he spent a half hour working the kinks and aches out.

This tour, he thought, and maybe I'll quit, retire to some backwater on one of the Territory Worlds, far from the Combined Forces, find an ignorant farmer's daughter for a wife and raise a litter of noisy kids.

He grinned to himself at the picture that thought evoked. Then again, maybe he wouldn't do anything of the sort.

The specter of that sort of stagnation was the primary reason, despite what he had told Rankin, that he hadn't allowed himself attachments in the past. There was a certain appeal to domesticity, but it had always been very secondary to his need for novelty, for freedom of action.

One of the primary attractions of his profession was that on the underpopulated and largely unexplored Territory Worlds there was to be found if not adventure per se, at least a certain amount of the exotica that could no longer be found on Terra or the more settled worlds in this age of more or less instant and universal transportation.

Some obscure outer world might give him enough variety to keep him interested in living and enough peace to make it comfortable, but even so, he wasn't ready for a wife and family—not yet.

Variety and peace. Even in the wide expanse of the inhabited universe, it was a rare combination. Of the forty-eight known inhabitable worlds, only ten were Terran protectorates. Those planets were peaceful but to Clay's mind overcivilized. A truly peaceful society was one that chose to be that way. Peace at the end of a leash was only outward peace.

The other worlds inhabited by humans belonged to the people who had settled them a century before Clay had been born, in the first years after it had been discovered that flinging an object into any handy pulsar would cause the same object to appear, only slightly distorted by the instant's exposure to rapidly changing gravities, in another place, ejected by another pulsar—or, rather, as the theoretical physicists contended, by the *same* pulsar, which just happened to be in two or more places at the same time. Which sounded rather unlikely to Clay, but he couldn't deny that it had worked so far as interstellar travel was concerned for more than a hundred years.

That process had caused untold headaches for the physicists, who for the most part couldn't accept the thing called simultaneity and made a tragedy of one of the few noble accomplishments of the fragmented governments of the previous century, a near-light-speed colonizing expedition begun ten years before the discovery of the pulsar jump.

When the colonists arrived, after a subjective flight of only a few years, they would find a planetary system overrun with the bureaucracy and population of several hundred years, compliments of relativity and a couple of invisible radio sources.

It was the sort of irony Clay could appreciate. There was also a certain inherent futility in being a soldier for hire, fighting battles for causes that inevitably lasted no longer than the cause they replaced.

But then, Clay thought, at least I get paid.

Rankin stood from his blanket with a groan and stooped to pull on his boots. "I suppose I'll go find the others and we can get this show on the road. Check those packs, if you will, make sure everything's stowed as it should be." In a lower voice he said, "And unlimber your weapon. Out here, better safe than sorry."

"Sure." He watched Rankin stride off toward the stone, mud, and thatch of the village proper.

Just as Rankin was midway through the pasture, Clay saw a movement against one of the nearer huts of the village and realized it was a small figure, possibly a woman, who had been watching them from a doorway. He squinted, but she, he, or it was gone, absorbed into the gray facelessness of the village. It disturbed him, though realistically there was little in the way of threat in the villager's actions.

Just curiosity, he thought, nothing more. He shrugged and forgot it. He stooped and went into the hut, leaving behind the small trace of unease, stepping into the cramped building's dark and airless heart.

While Rankin was gone, he inspected the gear, especially the satchel of plastique that Rankin had been leaning against, and prepared to move out in the countryside.

When the packs were arranged to his satisfaction, he saw to his own equipment, clearing the assault rifle, working the bolt to bring a cartridge up from the clip into the chamber, checking the safety.

The rifle was a reassuring weight in his hands. It was one of the best-made conventional weapons available, and he felt the smallest tinge of pride in the fact that it was of Terran manufacture. One thing that still seemed to be built with a certain amount of care was weaponry.

The rifle was Israeli; it fired a ten-millimeter caseless round and was recoilless, made for heavy desert use, built entirely of high-density plastics. There was very little about it that suggested the traditional rifle form of old-style weapons like Rankin's carbine and the rifle the guard on the bus had carried.

It was relatively short, the chamber and all but the muzzle of the barrel recessed into the blunt oblong that was the weapon's stock. Where the barrel of Rankin's carbine was thin and round, projecting out from the action like a blunt steel rod, the assault rifle was a simple modular unit without a distinctive projecting barrel, its barrel and action contained in a slim hard plastic casing from which a grip and trigger housing projected.

At the top of the plastic casing a range-finding scope was mounted. Looking through it, he could clearly see objects several hundred meters distant, and the range finder would accurately compute the distance to the target so he could adjust the weapon's elevation to compensate for the trajectory of a fired round.

A heavy silencer, a third again the length of the rifle, was mounted from the muzzle end of the weapon. The long silencer made the weapon barrel-heavy, and he swung it to his shoulder and picked up several targets in the range finder, testing its weight. Against his shoulder the rifle felt comfortable and balanced. All in all, it was an efficient and rather awesome example of the weaponeer's craft.

Rock and roll, he thought.

A megawatt laser might clear a wide path through a battalion or a wall, but the assault rifle's one-hundred-grain explosive slugs would be more than adequate in a routine firefight or against any of Ithavoll's nastier native life-forms. And he carried at least twenty kilos less than a Combined Forces infantryman would.

And slow-moving objects made great targets, even for natives with rocks and slingshots. The Forces, he reflected, were masters of inefficiency through excess.

The Combined Forces had been allowed, wisely, Clay

thought, to atrophy after the last Russo/American–Luna conflict some twenty years before, but it was still the major power in the known universe, and its generals were more the rulers on Terra and its territories than was the largely impotent United Nations government that had, in theory at least, consolidated the different nationalistic governments of Earth when it had become necessary to show a reasonable united front to the rebelling lunar colonies.

Now, twenty years after the heyday of its powers, the C.F. accomplished its goals more through covert "adjustments" of the type that Clay now found himself involved with than by overt military means.

It was secrecy, Clay reflected, that inevitably signaled the decline of any organized government. When a group's activities became too arbitrary or too destructive to meet general approval, it was only a matter of time until a different—though not necessarily better—organization replaced it.

In the United Democracies' case it would be a little-mourned loss, Clay thought.

But for now the U.D., or rather its Combined Forces, had contracted his services, and as with any client, for the duration of the project they had his loyalty, at least to the point at which the C.F., or, as with the case of the officer Clay had killed, one of its operatives, violated what he considered right—though "right" by his definition was not necessarily synonymous with "peaceful" or "just."

When Rankin returned with Greene and Fitzgerald in tow, they loaded the packs and equipment onto each other's backs, strapping the material onto pack frames. Clay slung Greene's pack up onto her back for her and received a quick grunt of thanks.

When he had been loaded with his share, Clay felt awkward but not overly burdened. Each of the pack frames weighed less than a kilo, and with the full weight of the goods Clay was carrying, it still weighed less than fifty, as almost all of the equipment, both the survey instruments that they carried to support their cover and the other weapons and such that went with their true mission, were made of extremely lightweight alloys and polymers.

Rankin, though carrying less bulk, was actually burdened

with more weight, as he had taken the heavy satchel of plastique as part of his lot.

Still, Clay felt less than ready for any quick action, and it made him feel vulnerable. But, he thought, there was nothing for it. He compromised with the awkwardness by keeping his assault rifle balanced across his forearm as they started out, walking single file down the worn extruded-plastic road that led generally west from the little village in which they had spent the night.

The uselessness of land vehicles in the continent's interior was made quickly apparent when, after about four kilometers, the plastic road surface gave way to dirt and the dirt road itself, after another six kilometers, petered out into side-by-side wagon ruts that themselves ended at a stream, continuing on only as a foot trail on the other side.

Greene stood by the stream, eyeing the narrow path ahead critically. "Where the hell is the road?"

"And why the hell are we going through that—" Clay gestured at the woven thickness of the jungle into which the trail disappeared. "—instead of using a copter or some sort of ground-effect hopper?"

The individual villages are more or less autonomous," Rankin explained. "Whatever commerce they do, they do by air shuttle. The woods are so thick, we'd miss a number of the smaller settlements if we traveled by air, and I'll wager there's not a ground-effect–type vehicle within a thousand klicks of here. No decent roads for it if there were. A survey party would have to walk it in order to do their job. So we walk. Less prone to miss anything of significance, anyway."

Still, Clay thought as they trudged up the trail, climbing steadily up into a series of heavily jungled foothills as they did so, a horse or some equivalent at least would have been a great convenience.

When Ithavoll had first been settled, he had been told, equines had been brought along, but their systems had produced insufficient enzymes of some sort for dealing with the local flora on which they had to graze, and they had failed to thrive. The closest that Ithavoll had to horses were the hybrid bovines that Clay had watched grazing in the field next to the stone hut. The beasts were adaptable to almost any sort of fodder, were acceptable food animals, and would pull a plow but were not suited temperamentally to be of much use to anyone as saddle animals.

So they walked, a not too unbearable hardship, Clay thought, but damned inconvenient nonetheless.

As he walked, he reviewed in his mind the mission as Rankin had outlined it aboard the portal-ship on the jump to Vega, Ithavoll's system.

Rankin's plan of action was simple: The team would play out the role of census and survey that they had taken as cover, moving from village to village, stopping at homesteads and squatters' settlements along the way.

After a reasonable amount of time they would go about the search more directly, dividing the area Fitzgerald had pinpointed into a grid of which each member of the team would take a sector to cover by foot until whatever was hidden out there was found and destroyed by whoever found it.

And if one member of the team failed to show at a preselected rendezvous, the other three would know with an ominous certainty in which sector the Emperor Shotoku had concealed his weapon.

If the search took longer than a week, they would radio ahead to hold back the copter, staying in the field until the objective was found.

But much more than two weeks, Clay thought, and I'll manage to make my own way back, even if I have to borrow some local chieftain's beaten-up cargo copter. He had agreed to a month; that was what they would get.

As the trail steepened, Clay was surprised at Rankin's agility. They kept a brisk pace even in the stretches where the trail inclined steeply enough that they had to grasp roots and branches to pull themselves forward, and Rankin showed no signs of fatigue or of slowing up.

Clay was forced to reevaluate his estimation of the older man's physical capabilities. Not only was the going rough, Ithavoll's gravity was about five percent higher than Earth standard, and even Clay, at least ten years younger and arguably a better candidate for the sort of climbing they were having to do, was feeling the strain. There was more to Rankin, he had to admit, than met the eye.

The trail rose, but the terrain was not particularly broken—yet—and Clay had time to look about at the countryside. The part of the planet they were hiking through was reminiscent, Clay thought, of the parts of the Tennessee Smoky Mountains back on Terra on one of the good days, when in the early morning the skies were clear and the air smelled clean—at least those parts that hadn't yet fallen prey to industrial development and the swarming population's need for housing.

The forest that loomed up on either side of the trail was thicker than the southern pine and kudzu of Tennessee, and though the trees were tall and straight like southern pines, they were broadleaved, with rough, broken bark the color of modeling clay, muddy gray and veined with brown. Roughly a meter back from the bases of the first trees next to the trail, the real jungle began in the thick viny undergrowth.

At one point Greene touched his arm and pointed upward and to the right of the trail. A great bird, its wings spread to support it on the thermal currents that rose from the hills, glided into sight above the tops of the trees. Clay guessed it was roughly twice as large as the models of the extinct eagles he had seen in museums. He was awed for a moment at its huge grace as it banked smoothly away.

Greene smiled. "Some bird."

"Beautiful," Clay admitted. He looked again where it had disappeared behind the trees.

"The locals call them *munin*. They're a lot like the pterodactyls of ancient Earth. Small brain, lots of wingspan, and a tail that's a continuation of the backbone instead of tailfeathers. Carnivorous, though they don't turn their noses up at carrion." She smiled again, damned prettily, he thought, shrugged her pack up a bit higher on her shoulders, and turned back to the trail.

Clay reminded himself that she was as much a professional as he and had probably killed as many men.

Still, he thought, she was appealing despite the muscle. Or, in a way, because of it. He had never cared for what Terran society considered the model for female appearance or demeanor. Soft, silly, and dependent didn't strike him as particularly appealing.

It was twilight before they reached the first camp, descending into a small valley to a squatters' village beside a river. They found a clear space away from the stench of the settlement's open sewers and set up camp.

Clay inflated his pup tent, stowed his weapon and his equipment inside, then walked with Greene down to the river, where they washed themselves and filled the water bags that had been emptied on the hike.

They did this upstream from the settlement, but Clay was still glad that the linings of the water bags contained a chemical that sterilized and purified the water. More than once he had suffered the machinations of some alien bacteria, and several times he had been deathly ill before the antibiotics had conquered whatever bug he had managed to pick up.

The water was cold with snow melt and reasonably clear, flowing down from the mountains. Clay stripped and eased into the crisp, biting current, letting the cold water wash off the combined filth of the city and the sweat of the day's march. After scrubbing himself vigorously with fistfulls of sand, he swam hard across the river and back, fighting his way against the current back to where Greene waited, filling the last of the bags.

Greene tossed the water bag up on the bank. "How's the water?"

"Cold as space." Clay floated, making only enough effort to keep the current from pushing him downstream. "It's invigorating. You ought to give it a try."

"Don't mind if I do." Greene stripped quickly, shrugging off her fatigues, and Clay was struck again by how shapely she was despite the well-defined muscle that rippled as she pulled off her fatigue blouse. She dived from the bank into the clear water and struck off for the opposite shore. She's a soldier, hard as nails, Clay reminded himself. But it was easy to forget that fact.

Green swam back against the current and floated beside him, barely resisting the current.

"What in the hell made you want to be a soldier, Greene?" Clay knew it was a question he shouldn't have asked. The code was much the same for soldiers for hire as it was for thieves—pasts were not open for discussion. Still, suddenly he felt the need to know. He expected Greene to tell him to go to hell and mind his own damned business.

Instead, Greene stopped floating, let her feet drop in the current, and stood in the waist-deep water. Clay felt the old, familiar—though long enough denied to be nearly forgotten—stirrings of desire and repressed them. It was not the time or the place.

"Damned if I know," she said simply. "It pays the bills. What about yourself?"

"Because it's what I'm good at, what I do best."

She pulled herself up out of the water, shook herself off like a lioness shaking off rain—at the same time sending a thrill through Clay's gut that felt as if someone had reached in and caressed something vital—and began to dress. She knew he was watching, and was obviously enjoying the attention.

"A vocation."

He nodded, watching her pull on her blouse. She flashed him a white-toothed smile. "It'd be a sin to deny a talent, now, wouldn't it?"

"Amen," Clay answered, grinning. "A sin, indeed."

Dressed again, she looked down at him from the bank and frowned, her face darkening. "I think the real reason I do it is because in battle you find the truest men—and women. The ones who don't have it inside scrub out or run. The rest are the only beings in this universe I would care to die with."

"Maybe that's what it boils down to for all of us," Clay said, and let his toes dig into the firm clean sand of the river's bottom. " 'The camaraderie of the damned,' I think they used to say of the old French Foreign Legion. Maybe you can only truly love someone who is ready to die fighting beside you. Or someone who is ready to die fighting against you."

"True enough, soldier," Green said, gathering the water bags. "True enough."

They returned with the dim sun setting behind them to find Rankin and Fitzgerald sprawled comfortably before a fire.

"Sit," Rankin said amiably. Clay complied, though a bit hesitantly. There were eyes in the night, all around, watching the men at the fire.

Rankin anticipated Clay's question. "Not much of interest usually happens at a squatters' camp. We're tonight's entertainment."

"Should we post guard?" Greene asked.

It was Fitzgerald who answered, his voice low. "No need.

They won't touch us. It would be a good idea, though, to secure anything you don't want spirited away while you sleep. If it's not tied down, they'll steal it.''

Clay nodded. ''They're not really an inherently violent people. Their leader is an exception, and they tend to be a faithful bunch, even these disowned wretches. They'll do as the emperor's people tell them, but up to that point we're just a free show. Just another bunch of nosy off-worlders asking how many babies they've had.''

Rankin grunted. ''Fitzgerald's right, however. These folks aren't quite as noble and honest as the herdsmen of the southern steppes that you're used to—hunger makes for a certain desperation. Button everything up in the tents with you while you sleep.''

He lowered his voice so that it carried no farther than the four of them. ''And for god's sake, keep one eye open even then. We can't afford to have some hungry fool ransacking through our gear and finding explosives and the like.''

Rankin rummaged in his personal gear for a moment and came back to the fire with a small leather flask. He uncorked it and passed it around. Fitzgerald took a long swallow and passed the flask to Clay. Clay tilted his head back and swallowed, the liquid burning down his throat.

''Damn!'' he said, and Rankin grinned hugely.

''Not Kentucky bourbon but not too damned bad, either. Terra could learn something from these local bootleggers' bathtub distilleries.''

Clay offered the flask to Greene, and she waved it off. ''No thanks. I tried it this morning. I'd rather drink cleaning fluid.''

They passed the bottle around a few more times, then secured the camp and settled into the tents. The liquor had made Clay drowsy, and he drifted off quickly, but he slept uneasily, dark faces outlined by firelight flickering in his dreams.

CHAPTER NINE

*Clay woke suddenly, disoriented. He reached instinctively be-*hind his head, drew the pistol that he'd left loaded and cocked under the change of uniform that he was using for a pillow, and flipped off its safety with his thumb. He shook his head to clear away the cobwebs, then lay back again and listened for the sound that had wakened him. He heard it again, low and far away, though it had seemed close in his dream just before he had awakened.

He pulled on his fatigues and boots and slipped out of the tent. The night was cool and humid, the fire had burned down to coals, and the audience of indistinct faces was gone. Clay looked around.

The other three tents were still sealed against the wet night air. The sound hadn't awakened the others, then. He heard it again, a sound low and tremulous, like a sustained note from a pipe organ.

He holstered his pistol and ducked back into the cramped interior of the tent. He pulled the assault rifle out and sealed the flap, then loaded the weapon and slipped an extra clip into a pocket of his fatigues. He took a step toward the sound, then stopped, knelt by the dead fire, and scooped a handful of cold ash from the edge. He smeared the black, damp ash across his forehead and cheeks and the backs of his hands. When he had finished, he rubbed his hands on his pants leg and hung the rifle muzzle down across his shoulders by its strap.

He waited, listening for the sound, and when it came again, he padded out into the darkness toward its source.

As he stepped into the cover of the forest, even the thin light from the sliver of moon was lost, and he walked in a thick tangible darkness, stopping now and again to orient himself by the pealing note.

The ground there was reasonably flat, though, and he made good time, sprinting across the cleared and plowed fields where the moonlight gave him some idea of the footing. Though Ithavoll had two moons, one rose during the day through this time in the planet's year, and the second was reaching the end of its period, faded to a narrow crescent. In a few nights, he knew, it would be nearly impossible to travel after sunset without lights across the broken and treacherous ground they'd be covering. It wasn't a thought that cheered him. A man with a torch in his hand was the easiest possible target.

Almost a kilometer downriver from the squatters' settlement he found what he was looking for. There was a flickering of torches near the river's bank, a murmuring of voices. He moved cautiously toward the place, running at a crouch through an outlying field and ducking into the dense cover of a thicket of trees.

As he approached, moving cautiously through the tangled underbrush, he could see by the light of torches that there were some two or three hundred people, probably the entire population of the squatter's settlement, gathered around something hidden from view in an area cleared of the trees and undergrowth of the forest but not plowed or planted.

He approached quietly to within twenty meters of the edge of the crowd but still couldn't make out what it was that they had come that far from the settlement in the middle of the night to watch or take part in. Too little light, too many bodies milling in the flicker of torches.

He stood fully upright and strained to see as the crowd surged forward for a moment with a collective gasp and mutter. The sound came again, so close that Clay started, a loud moaning note on some sort of instrument; then he spotted its source, an elderly villager who held in his hands what looked to be a large snail shell. Each time the crowd surged, he held it to his mouth and blew a single mournful note for a long moment until whatever it was that held the crowd's attention ceased or slowed.

Clay tightened the rifle's strap so that it wouldn't bang or rattle and pulled himself up into the lower branches of one of the tall, straight trees. He felt around the tree and discovered that the branches were in groups, farther apart than he was tall. He had to shinny up to the next group, the rough bark crumbling between his knees as he pushed. He took hold of the lowest of the next grouping of limbs and swung his leg up over its neighbor, pulling himself higher.

He climbed as high as the third set of limbs, then wedged himself in the space where a limb met the trunk and looked out over the crowd of squatters.

They were gathered around a shallow dirt-sided pit in which there were three men, one already dead, Clay guessed, sprawled to one side in a bloody heap. The other two men were fighting, each with a knife or short sword that Clay estimated to be easily three-quarters of a meter long, slashing and feinting at each other. The men fought wordlessly, the only sounds the grunts of effort and the clash of metal. Each was clothed only in a breechclout.

As Clay watched, one of the men lunged and slashed up at the other's midsection, wounding him slightly, opening a thin gash across his belly. The watching crowd surged forward, the spectators in front pushed by those behind seeking a better view, and the old man blew his horn. Clay noted that each man had already been wounded several times; one man was favoring his side where a deep slash bled profusely.

Clay watched for a few minutes more. The men were evenly matched, but the one with the wound in his side was losing enough blood that he would weaken quickly.

The men fighting knew this, too, Clay thought. The stronger one was not pressing the battle, only harrying his opponent with occasional attacks meant more to tire than to injure. And the weaker was doing his best to protect himself from the quick attacks.

He is getting desperate, though, Clay thought. It will end soon.

Suddenly the wounded man feinted low, then threw his shoulder into his opponent as the other man parried, throwing him off balance.

The move might have worked, Clay mused, if he'd had the strength to carry it off.

As it was, the stronger man reeled backward from the blow but didn't fall. He caught the blade meant for his heart on his forearm and twisted it away, then moved under and disemboweled the other with a short twisting thrust of his long-knife.

The crowd roared frantically, and Clay thought they would surge into the ring, but they held their ground at the edge as the victor grasped his dying opponent by the hair and tilted his head back. Then, with the keen, sharpened edge of the long-knife, he sawed at the man's neck until the head was free. He held it high, the blood running in rivulets down his arm and across his chest, mingling with the blood from his own wounds.

He tilted back his head and shouted one word that resounded above the chaotic roar of the crowd. The sound sent a curious thrill down Clay's spine, making the hair on the back of his neck stand up.

"Hachiman!" the warrior below shouted again, turning slowly to display his prize.

The crowd roared its blood lust, and Clay felt his gorge rise into this throat. The sensation he had felt at hearing the warrior's shout faded and was replaced with simple repugnance. He had seen many things in the past that were more atrocious, but he had yet to become inured to the mutilation of the vanquished or to the mob mentality that delighted in it. When a man had died honorably in battle, his remains deserved the respect accorded any warrior.

The crowd lifted the victor and his bloody trophy to its shoulders and carried them off into the night in the direction of the squatters' settlement. The bodies of the dead were left as they lay.

Clay waited for the few hangers-on to clear out before he left the tree, then he climbed gingerly down and unstrapped the rifle. He checked to make sure it was loaded and ready to fire, then walked carefully to the arena.

It was largely dark around the pit, the crowd having taken most of the torches that had lighted the combat with them, but there was enough light that Clay could see the two corpses in the arena. He walked around its perimeter looking for clues as to the purpose of the contest but found none. Sport, he supposed. There were worse things done in the universe in the name of entertainment.

He heard a stone roll in the darkness behind him and whirled. A black form rushed out at him from the inky blackness beyond the light of the remaining torches, a sword held high for a stroke that would have decapitated Clay.

With desperate speed, Clay swung up the assault rifle to block the long blade that strove to reach his throat, the force of the blow hacking a fingerlong sliver of plastic from the rifle's butt.

His first attack stymied, the attacker took a quick half step back—not enough for Clay to bring the rifle to bear—and slashed at Clay again. Clay caught the blade with the rifle's long silencer and forced it down, then in the same movement brought the butt swiftly up and clubbed the attacker with it under the chin, making his teeth snap together with a dry, chipping click and making him stagger. As he stepped back, Clay swung the rifle again and smashed the strong plastic stock against the man's head.

The man stumbled and fell to his knees. Clay trained the rifle on him, then stopped without firing.

He dropped the rifle, stepped behind the black-clothed figure and brought his forearm across his assailant's throat, then twisted the head sharply to the side. The man's neck broke with a crack of ruptured bone, and he jerked once and went limp. As Clay released him, his body slid loosely over the rim into the fighting pit, sand and small stones cascading down with him.

Clay caught his breath, then retrieved his rifle. He fought back the adrenaline panic and forced his hands to loosen their knuckle-whitening grip on the rifle.

He considered for a moment simply leaving the body, letting it rest in the darkness with the other two in the pit, but someone was bound to find it soon after sunrise and wonder why he had been killed and by whom. Clay slung the rifle once again across his shoulders and eased over the crumbling edge into the pit.

The darkness in the arena was thick and tangible, and Clay stood at the bottom for a long moment, allowing his eyes to adjust to the deep shadow.

Vaguely, he could see the three forms that lay on the floor of the arena, one headless. He went to the nearest one, the one he had killed, and, squatting, lifted him up. The man smelled rank and unwashed, and his body was slippery with sweat. Clay faced the pit's side and heaved, throwing the limp form up and onto the ground above; then he followed it out, scrambling for foot-

and handholds in the loose gravel and sand of the pit's steep sides.

Once he had pulled himself over the edge, he stood, panting for breath, over the body. He thought for a moment, then knelt and quickly searched the inert form. He found a knife and a pouch of something he imagined to be either tobacco or some native herb—probably hallucinogenic—and nothing else.

Something gleamed in the dim moonlight on the dead man's breast, and Clay pulled back the loose shirt and touched the object. It was strangely cold despite the heat of the still warm body, metallic and indistinct to his touch. He hesitated, then, almost despite himself, he drew his knife and cut the leather cord that held the thing, then slipped it into a pocket.

Clay grasped the body by its feet and dragged it quickly to the river's edge, then rolled it down the shallow bank into the water. He waded out into the chill water, pushing the barely floating body ahead until he felt the pull of the current, then shoved it out into midstream and watched it wheel away from him downstream into the darkness.

He washed his hands and face in the river water, not pausing to worry that he was standing in the polluted water downstream from the settlement. When he felt reasonably clean again, he started up the embankment, then dropped flat as he heard a sound near the pit.

He cursed his luck under his breath, then eased up on his elbows and looked out. In the light of the one torch that remained burning he saw one of the great birds he and Greene had watched that morning hop from the pit's edge down into its depths.

Just cleaning up the mess, Clay thought. Two more of the birds alighted beside the pit and folded their wings. From the pit he could hear the first of the birds—the name Greene had given them came back to him suddenly: *munin*—thrash around, beating its wings to give it leverage as it began its grisly meal.

Clay pushed himself up and brushed off the sand. Upriver he could see the lights in the settlement, and faintly, he thought, he could hear the voices of the crowd. He oriented himself and turned to walk into the brush.

The two carrion eaters beside the pit squawked suddenly and rose up, flapping their broad wings furiously. Clay began to turn, then felt the wire loop of a garrote fall across his throat. In the instant before his new assailant could pull the noose tight, he shoved his open hand between the wire and his Adam's apple.

I didn't even hear a sound! Clay thought with panicked amazement.

The noose snapped tight, and Clay could hear the man behind him grunt with the effort of pulling the garrote tight. The wire sliced a thin burning line across the palm of his hand and the sides of his neck. The wire twisted as the pressure increased, and he began to choke.

Clay fell to one knee, bringing his assailant up close against him, and thrust back hard with the elbow of his free arm into the man's ribs. The man barked with pain and fell but without losing his grip on the garrote's handles. Clay felt himself being dragged down by the throat, then rolled suddenly over, face-down in the grit and dirt.

The man coughed and cursed and pushed himself up until he was sitting in the center of Clay's back. The pressure on the noose increased once again, the wire slicing into Clay's trapped hand, forcing his knuckles into his esophagus and shutting off his air.

Clay strained for breath and could draw none. He gagged and clawed desperately up with his free hand, but his attacker was beyond his reach. The man jerked the noose tighter.

As he felt consciousness begin to fade from him, a surge of heat seared across his back and his eyes burned in a sun-bright flash of light. The weight on his back jerked and fell away, the noose loosening suddenly from his closed-off throat, letting his lungs fill convulsively with the sweet, wet night air.

He gasped, drawing in air in ragged gasps. His head spun, and he smelled the sweet-sick odor of burnt flesh and cloth mixed with the rancid sweat smell of the man who had been strangling him. He pulled at the loosened garrote, tried to rise, and passed out.

He awoke a moment later flat on his back, staring up into a narrow face smeared with ash.

"Greene?"

"Yeah. Are you all right?" she whispered. Her intent face looked strangely comical staring down at him from above, the ash smeared across her cheeks, nose, and forehead startlingly like the war paint in museum pictures of Indian warriors.

Clay forced a grin. "Yes. And damn glad to see you."

It was a true effort to speak. His voice croaked hoarsely up from his battered throat. He turned his head and peered in the darkness at the still-smoking heaped silhouette that had been his assailant.

Greene straightened and settled the heavy laser rifle across her forearm.

"Easy shot. He was too busy to notice me. I got up to about a dozen meters and took him out." She patted the infrared spotter's scope mounted on the rifle's upper receiver.

Clay coughed and sat up. "Well, I'm glad you took your time and got it right. That damn thing is hot." He could still feel the scorch across his back through his fatigues like a mild sunburn.

He took several deep breaths and rolled painfully to his feet. He touched his throat gingerly, then studied the deep slash across his hand as carefully as possible in the dim light. He flexed the hand, made a fist. The wound burned like the devil, and his hand was already beginning to stiffen somewhat, but the tendons were intact. It was still usable.

"Let's get this grubby bastard into the river," he whispered hoarsely. He grabbed the dead villager's feet and began to tug him toward the river's bank.

Greene watched while he pulled and tugged the corpse to the water, scanning the surrounding trees through the night scope. When the river's current took hold of the second body, wheeling it away in the concealing darkness, Clay dragged himself from the water and used a branch to smooth out the evidence of the two bodies' passage through the sand. When he had finished, he tossed that into the river, too.

"What the hell were you doing out here?" Greene whispered to him when he walked up.

"Long story. I'll tell you when I tell Rankin and save myself the breath," Clay answered dryly.

"Soldier, you're going to get us all killed with this gung-ho bullshit."

"Maybe. We'll find out soon enough."

Greene stared at him quizzically, then jerked her head in the direction of the camp. ''Well, let's get the hell out of here, then.''

Clay nodded and gathered up his rifle. Greene turned and wordlessly jogged into the thick darkness beneath the trees. Clay followed behind, his mind working.

CHAPTER TEN

Clay climbed quietly into his tent, watched Greene disappear into her own, then sealed the door flap and tapped the glowbar embedded in the material of the tent's ceiling twice, turning it on.

Under the thin greenish light he treated his wounded hand with antibiotics and a quick-healing salve and bound it with a strip of gauze. He gritted his teeth and flexed it, making a half fist. With the drugs, the hand would be for the most part healed in a day.

When that was done, he tore down the assault rifle and cleaned it, then checked the handgun and slipped it back under his make-shift pillow. The burn and itch of his healing hand were annoying, but he ignored them and tried to sleep, the noise of the insects outside in the bush rising in the darkness as loud as a scream.

Clay slept fitfully. In the morning he told Rankin what he had seen.

Rankin pursed his lips and looked puzzled, then looked annoyed. ''You shouldn't be running around out in the wilderness by yourself, John. Not good business and damned poor public relations, you killing two of the locals—though I'll grant that it was probably the best thing you could have done under the circumstances.''

Clay didn't object that it was the only thing he could have done under the circumstances. He also saw no need to mention that Greene had burned one of the two villagers. If she wanted him to know she had been in on his foray the night before, she would tell him.

Rankin turned on Greene as if he had read Clay's mind. ''Well, soldier, what was your part in this?''

Greene shrugged. ''I heard a noise, saw the lieutenant here fade into the woods, and trailed him out to see what he was up to. I lost him once—it was darker than Hades out there—and by the time I caught up, a local had him wrapped up pretty good. I lent a hand.''

Clay smiled at her wryly. One hell of a hand. He made a mental note to repay her, if possible, before the detail was finished and to look her up next time he had to put together a mercenary assault team. She was a hell of a warrior, and a fighter one could trust was a precious commodity.

''Neither of you saw fit to let Fitzgerald or myself in on the fun?''

''I didn't think it would take more than one of us to take a look. As it is, I don't think we all could've climbed that tree.'' Despite himself, he glanced meaningfully at Rankin's paunch.

''Eh? Don't worry, I'll take care of any trees I need to climb.'' His face screwed up in thought, and he stared intently at the ground. ''If what you're telling me about is what I think, it's a bit worrisome but not necessarily dangerous to the mission.'' Rankin closed his eyes and rubbed a hand across his face as if calling forth a dimmed memory. ''John, you've served here before.''

Clay nodded.

''On that tour, did you happen to hear anything about a group of men, of warriors, ghosts, whatever, that the locals call the *yamabushi*?''

Clay nodded again. ''The mountain warriors. Ghosts that come and go without being seen, leaving death behind. Campfire stories.''

Rankin shook his head. ''More than that, and less, too.'' He stood up. ''Hold on a minute.'' He went to his tent, pulled out his personal kit, and rummaged through it as he'd done the night before for the liquor. This time he drew forth a thick book. Clay marveled to himself that the older man had brought such a heavy item along. Rankin sat and flipped through the volume, searching.

Clay frowned. "What have you got there?"

Rankin looked up for a second. "Ancient history. The Japanese of Old Terra, back even before anyone thought of calling North America the United States. The people of the island of Japan, in some part these folks' distant ancestors, by the way—" He nodded toward the crowd of villagers that had returned with the morning. "—were a vicious lot, good fighters. It always pays to know something of the background of the people that you're dealing with. Especially if you have any intention of keeping body and soul together."

" '*Bushido*,' " he quoted, " 'the "way of the warrior"—a martial, cultic belief in the rituals of war, particularly single combat. As an outgrowth of a feudal hierarchy, it persisted as a nearly sacerdotal subculture on the islands of Japan until early in the twentieth century. Practitioners were notably selfless and notoriously merciless, and proved their worthiness through acts of violence often bordering on wanton mayhem.' "

He closed the book and looked up at Clay. "The *yamabushi* were the most ambitious of the *bushido*. Most, if the histories are any indication, were monomaniacs whose lives consisted of finding a particularly bloody and spectacular way to die. Gave them credibility, they thought, when they faced their ancestors to beg entry into heaven.

"The group that led the colonization of this planet was of more or less pure Japanese stock, from the islands off the coast of southeast Asia, back on Earth; that group has since interbred to a certain extent with the mainland Asians imported here as labor. Centuries ago, the cult of *bushido* flourished there, in Japan. It makes good grist for the mills of legend, myth, superstition. And like your friends to the south, the common man in this hemisphere thrives on that sort of thing, though for different reasons. Here, it's because it's the kind of idea around which those who live hopeless lives can build faith, hope for something better. The more pure Japanese blood a man has here, undiluted by Chinese or Occidental, the higher his status. The next best thing to being of pure Nippon stock is the veneration of all things Japanese. Old religions are handy pegs on which to hang racial obsessions. Most of these folks have nothing but their illusions and their faith.''

Clay was catching the direction of Rankin's thought. ''And a faith requires sacraments. Worship of some kind, ceremonies, priests, and the like.''

''So?'' Greene piped up. ''Does that mean that that fighting pit was some kind of church, and the fight was like a mass of some kind? I don't think I buy that.''

Neither did Clay, though for different reasons; there was more to what he had seen, he was sure, than veneration of an ancient code or cult. But he kept silent.

Rankin shook his head. ''Not a mass. A sacrament, yes. A weeding out of sorts. The men in the pit were supplicants, I believe. Not to a god exactly, but to an idea. Or maybe more to a state of being. They were vying to become *bushi*. All of the Asian cultures that form the rootstock for this world's population have a mythology of semidivine warrior cults. The Emperor Shotoku is, I'll bet, keeping a personal guard, an elite group of assassins and warriors. He isn't the first emperor of Ithavoll to take advantage of superstition and blind faith. This is, maybe, the method by which he selects candidates for his own guard.''

''And maybe not,'' Clay commented. ''I think it's more than that. There's something strange about the way this business is carried out. It seems more than civic pride or nostalgia to me, the pure violence of it. You don't kill off your own sons for simple civic pride.''

''It does seem like a rather murderous way to build a team,'' Fitzgerald said. ''Why do the villages go along with it? It's their own sons and brothers dying in the pit.''

''Don't underestimate the power of ceremony, friend. Poverty makes for devotion; these people's lives are so squalid and so desperate that the next life is their only real hope for any contentment or joy. And only the devout and the self-sacrificing make the grade and end up with their ancestors in the hereafter, wherever that is. Besides being a religious rite, it gives a village prestige to contribute one of the emperor-god's chosen to the ranks, and the people, whose real lives are of the most mundane, desperate sort, can then live vicariously through the relative success of the one victor—and maybe share a bit of his immortality.

"In a sense, a village that can contribute a warrior to the emperor are all *bushi* in a small way. And the emperor gets an elite guard in which each man will not hesitate to die at his smallest whim in order to assure a place of honor in the afterlife. When I fought here before, against you and your men, Clay, there were no *yamabushi* other than those in the legends; at least, if they existed, they were never used in battle where we could see 'em."

Clay scrubbed his boot aimlessly in the dirt, thinking. "I don't buy it. It's too clean, too easy. I wonder if your emperor has anything to do with this at all. These people were doing more than selecting warriors for some ruler they probably despise. What about what happened in the city, the *gembuku*? What did that have to do with this?"

Rankin shook his head impatiently. "I don't know. Some precursor to it, an initiation, maybe. But the cult of *bushido* has raised its hoary head here before, fifty, seventy-five years ago, and they were a vicious, bloodthirsty lot. Ithavoll's rulers have never been loath to play the cult to their advantage in the past. What you describe is straight from the local histories. And it makes sense. Not only does the emperor get his personal breed of invincible warriors, he weeds out the strongest in the local villages, cutting out any possible uprising at the roots. And the best warriors traditionally come from hungry, desperate stock. These people have been hardened to pain, and they have nothing to lose and everything to gain, at least in the afterlife. Shotoku has built himself a hell of a breeding ground here.

"Still, it's nothing to worry us, I think, at least for now," Rankin continued. "The settlement's made itself a *yamabushi*. All we care about, so far as they're concerned, is census and survey, making maps and counting babies. Unless of course they figure out you were snooping around, watching their private sacred ceremony. In that case they might well hang us by our privates from the nearest tree and use us for bayonet practice."

Clay shook his head. "Only the two men saw me, and they're not talking."

"Well, that much is good. Still, it might be best if we did what we're pretending we came to do as quickly as possible and then move out double time. Those two are bound to be missed, and soon someone will wonder if we had something to do with it. Or worse, the bodies might be found downriver. I know you've had an interesting night, but we've work to do,'' he said, closing the subject.

"You—" He pointed to Clay. "—are officially in charge of baby counting. Get names, ages, general health for every family you can find. Be thorough; make it look good.

"You—" He gestured to Greene, who had been squatting nearby, listening to Clay's report. "—and Fitzgerald do a scratch survey of the general area. Hit up the local chieftain, if they've got one, and find out how much of the area the settlement has cleared and bonded legally and how many squatters have been here long enough to own the piece of jungle they're working.''

"Aye, aye.''

Clay watched the two gathering equipment while he finished his coffee. When they had gone, he walked to Rankin's tent, said, "Colonel,'' and waited until Rankin had unsealed it and pulled himself up and out once again.

"What?'' Rankin asked gruffly.

Clay answered him calmly. "I got the impression you were more worried about the action I ran into last night than you were letting on. Something maybe we should know? I don't much care for being left in the dark.''

Rankin shook his head slowly, "You know what I know, for the most part. Well, except that that little ceremony you saw confirms something for me.''

"Yes?''

"That this time we're on the right side instead of just the politically justified side. Whether you believe it or not, I'm gratified to know it.''

He squinted up at Clay. "Lieutenant, don't you have work to do?''

"Aye, aye, Captain.''

Clay dumped the dregs of soya-coffee from his cup, collapsed it, and gathered his recorder. He grimaced to himself. A day with the native sector was not at its most optimistic a prospect to which he looked forward.

* * *

It took Clay the greater part of the day to canvass the dozens of widespread families that made up the settlement. For endless hours he walked from shack to shack, asking his questions about births and deaths and relatives and the generally inane things that census takers asked. The living conditions he saw were generally squalid. The women were amazingly fertile and for the most part reluctant to answer Clay's questions, though all spoke idiomatically the more or less universal Terran Standard.

Clay dutifully entered it all, punching the useless information into the tiny microcomputer he carried with him, hanging around his neck by a strap.

The men were not in evidence at all. Clay supposed they were in the fields just beyond the settlement, in which the locals grew hybrid soybeans both for their own consumption and for market, though he was sure they ended up with very little at harvest to sell for reasons that were simple enough. Though they grew high-yield plants from hybrid seed that had taken generations of Terran science to perfect, the only tools they used were of the most primitive sort, for the most part consisting only of what was known to the locals as an *ard*, a simple wooden, ox-pulled plow, and a simple stick for poking shallow holes in the soil of the rows for the seed. It was an inefficient, time-consuming, and backbreaking process.

The discrepancy said much about the dictator mentality—make the show of obtaining for the people the most productive food source ever developed yet neglect to give them any way in which to cultivate it effectively. He felt revulsed by the pure waste of it.

The squatters' houses were for the most part hastily built timber-framed shacks, some stone-walled but most with walls of cut turf and roofs of thatched leaves and straw. The floors were clay that had been stomped smooth and hard by bare feet. They were low, musty dwellings, dark and usually windowless.

He stopped at the last shack he could find, a tiny one-room hovel tucked into a cane grove that he found only by asking several of the generally unhelpful squatters' wives, questioned a toothless old woman who seemed honestly ignorant about the number of children she had borne, then headed back to the camp, wearied and frustrated. Ithavoll's sun was already dipping behind the trees, flooding the sky with orange and purple.

Beyond discovering that a mutated and not particularly vir-
ulent form of cholera was a common childhood disease on
Ithavoll, he had found out little, partly, he was sure, because
he didn't dare ask direct questions.

It was difficult to tell if the general attitude of suspicion he
had encountered was simply a product of his status as stranger
and off-worlder or if the squatters had something to hide.

At that rate, Clay thought, it would be a long and unproduc-
tive two weeks unless other methods of data collecting proved
better at prying loose the locals' tongues. Still, at least they
knew more or less where the objective was, even if they didn't
know what it was.

The others, though more likely to have found something significant while doing their cursory survey, had also come up
empty-handed.

Rankin was unperturbed. "Time. And we've enough, I think,
if we don't expose ourselves prematurely." He looked meaningfully at Clay.

Clay shrugged. He had worked well alone his entire professional life, and he knew he could depend on his own instincts
whether Rankin trusted them or not.

Besides, he had discovered something during his late-night
sortie that was at least of minimal significance. He had nothing
to apologize for, even if Rankin was a little ruffled by his in-
dependence.

Later the four of them spent a few hours around the campfire
passing war stories and trying to ignore the staring audience that
had gathered to watch them just beyond the fire's light. Clay was
amazed at the candor with which Greene discussed her rather
bloody success with an antipersonnel mine she had designed
herself, evidence, he supposed, that the chauvanism that had
survived since prehistoric Terra wasn't to die out in his genera-
tion, at least not so long as he survived. The group broke up,
and Clay stretched out, bone-tired, on his air mattress and tried
to sleep.

As he lay, trying to empty his mind and relax, he noticed a
small spot of burning coldness on one thigh. Puzzled, he reached
to touch the spot and felt the irregular form of the amulet he had
taken from the man who had attacked him beside the battle pit
the night before. It seemed, he thought, almost to radiate a

strange cold that reached up from the spot on his thigh to chill his soul.

He dug the amulet out of his pocket and held it by the broken thong, studying it in the thin moonlight that filtered through the opaque fabric of the tent. It turned slowly on the cord, seeming to absorb the moonlight and radiate back a dim, cold metallic glow. It was a simple, abstract oblong of metal; the basic shape was cylindrical, but the form was twisted, as if before the molten metal had cooled it had been grasped and wrenched out of true.

Clay had no idea what it meant, but somehow, in some deep, inexplicable way, it disturbed him. He rose from the air mattress and pushed his way out of his tent, then stood in the chill night air, holding the amulet in his palm, feeling the strange coldness seep from it through his hand.

With all his might he threw it into the dark wall that was the jungle, hearing it whip through the leaves and branches and come to rest somewhere out in the darkness.

He stood for a minute listening, almost expecting to hear something, some movement, some signal from the deep shadows under the trees. Then he turned and crawled back into his tent.

Once again he tried to sleep but found that his mind insisted on wandering, replaying the events of the night before. The man he had killed bothered him no more than any other he had had to kill in the line of duty and considerably less than some.

But he still lay awake a very long time, listening to the rain that had begun to fall as it rattled on the taut surface of the tent. Only much later did the welcome oblivion of sleep come.

CHAPTER ELEVEN

His name was Tind. He couldn't remember his patronymic— he'd dropped it long ago from the small group of memories he chose to keep. What family he had had no longer mattered to him; ancestor worship was for peasants. He worshiped only *Hachiman*. Even the vague memory of the peasant villages no longer disturbed the pure tranquillity of his given purpose, to serve, to fight, to finally and gloriously die.

Only a very few things mattered to the *bushi*.

One—the most important—was a good death.

Tind spun, his weight on his toes, and drove the length of his long-knife into the battered carcass hung by a crosstrees in the center of the arena. The carcass was that of a bull dead for two days, pierced and torn under the blades of the *yamabushi* who served *Hachiman* and trained here in the emperor's arena.

The stroke was good. He relished the shock of the blow through his hand and arm, the subtle sensation of the blade slicing between ribs and into flesh, but he grimaced to himself as he tugged the soiled blade free and wiped its length on the drying hide.

There was no glory in pretending to kill dead cattle. He kicked the torn carcass viciously, sending it swinging, crosstrees creaking with the moving weight. The strong musk smell of the animal and the sickly-sweet odor of the rotting carcass rose in his nostrils.

He felt galled by the drill and practice. A man, like a blade, could be sharpened only so much before he wore away to nothing. The first lesson learned as a neophyte was that waiting for glory was the quickest way to be damned. A *bushi* had to grasp it in his fist and take it for himself.

He chafed under the necessity of inaction. Battles had been too few for too many years. What fighting there was, his lord saw fit to withhold from the *bushi*. Commoners fought. *Yama-bushi* waited, too precious to risk in petty warfare, where modern weaponry consumed lives wholesale and without discrimination.

Only the constant sparring and the occasional *Talc*—the testing battles with the hopefuls from the villages—kept Tind from growing soft. And unlike the villagers' *Talc*, only minor wounds were allowed in here, except on the rare occasions when *Hachiman* asked for souls; only then could Tind gather souls to sit at his feet and serve him in the afterlife. Very few—only a handful in his lifetime—could be *yamabushi*, but those skilled enough to attempt the rituals were valued as grist for the emperor's infantry. Those slaughters he considered poor enough tribute to his god. He spit in disgust into the arena dust.

He spun again, his weight on the heel of one foot, then the ball of the next, and thrust into the bull's carcass. He pulled the blade free again. Then, in sudden anger, he raised the gory blade high and hacked at the carcass, the knife's sharp edge cutting through stiffened flesh and bone, tearing loose an entire hindquarter. The carrion birds grouped on the edge of the pit stirred and flapped.

"Have it, then!" he shouted. Two or three of the birds flew up, startled at the noise, circled, then settled again. Tind turned away disgusted and strode toward the open gate that led to the rooms carved into the native rock that were given over to quartering the *bushi*.

He stopped. He felt a disturbing presence and traced it quickly to the vaulted entrance to the catacombs.

"Who?"

There was movement. A figure in the gray robes of a mendicant priest—the only holy men who ever left the temples—stepped into the light, shading his eyes with a pale hand. Tind felt his muscles tense involuntarily.

"I would speak with you." The voice was deep, disconcertingly resonant.

Tind sheathed his knife, trotted up to the man, and bowed low.

"Brother."

The man touched a hand to Tind's head. The smell of incense blended with the subtle odor of *Maki* overwhelmed him, the drug smell making him flush with complex remembered emotions. Many years, many dreams . . .

"You are to go to the First Temple. Go quickly."

Tind raised his eyes. He had not crossed the threshold of a temple since he had reached majority. He was confused. "May I ask—"

The priest interrupted, shrugging primly. "An assassination."

An assassination! Tind grinned, elated, then as quickly stifled it. *Hachiman* was good; perhaps the waiting was to finally end.

The gray-robed figure turned away back into the tunnel. Tind touched the hard, reassuring solidity of the grip of his long-knife and followed.

He yielded the long-knife reluctantly to the underpriest who stood as attendant in the cavernous anteroom of the temple. The young student priest bowed his shaven head and took the weapon, handling it correctly without touching the blade, and placed it in a stone recess, nodding to Tind as if to reassure him of its safety while he was inside.

Tind followed the priest through the first anteroom, prostrated himself at the entrance, kissed the rough stone, and muttered the proper words of reverence. The priest pulled back the enveloping hood of his cloak and did the same. They both stood and walked slowly, eyes lowered, into the Mystery of the temple of *Hachiman*. A cool, damp hand touched Tind's forearm, and he had to fight to keep his eyes on the rough pavement; to look up would be to profane the secrets of the temple, possibly to lose one's soul. Tind gritted his teeth at the touch and followed.

Tind was led across an open space and into a narrow passage. The torchlight that flickered on the temple floor faded into a dim fluorescence that emanated coldly from the stone walls themselves.

The guiding hand pressed him to a stop, and a bowl of smoldering powder was held under his face. Tind obediently breathed deeply of the hallucinogenic *Maki*, felt his head lighten, his attention contract as if drawn tight by a string to the pale hand that held the bowl. He thought, without conscious volition, Fine skin, high caste.

After a moment the bowl was withdrawn, and the hand drew Tind onward, then down a spiraling ramp. The stone grew cold, and he knew they were descending into the catacombs beneath the temple. A tiny edge of doubt raised itself; no one went into the catacombs but the priests. The *Maki* drew the thought away, clouding his mind with images, colors. With eyes unfocused, the stone of the passage floor becoming a blur. The hand drew him on.

His head lolled, and he stumbled. The hand that was guiding him steadied him, and other hands touched him, held him up. He walked ahead mechanically, his head burning with the twisted shapes of the *Maki* waking dream. Strangely distorted animals— serpents and bears—twisted themselves in a roiling miasma before his eyes. He steeled himself, felt the brushing touch of scaled skin against the flesh of his face. Though he knew his jaw to be clenched shut, he felt the sudden sharp taste of a bitter root he had foolishly tasted as a child bloom on his tongue. The same nausea he had felt then washed over him, and he heaved dryly, his stomach knotting in spasms.

After a time that seemed days long, a hand grasped his chin and held up his lolling head. Through a roaring like surf in his ears, he heard his name called.

He strained to focus. After a moment, vision began to return, though the shapes before him swam sickeningly as though seen through jelling oil. A voice muttered at him from a bright, quivering shape in the near distance, and he concentrated, trying to make out the words. He felt the sting of a blow on his cheek, and the muttering clarified and became words.

"Do you serve your god?" a voice demanded in his mind, and he realized suddenly that he had heard nothing with his ears but the low hum of the priests' mantra since they had brought him into the catacombs. *Hachiman* had entered him and now possessed his soul.

Tind tried to speak, could not form the word, and nodded weakly against the hand that held his chin.

The shape before him moved closer, resolving itself for an

instant into a shape that twisted and roiled but was not *Hachiman*, for *Hachiman* was within him, roaring like a wasp in his mind. A priest approached through the haze, his white robes burning with fluorescent brightness, a long knife in his open hand. The hand closed into a fist around the knife's grip and this disappeared from the tunnel that was Tind's field of vision. He felt the steel touch him as the blade etched a burning line across his chest.

"Do you feel the pain your god gives you? Do you relish it?"

Tind bobbed his head weakly. Something hard and damp struck his cheek. The smell of the *Maki* became strong again, and Tind's eyes suddenly focused, crystal-clear, on the burning herb in the bowl held before his face. He inhaled deeply, and a new strength replaced the weakness and nausea. He remembered this sensation; deeply, viscerally he remembered it, though in no part of his conscious mind. He swayed, not in weakness but in time to the chant being taken up by the dozens of priests he now realized surrounded him.

The priests went suddenly silent. Tind held out his hands, palms up, as if ordered to do so, though no one in the room had spoken. The white-robed priest placed in his open hands a long-knife, and Tind knew, without knowing how he knew, that it was his own. He grasped the knife by its handle and followed with his eyes the blood-red runes that had been painted on the blade.

"Do you feel the pain of your god in your very soul?" the priest intoned.

"Yes," Tind answered, his voice little more than a sigh. And he did. *Hachiman* touched him again, deeply, and it was as if flame had touched tinder and set it afire.

"Is your blade *Hachiman*'s blade?"

"Yes."

"Will you kill for your god?"

"Yes."

The priest grasped Tind's empty hand, held aloft a small skin bag for those in the room to see, then thrust it into Tind's hand. "This is the holiest of holies, the mind of your lord. Do you understand?"

"Yes." Tind drew the blade of the long-knife across the scarred back of his hand, feeling nothing but the sensation of the steel against the flesh. He watched the blood run down and across the pouch the priest had given him. He could feel, he imagined, a pulse coming from the substance inside the leather.

Hachiman spoke again, and he felt the presence flow through his hand and up his arm to his heart. The blood ran down the sides of the pouch, collected at the bottom, and began to drip steadily onto the worn runes cut into the stone of the floor, filling them so that they appeared to be written in red on the stone as they were drawn on the knife's blade.

"It is done," the priest intoned.

Tind lay on his back on the bed he had made with straw and dreamed. In his dream a man with black hair and yellow skin like his own but with full eyes, rounded almost like a Terran's, touched him very softly, but it made Tind tremble as if he had touched a nerve.

Tind realized suddenly with a shock that he feared this man.

In the dream Tind suddenly had a great gleaming long-knife in his hand, and, exulting, he thrust the knife through the dark-haired man, but the man was as suddenly gone. The knife passed harmlessly through air, and then the knife was gone, too, and Tind stood alone and naked, frustrated and defeated.

Tind woke trembling and nauseated. He pulled himself up from the leaf bed and crawled out of the lean-to he had made with limbs from the same trees. The night was cool and black with rain.

The blood pulsing through his temples seemed gradually to slow. It was a bad omen, that dream. When one dreamed before entering into battle, it was always bad, but he was deeply disturbed. He had dreamed before, but he had never dreamed defeat.

The chill drops of rain beat down on his shoulders, but he refused to feel it. He was a *bushi* warrior. Cold was nothing, pain was nothing, and this dream—this dream he would forget, for a *yamabushi* could not acknowledge the possibility of failure.

His body shuddered involuntarily against the chill and the dream, and he fought it, stopping the shaking through pure force of will. He stood outside the lean-to for another few moments, then ducked back inside.

With the light he would move on, and in the following day he would do as he had been commanded or he would die as all men are meant to die, but he would die hard and with much glory. He lay back on the pallet, and the rain beat heavily on the waxy, overlapping leaves over his head.

When he slept, it was dreamless.

CHAPTER TWELVE

"Mount up!"

Clay shuddered awake from a dream that was already fading and opened his eyes to the lightening darkness of premorning filtering through the material of the tent. A hand slapped his tent door.

"Up!" It was Rankin's voice, gruff and loud in the morning stillness.

Clay rolled up from his air mattress and pulled on his boots, then unsealed the tent and stepped up and outside. The sky had lightened to a deep purple.

He looked around, peering into the still-deep shadows of the nearby jungle. Even now there seemed to be a certain malevolence in the thick underbrush into which he had thrown the strange amulet.

He looked to the sky again, guessing it would be full daylight in less than a half hour. The others had already collapsed their tents and were packing away gear. Clay stretched and yawned, taking a deep lungful of the cool damp air, then opened the tent's valve and began stuffing his personal gear into his pack.

He looked out toward the squatters' village a hundred meters or so away. There was a bustle of activity beginning in the narrow walks between the sod-walled huts; men with tools, women with children beginning the day. There was little about the scene that seemed threatening.

Still, he was glad to be putting some distance between it and himself. The two men he had killed had doubtless been missed by now. It was probably only a matter of time before a fisherman or someone watering cattle downstream came across one of the bodies, and once they were out of sight, they were less likely to be connected to the murders.

Violence was commonplace enough on Ithavoll. That would work to their advantage.

When he had finished with the tent, he stripped the bandage off his hand and examined the reddish-pink scar across the back. The new scar was only one more in a numerous collection of scars scattered randomly across his body.

Though he could have had them all removed at minimal cost in any outpatient plastic surgery clinic on Earth, he had never bothered, mostly, he admitted to himself, because he enjoyed the way people usually reacted to the road map of scars that lined his skin. For women it was often shock at first, then curiosity, then, occasionally, arousal. Men were usually impressed as well, though on the most civilized worlds it made most eager to keep him at a distance—which, Clay reflected, had always been just fine with him.

He flexed the hand, made a fist. The range of motion of the fingers was nearly as good as ever. He tossed the bandage into the remnants of the fire and shouldered his pack.

In less than five minutes they were ready to move out, each with a bulky kit strapped to his or her back.

Rankin shouldered his load and indicated the narrow band of the river with a gesture. "That's the western boundary of our original search area. From here, we turn north."

"The numbers could be wrong. It could be beyond the river," Fitzgerald suggested. His brow furrowed, and Clay could almost see the gears working in the man's head as he thought back across his calculations and figures.

"Then we don't find it, and this planet goes to hell in a hand basket. We're all that's between these people and the Armegeddon Shotoku and his ilk are likely to bring on."

Clay snorted loudly enough for Rankin to hear, though he

hadn't intended that. He shifted his pack on his shoulders and gestured northward with his head. "Are we going to get the show on the road, or what?"

"Comment, John?"

"Look, I've been to most of the protectorate planets. Nine times out of ten, U.D.-controlled puppet governments are no better than what they have here with Shotoku. Or at least damned little."

"That's where you're wrong, Lieutenant. The U.D. doesn't control those planets. They're free. And they're damned sure better off than these wretches. The presence there is advisory for the most part; sometimes circumstances call for a certain amount of interference."

"Of the sort we're up to here?"

"If necessary."

"Do they consult the local populations before meddling? Strikes me that there's damned little in what they do on the out-planets that resembles democracy. For them, it's just a word. All they do—no, all *we* do for them is substitute one dictatorship for another. These people have no choice. Instead of a despot they get a somewhat more benevolent big brother in the form of a governing body controlled by men who will never so much as visit a backwater like Ithavoll. They'll eat better, maybe, but they won't be free. And if they attempt to govern themselves, the U.D. will televise the hangings."

Rankin sighed heavily. "Lesser evils, Lieutenant. Lesser evils. We could depose genocidal lunatics like Shotoku, then blast happily away back to Terra while a million people died in the ensuing struggle between the dozen or so aspirants among the locals who want to take his place. You don't leave children in charge of a planet."

"And who the hell are the United Democracies and the C.F. to make that call? Those bastards—" He stopped. He had no good reason to feel the anger that suddenly swept across him, making his face flush hotly.

He forced his hands to unclench. He knew as well as anyone what happened when revolutionaries become bureaucrats. One evil was replaced with another. Absolute power corrupts absolutely, they said, and he had seen nothing to dispute the maxim during or after the dozen or more wars in which he had fought.

He examined his own motives and could find no adequate rationale for the rage he felt. Yet it was there.

"Perhaps the difference is intent, Lieutenant. The U.D. works toward order. Chaos is a dangerous state of affairs for everyone involved, and a world run by one man or by a group of ignorant men is one a small degree better. Peace is obtained, even if the methods used to obtain that end have something of a foul flavor about them."

Clay nodded. "Cattle are peaceful."

Rankin grunted. "I suppose they are. Look, son, I empathize with your feelings about it." He stared intently at Clay, and Clay met his eyes without wavering. "Still, it seems a strange philosophy for a mercenary to hold. A tool criticizing the carpenter, so to speak. A willing tool."

Clay didn't answer. There was a long, painful silence. Clay kicked himself mentally. There was no place in the field for philosophical arguments. Unity was often the key to the survival of a team. Even the smallest rift was too large when acting as a harmonious unit could be the difference between success and death.

It was simply that injustice was a thing that bothered him deeply, subliminally. And there was nothing more unjust than taking away a man's ability to decide his own fate, to direct his own life.

It was something he had learned very young from the stories his grandmother would tell him of the North American Sioux Indians. Theirs was a primitive society as well, and compassion and morality were not standards by which they ruled themselves. But justice was. If a man took another man's life without good cause, the dead man's responsibilities fell to him. The dead man's children became his own. By the same token, though prisoners were most often killed—fortunes of war—they were allowed to die with dignity, demonstrating their bravery by welcoming the lance or knife.

A man's dignity was his own; he was allowed to choose if not the method of his death the *way* he would die. It wasn't a peaceful society, but it had functioned in a way that Clay knew viscerally was preferable to the peace of the herd that the U.D. brought. Then the Sioux had been civilized into extinction, and when they had lost their true freedom, they had lost their nobility. But the hunger for justice was still in his blood.

Rankin filled the awkward silence. "We're fairly certain the site isn't beyond the river. Reconnaissance is difficult . . . Shotoku isn't about to allow any more observation satellites to get into orbit. Even a ship that varies its orbit to any great extent is liable to find itself shot down as a spy. Still, we've got what Fitzgerald squeezed out of that box. They've been pretty discreet by their standards—they know that if the Combined Forces could come up with hard evidence of stockpiled atomics or some other weapon denied them by treaty, the U.D. would sever any and all diplomatic ties and would probably send in a strike force to bomb the place to kingdom come.

"Of course, the U.D. doesn't want that to happen any more than Shotoku. Discretion is the key word. Keep it peaceful. That blasted machine, or whatever it is, is in this area; we just have to find the bastard and do it in, and we have to do it without the U.D. or the Combined Forces getting involved in any overt fashion."

"Sorry I said anything," Fitzgerald said ruefully.

Rankin smiled. "I never asked anyone to agree with me, only to do the job."

Clay met his eyes. "Fair enough."

"Let's move it out, then."

As they traveled, Rankin kept the river to their right. The trail began once again to climb, and the river fell away into a steep-sided gorge until finally one had to stand on the cliff's edge to see the blue-brown strip of water at all. The path skirted precariously close to the precipice, and Clay took care to watch where he put his feet.

At one point Clay heard the roar of a falls rising from the depths of the gorge, and he peered over to see the water spilling out, falling from a dizzying height to be churned white even farther down. The water shot over the edge of the drop below in a feather-white arch, ballooning back up in clouds of mist, obscuring the river for fifty meters or more downriver.

That was the way Terra had once been, he mused, and it was a saddening thought. Very little of his home planet was still wild, and none of the old range of his grandmother's people had been left intact. The symbols of that people—their gods in animal form, the buffalo and the eagle—were long extinct. The plains and the sacred Black Hills were domesticated and covered over with crops and high-rise housing.

Still, the falls were a breathtaking sight, and he felt invigorated by it.

When they stopped to eat, Clay found to his surprise that he had a voracious appetite; though the dehydrated rations they carried were not gourmet quality by any stretch of the imagination, he ate heartily of soya beef substitute and made a nearly acceptable drink of Rankin's local booze and powdered orange juice.

He relaxed against a rock outcropping at the gorge's edge and watched the water far below, thinking that he was getting paid mighty well for what seemed to be rather soft duty. As long as he could keep a distance from the locals, there seemed little peril. Shotoku's people wouldn't dare make any overt move against a Terran survey team. And the more he saw of the northern continent's broken and thickly arboreal terrain, the less he thought it likely they would even find what they'd been sent to find. And if they didn't find it, then they were in fact as well as in appearance nothing more than an innocuous United Democracies census and survey team.

Too soon, Rankin had them ''mounting up'' and back on the trail, which, though it had narrowed and still climbed, was less steep than it had been.

As they climbed, Clay noted that the forest on the side of the trail opposite the river had not thinned appreciably, and he wondered at that as he walked. As a general rule, altitudes much beyond sea level on inhabitable Earthlike planets tended to discourage the sort of rampant, near-jungle growth though which the trail and the river gorge wound.

The planet's atmosphere was somewhat denser, Clay mused, and certainly more opaque than Terra's. It made for something of a constant greenhouse effect. Because of that the climate was generally damp and constantly warm, even at fairly high altitudes. Regardless, the land was lush and idyllic, a place of overgrown splendor.

The surroundings, the seeming lack of threat, he thought later, had made him more lax than he ever had a right to be in what was essentially a combat zone. He had just tabled the debate with himself on the local flora when something large and apparently furred dropped out of an overhanging tree limb directly over Fitzgerald.

It took Clay a full second to realize that the something was a man clothed in some sort of fur vest—he was third in line behind Fitzgerald and Greene, Fitzgerald having taken point—and even then he couldn't bring his rifle to bear with both Greene and Fitzgerald in the line of fire.

Greene shouted and brought the laser around to cover the squirming pile that was Fitzgerald and his attacker but held her fire.

"God*dammit*!" she shouted in frustration. She threw aside the laser rifle, tugging at the harness buckles and yanking free the heavy battery pack and its cable in the same movement.

Clay rushed clumsily forward, the pack making him awkward and slow, as Greene reached Fitzgerald and his assailant, her combat knife in her hand. She stabbed at the hunched back, the knife held high to give the thrust strength.

The figure that had dropped on Fitzgerald whirled, slashing at Greene with something that was long and bright in the diffused sunlight. Clay fired as she fell, and then the man was as suddenly gone, rolling away from the burst with startling agility, throwing himself into the tangled thick growth beside the trail.

Clay sprayed the underbrush with fire, hearing Rankin open up behind him with his carbine at the same moment. He emptied the rifle's clip, tearing holes in the forest cover beneath the trees, but he had no confidence he had actually hit anything. The figure, the man, had moved too quickly, knowing he was protected from Clay's fire first by Fitzgerald and Greene, then by the density of the forest.

He deftly ejected the spent clip from the rifle and slammed another home.

Greene had dropped to her knees before the prone form of Fitzgerald. Clay ran toward her awkwardly, trying to crouch and keep his rifle trained on the spot where their assailant had disappeared, fighting the unwieldly bulk of the pack on his back. He had no way of knowing what other weapons the attacker might have or whether he was alone. For all he knew there was a battalion of loinclothed foot soldiers hidden in the blue-green shroud of the forest.

He stepped quickly around Greene, unbuckled and shrugged off his pack, and knelt beside Fitzgerald. Fitzgerald lay face-down in a shallow pool of his own blood. Clay rolled him over to check his pulse and found that there was no need to—a huge grinning wound stretched across his throat, almost from ear to ear, cutting through his esophagus and both carotid arteries. His heart had already stopped, and the blood, though it no longer gushed, flowed thickly to puddle in the dust of the trail.

Clay let Fitzgerald's body fall back and turned to Greene. She was hugging her midsection with both hands but raised one arm to let Clay see the wound.

Clay touched the area above it, and she groaned under her breath.

"Bad?"

Clay nodded. The knife's blade had come in low, slashing upward, and had lifted her protective vest aside as she rose, cutting through her fatigues and into her abdomen before it skidded up across the vest and her unprotected upper arm. The wound on the arm was superficial, but the abdominal wound had cut through the skin and muscle. Part of a veined loop of intestine protruded past Greene's fingers.

Clay opened his pack and took out the medical kit. He could close the wound and protect it against infection, but there was a good chance—especially if the knife's blade had nicked the intestines—that peritonitis would set in soon enough anyway. If that happened, chances were good that it would kill her before they could get her to medical help.

Clay heard something crash into the brush behind him, and he turned to see Rankin force his way into the undergrowth at the point where the assailant had disappeared into the verge of the forest.

He looked back to Greene and saw that her face was composed and that there was no real sign of shock yet, but he popped a syringe open and injected her with antishock anyway. He rummaged in the medical kit and took out a bandage, then lifted her hands and pressed the spun gauze gently against the wound, placing her hands back across it.

"Back in a flash, sweetheart."

She nodded wordlessly, and he retrieved his weapon and followed Rankin into the underbrush.

CHAPTER THIRTEEN

Clay quickly found that even though he was following a clear track made by Rankin and the man they were chasing, it was slow going through the thick semitropical undergrowth. He could tell by the cut vines and brush along the fresh trail that the attacker had prepared an escape route ahead of time, and that made him wary.

A few meters farther along the trail his caution paid off. A length of twine made from, so far as he could tell, fibers stripped from the bark of a nearby tree stretched across the trail at the height of his ankles. It was the same color as the underbrush and was almost indiscernible against the trail.

He stopped for a moment to inspect it, noting that Rankin had apparently also avoided the trip wire.

It was a simple enough device, a sapling cut and wedged in the low crotch of a tree, then bent back and snagged by another length of twine to a notch cut into a stake pushed into the clay. Another stake was lashed with yet another length of jute twine to the far end of the sapling pole. When someone stumbled across the trip wire, the twine binding back the sapling pulled loose from the notch, and the sapling whipped forward, driving the stake through the careless victim's midsection.

He had seen the same basic design many times before on a half dozen different planets. Simple and relatively effective if the victim wasn't looking for it.

Clay didn't bother disarming the trap. He knew where it was

now, and the rest of the team was in no shape to follow and blunder into it. He stepped carefully over the stretched twine and jogged along the trail as quickly as the packed undergrowth would allow.

He pulled up suddenly at the sound of gunshots, ducking into the brush to the side of the indistinct trail. He listened to the muffled staccato reports and placed the weapon instantly as Rankin's carbine—Rankin's weapon was unique, an antique metal-barreled, small-caliber carbine. The weapon had a distinctive popping report, and Clay was glad Rankin had also been stubborn with the armorer in choosing his weaponry—the unmistakable sound of the carbine identified him as surely as his own voice would.

He waited for a moment, then moved toward the sound of the gunfire. He heard one last sputtering burst from the carbine, then nothing.

Clay moved faster through the brush, forgetting caution, and burst through the bushes into a dry streambed, one of the many, he was sure, that fed eventually into the gorge river they had been traveling beside. He saw Rankin almost immediately, leaning with his back against the far bank, tying a bandage torn from his fatigue blouse around a wound on his upper arm. His carbine lay against his knee on the bank beside him.

Rankin didn't react when Clay came crashing into the streambed, and Clay was gratified by his nerve. In the same position he more than likely would've shot whatever moved and made friends later.

"Been expecting you." Rankin continued with his chore. "He nicked me with that damned meter-long frog sticker. That bastard's good, faster than any goddamned human being I've ever seen, but I think I might have winged him. How's Fitzgerald and Greene?"

"Fitzgerald's dead," Clay said bluntly. "And Greene is probably just as dead in the long run. Belly wound; opened the peritoneal cavity."

"Damn. I was afraid of as much." He used his teeth to pull the makeshift bandage tight, cursed at the pain, then spit with frustration in the sandy creek bottom.

Clay turned away and studied the streambed for a moment

and found the stranger's tracks, heading upstream away from the gorge.

He rechecked his rifle and started out upstream after the man who had killed Fitzgerald. "I'll pick you up on the way back."

"Whoa, son. Leave him be; he's probably not going to stop running until he's well clear of us now. Hell, the son of a bitch was only armed with a knife! We've still got an objective to accomplish, even if the evidence points toward the proposition that our cover's blown all to hell."

Clay shook his head. "No dice. Do what you want, I'm after him. I'll bring you back his ears."

Rankin finished the clumsy knot he was tying and casually picked up his carbine. The barrel swung around to cover Clay.

"Uh uh. I'm still in command, believe it or not. We don't have time to fool with it."

Clay hesitated, then relaxed. "Sure."

There was no percentage in having it out with Rankin, and he was still for all intents and purposes a member of the Combined Forces, subject to their laws and to their penalties for insubordination.

Rankin groaned and pulled himself upright. "Let's go see what we can do for Greene, then." He slung the carbine over his shoulder.

Clay nodded and fell in behind him.

The stranger had beaten them back. When they pushed back through the brush onto the trail, they found Greene still on her knees, holding herself in with both hands, but nothing else. Fitzgerald and all the equipment had vanished.

Clay knelt beside Greene, and she opened her eyes to look at him and spoke calmly.

"He was here." He threw all the gear over the cliff into the gorge. Fitzgerald's body, too. He told me—" She stopped for a moment, and Clay saw her shudder. "He told me that he wouldn't kill me because you would be easier to kill if I slowed you down."

Rankin cursed fluently and peered over the cliff's edge into the gorge. "It would take us most of a day to climb down there, another to climb back out. If he could scrounge up any sort of

projectile weapon at all—a crossbow, a slingshot, anything—
we'd be damned easy targets on that rock face.''

Clay helped Greene lie back on the packed clay of the trail.
He tore a strip of cloth from his blouse and tied it around her
midsection to bind the soaked-through bandage she had been
holding. Now that the kit was gone, he had no way to redress it
without increasing her already high chances of infection.

"He was right," Greene said without inflection.

Clay glanced down at her, and she grimaced with pain.

"About what?"

"About me. Either kill me now or leave me here. That's SOP,
and you know it. You're a professional just like the rest of us.''

"No. We all get out of here. Together.''

"Oh, God. Don't be such a sentimental ass. I don't feel up
to much traveling, anyway, so why don't you or dear Dr. Rankin
do the right thing by a lady and shoot me.''

"Don't worry about it," Clay said softly. "We outgun the
bastard. No need for heroics yet.''

"Ass!" Clay heard a sincere tone of disgust in her voice and
chose to ignore it.

Rankin called, and Clay walked over to the gorge's edge,
where Rankin was still peering into the depths. He squatted
down and looked at the river, shrouded by distance and mist,
wild and torn into whiteness by the rocks below.

"Options?"

Rankin shook his head wearily. "For me, only one. Find the
weapon, then get back to the nearest C.F. command with the
location and blow it to hell and gone some other time. For you,
two. Leave Greene here and go after that wily bastard or hope
he sticks to me while you take her back to that village and hunt
up a radio—the village chieftain has one, I think—and call in a
copter. Either way, I've changed my mind—this is our parting
of the ways.''

"I don't think Greene can be saved.''

Rankin shrugged. "Your call.''

"All right. I'll take her back, at least as far as she lasts. Then
I'll be back.''

"Good enough.''

Clay hesitated. "One thing. Why was there only one of them?

I mean, if they knew about us, what we were up to, why not a battalion with modern weapons?''

"Christ, I don't know." Rankin screwed up his face in thought. "I guess the simple explanation is that they *didn't* know about us, really, at least not as a certainty. One man, a rogue religious fanatic, whatever, kills off a small survey party; it isn't the sort of thing our people, at least officially, can get too heated about beyond demanding the fellow be brought to justice. I suspect, too, after seeing that crazed bastard, that they thought one was enough."

Rankin picked up a stone and slung it with all the might of anger over the cliff edge into the gorge. "And he damned near was," he added.

Clay waited for the sound of the stone hitting the bottom, but it never came, the small noise swallowed up by the immensity of the gorge. Rankin's explanation made sense. Still, a worm of doubt worked its way into his mind. There was something more to it than that, he knew, without knowing how he knew.

But he couldn't worry about it. He had to save Greene if he could. Even as he thought it, his heart was heavy with the certainty that it was a task already doomed to failure.

While Rankin covered him, watching the forest, Clay cut two sapling poles with his boot knife and then cut the remains of his blouse into strips, which he tied so that they stretched across the poles, leaving a half-meter space. When he had finished, he possessed a functional if somewhat unsturdy travois.

He rolled Greene onto the makeshift stretcher as gently as possible, but he still managed to reopen her wound, and fresh blood began to soak through the clotted bandage.

At this rate, Clay thought, the blood loss will kill her long before infection can.

With the last strip from his shirt he tied her as securely as possible onto the travois. He pulled the outer protective vest back on and set the ends of the poles on his shoulders, shifting them until they rested fairly comfortably.

He couldn't pull the contraption and keep his rifle at the ready, but he arranged the rifle's strap so that it hung below his arm within quick reach. It was the best he could do, and he tugged the travois and Greene into motion without worrying about it further.

Rankin didn't wave; he simply faded into the brush beside the trail and was gone. Clay listened for a time even after he could no longer hear Rankin's passage through the brush, waiting for the sound of gunfire, which never came.

Good enough, he thought.

Rankin would travel for a distance through the underbrush, leaving as little trail as possible, then cut back to the main path farther up, where, if necessary, Clay could pick up his trail and follow, after Greene had been taken care of, for better or worse.

The going was rough; the trail that had seemed relatively smooth while hiking up became pitted and rocky, the travois jarring roughly across the stones if Clay moved faster than a very slow walk.

After a time he made some distance, but the going was painfully slow, and the itch between his shoulder blades was nearly unbearable, though he knew that if he were attacked, that particular spot would be best protected by the vest he still wore.

After a couple of tortuous kilometers, he stopped and eased the travois's bars from his shoulders. He pressed his fingertips against Green's throat, feeling for a pulse, and found one, though it seemed dangerously weak and thready. He surveyed the path ahead as he rested and thought it was a blessing that she had passed out sometime before. The road wasn't going to get any easier.

When some of the ache had left his arms and shoulders, he lifted the travois's ends and started carefully down the trail.

He had gone only a few meters when he heard a rustling in the brush he had just passed. He quickly lifted the travois from his shoulders and set Greene down as quickly as he dared, then unslung his rifle, bringing it to bear on the still-hidden source of the noise.

There was another rustling in the brush, and a broad gray snout poked through the brush, followed closely by a head that Clay guessed spanned a half meter across from ragged ear to ragged ear.

The beast snorted and pushed farther through onto the trail, and Clay saw that it was one of the wild piglike animals that had been one of Ithavoll's more dominant life-forms before man had taken over. He had hunted the same sort of animal for food when he had fought as a mercenary on the southern continent.

From its stump of a neck forward, it looked much like a Terran hog, but. its thick-haired torso and humped shoulders reminded Clay more of the pictures he had been shown when he was young of the ancient bison various of his ancestors had once hunted on the Oklahoma plains, its hide caked with the mud from a wallow.

And this one was big, easily twice the size of the animals Clay had seen on the southern continent. It snuffled at the trail where Clay had dragged the travois.

It smells the blood, Clay guessed.

The animals were omnivorous, and while roots and vermin were the mainstay of their diet, they were also hunters if the prey seemed easy enough.

Clay watched the beast lift its head from the trail and look nearsightedly at Greene where she lay on the travois, yellowed tusks weaving left and then right as he looked at them with first one eye and then the other. *We must seem fairly easy game,* Clay thought.

The beast took a step forward, swinging its head, and Clay raised the rifle and took careful aim between the wide piggish eyes. When it took another slow step, he squeezed off a single round.

The rifle was silenced, but the muffled report was still loud as it echoed between the trees. The giant boar staggered to one side, and Clay thought it was about to fall. Then it steadied itself, blood running in a rivulet from the wound between its eyes where the big bullet had gouged through the flesh then richocheted without exploding off the thick, hard bone of the animal's skull.

It snorted, shaking its huge head. It gazed stupidly in Clay's direction, dazed by the impact of the bullet. After a moment it took an unsteady step forward and shook its head again with a snort. Then it gathered itself, the muscles bunching across its chest, and charged suddenly, its great bulk moving with surprising speed.

Clay fired again, this time with the rifle on full automatic. The bullets struck the boar in a line of quarter-sized wounds across its flanks, and though it didn't slow, Clay believed it was dead before it covered half the ground between them.

But its legs kept churning forward on their own, only the impact of the big slugs saving Clay from being impaled on the long dirty tusks. The animal swerved with the force of the blows to its side and rushed headlong past him into the brush, crashing through to come to a stop out of sight in the thick undergrowth beneath the forest trees.

Clay released the breath that he hadn't realized he'd been holding.

He reslung his rifle and considered for a moment carving a ham from the huge beast; the food they had brought had gone the way of the rest of the gear, broken on rocks at the bottom of the gorge.

But time was more important. He could easily go without food for the two days it should take him to get back, and Greene was in no shape to eat anything. He shrugged and left the dead boar for the *munin*, the carrion birds.

He checked Greene, and she had regained consciousness. She smiled weakly up.

"You got it."

Clay nodded. "How are you doing?"

"Not good. Hurts like hell." Her eyelids drooped, and he could tell she had almost passed out again.

Clay wished passionately that he had some sort of painkiller to give her, but that too had been thrown to the bottom of the gorge. He added that to the list of personal scores he had promised himself he was going to settle.

"Why don't you try to sleep." He pushed her hair gently back from her forehead, and she smiled again, though only slightly.

"I forgot before. He told me to tell you his name was Tind. He said I was to tell you specifically. The man with the dark hair, he said." She looked up at Clay, suddenly more alert. "Why?"

He shook his head. "I don't know."

"I think he fears you."

Clay smiled humorlessly. "He has reason to." It wasn't bravado, it was simple fact.

He checked the strip of cloth that held her to the travois, then squatted and lifted the bars to his shoulders. He started carefully down the patch, the ends of the bars banging painfully across the ruts and stones.

The rain had begun again, but Tind ignored the cold wetness that seeped through the shirt made by a village priest from the skin of a bear Tind had killed with his own hands when he was young.

He remembered the animal and the hunt with pleasure. His "bear" was an animal that only vaguely resembled the ravening ten-foot monsters that he had heard the *skald*, the village story-teller, claim used to roam Terra like a plague. But it had been a worthy foe nonetheless, with claws as long as Tind's fingers, tipped with poisons that made the living flesh rot away from the bone unless an antidote was quickly given to the one who had been mauled.

He absently stropped the blade of his long-knife against the thick rank fur—he still had the scars across his chest and belly where the old boar had mauled him after running itself completely up the pike he had held against its enraged charge.

It had died soon enough, but Tind had spent many long days in the fever of his wounds. He let the memory pass, concentrating on the present.

He had watched the two men return to the girl, had watched her tell them what he had instructed her to tell them. It soothed somewhat the rage he felt for allowing himself to be distracted by the sight of the dark-haired man enough that he had brought his stroke short, wounding the woman instead of disemboweling her.

He ruminated over the dilemma he now faced, holding back the inner rage, trying to think clearly, to focus on his purpose. The man he wanted most to kill, the dark-haired-but-round-eyed one, was traveling with the female away from the place he had been commanded to protect.

And the old man was moving toward it.

The red hate that churned through him spoke one course; duty demanded another. He felt frustration rise like gall in his throat.

He watched the rain falling in sheets through the yellow light. The day was dying. He had to act.

If I can kill the old man quickly enough, he thought feverishly, I can return for the black-hair.

And then one of us will die.

He left the cover of the forest without hesitating further and trotted up the trail after the old man, ignoring the sharp pain that came with every step from the bullet wound in one thigh, the blood seeping through the bandage of herbs he had made, running down his shin and across his bare foot.

CHAPTER FOURTEEN

When the rain began, Clay debated with himself for a moment, then took off his vest and spread it over Greene's midsection. She was unconscious again and hadn't stirred when he'd lowered the travois to the ground.

He checked her pulse and found it weaker, and felt the smallest part of anger rise in himself at her, both for the fact that she was dying and, unreasonably, for the fact that she had not yet died, and he was ashamed. He touched her forehead and it was hot with fever.

He rested for a minute beside the trail. When the rain began falling in earnest, he picked up the ends of the travois and dragged Greene through the wiry brush into the depths of the forest.

He found a place to his liking and pushed the travois against the wide trunk of one of the large-leafed evergreens. He wrestled and twisted down a few of the lower limbs and, using the broad waxy leaves for thatch, quickly built a rickety, makeshift shelter over the travois.

When he was finished, he was soaked through. He shucked off his fatigue trousers and crawled under the leafy shelter beside Greene, only to crawl back out a few minutes later; a number of the smaller denizens of the forest, insects about as large as the ball of his thumb, had chosen to join them in the relative dryness of the shelter he had built. And they bit, lighting on whatever parcel of skin was uncovered and biting through to the blood.

Clay found a place between the raised roots of a tree where there was soil that had been exposed to the rain. He scooped out a double handful of the rank mud and smeared it on his torso, face, and arms, then took up another double handful and crawled back into the tent.

He smeared the mess as well as he could in the darkness on Greene's feverish face and arms. He hesitated, pulled open her fatigue shirt and applied the mud to her chest and neck, then pulled the shirt as closely as he could around her without disturbing her wound. When he had finished, he built up a pillow of leaves and lifted her head and pushed it under, letting her settle back against the relative cushion of the leaves.

She remained unconscious throughout his machinations, and he knew the chances she would ever become conscious again were small.

He settled beside her and forced himself to relax against the dead, punky-smelling mulch of leaves. He chanted a slow mantra, letting his jaw muscles sag, then his tongue, his shoulders, down to his feet, breathing slowly.

In a few minutes he had fallen into an exhausted, troubled sleep.

When he awoke, it was completely dark. The rain had stopped, though drops still fell heavily from the forest trees. He touched Greene, and her skin was cold.

He sat up and felt her throat for a pulse, and there was none.

Clay crawled out of the lean-to into the open and took a deep, shuddering breath. Then he squatted down in the thick leaf humus beside the lean-to and waited for dawn to lighten through the trees.

With dawn he dragged the travois from the shelter and lifted Greene's body gently from it. He removed the strips of his shirt from the poles and with them bound her legs together and tied her arms to her sides, then wrapped her head, covering her face as best he could. From under her shirt he pulled out her identity plate, a three-centimeter-square wafer of plastic that gave her age, sex, and blood type and claimed her as a U.D. surveyor.

He undid the clasp that held it to its chain and tucked it into a pocket.

Then he pulled the laces from her boots and cut them into lengths, then used them to bind limbs he pulled from a deadfall crosswise to the poles.

When he had finished, he possessed a rough ladder of sorts, the rungs closely spaced.

He then searched the area around the lean-to until he found a tree that would suit his needs. It was one of the tall evergreens, an old man of the forest that towered above the rest. Its lowest branches were a little more than two meters from the ground.

High enough, Clay thought, to keep her from scavengers like the boar he had killed.

He lifted the ladder and struggled to place it across two of the thick lower branches, balancing the awkward weight precariously on his shoulders until he managed to get both ends up on the branches. Then he wedged the ladder securely against the tree's trunk.

Bits and pieces of the old burial lore he had heard and absorbed unconsciously as a child came back to him, and for a moment he hummed a song to the dead he seemed to remember he'd heard his grandmother sing, though he couldn't remember when or why she had sung it or even with any certainty that she ever really had. He had never seen her outside the Miami flat she'd lived and died in.

He went back to where Greene lay, carried her back to the tree, and after a few false starts lifted her body up above his shoulders and rolled it onto the platform he had made. Then he pulled loose as many of the wide green leaves as he could carry and covered her as best he could, tucking the ends of the leaves into the ladder.

He could only hope his imperfect attempt at camouflage would be enough to discourage the carrion birds she had thought so beautiful.

Then he stood back and surveyed his work. As he watched, a breeze blew up and pulled one of the leaves free, sending it fluttering to the ground.

I'm sorry it couldn't be better, he thought. Which was foolish, he knew. She was a soldier. She had expected no more.

He felt grief, but it was a familiar and weathered grief; he'd lost comrades before, so many that he could remember only a few faces and fewer names.

But he would remember Greene, he thought. Yes, he would remember her and make sure the debt owed her was paid in full—paid with interest.

As he pushed out of the forest onto the trail, the rain began again, falling in a gray drizzle.

CHAPTER FIFTEEN

With the new rain Clay was reminded of the thirst that had been building in his throat for hours, making his tongue feel thick and swollen. He had no container but his mouth with which to catch the rain, and even then the drizzle was too thin to do much more than dampen his tongue and the back of his throat.

He stayed on the trail, climbing steadily again, for about another two kilometers before he cut once more back into the forest.

It was only a few minutes before he found the tree he was searching for, a medium-sized evergreen that had, sometime in the past when it had been little more than a sapling, been struck by lightning. About a meter and a half from the ground the tree split where it had been scarred by the bolt into two separate trunks.

At the juncture of the two trunks was a small hollow filled with rainwater.

He scooped up the water with his palms and drank deeply, his throat constricting against the dryness as he swallowed. The water was bitter and musky with tannin and doubtless, he thought, full of nasty native microbes that would catch up with him later, but there was nothing for it. The only way to purify the water was to boil it, and though he had no doubt he could quickly make a fire, he didn't have any sort of container handy in which he could heat it.

When he had taken in as much of the water as he could hold, he pushed back through to the trail and set off again at a loose jog.

Before long he came to the place where Fitzgerald had been killed, and he hesitated. If the man, the _yamabushi_, who had attacked them was still around—and from what Greene had said, Clay strongly suspected he was—he had obviously followed after Rankin instead of Clay.

Which meant that as long as Rankin was alive, Clay was relatively safe from attack.

Clay found no comfort in the thought. He was willing—no _eager_—to face the backwater warrior as quickly and as violently as possible. All else, Rankin's mission in particular, was secondary.

He considered for a moment climbing down the cliff face for the weapons and explosives. He doubted it would take as long to make his way down and back up as Rankin had estimated—the cliff was steep but not sheer, and he was a better than average climber—but it still would take a certain amount of time, time he could not afford.

If Rankin died while he was down in the river gorge, the man, Tind—the name sounded strange in his mind, alien and deadly—would be hunting him, and if Tind found him before he could climb back out, there would be no way Clay could defend himself. He would be a target, exposed and helpless. The _yamabushi_ would kill him with a minimum of effort.

It was a prospect he didn't relish.

And if Rankin faced the man alone, Clay felt suddenly, there was a fair chance that the colonel wouldn't survive.

Clay decided and jogged on past the place. The rain had washed the stain of Fitzgerald's blood from the stone, but Clay looked for it irrationally anyway as he passed.

The day grew hotter, though the planet's perpetually hazy atmosphere kept it from becoming uncomfortably bright, and he felt the sweat running in rivulets down his face and chest. He slowed his pace, though he was in good enough shape to continue at a relaxed run for several kilometers.

As the day grew hotter, he knew, it would become more and more difficult to find the hidden pools of water from which to drink as the night's rainfall evaporated into the already humid air.

Unless, of course, he found a more permanent source of water.

As he traveled, he had been keeping his attention on the forest to his left, watching for a sign that Rankin or the *yamabushi* had left the trail. Now he watched for other signs as well.

Soon he found what he had been looking for, an indistinct low game trail that branched away from the main trail and led off into the forest's deep undergrowth. Clay stooped down and peered into the narrow path that had been hollowed out in the bushes.

There were small hoofprints in the damp soil, and he studied them for a moment, then decided that whatever had made them wasn't of a size to pose a probable threat—though he knew of animals on other planets not much larger than his outstretched palm that could kill a man in seconds. Size and strength were not the only attributes by which a thing became deadly.

He knelt and crawled into the opening on his hands and knees.

After a few meters the small trail emerged from the briarlike bushes through which it had been traveling, and Clay stood and pushed his way through the somewhat thinner growth that flourished under the wide, shadowed canopy of the trees. The game trail was even more indistinct there, meandering through the tangled deadfalls and undergrowth in a random, unguided way.

Twice the path disappeared entirely where it came to wide—fifty meters and more—hollows that seemed to be filled with layer upon layer of dead leaves and debris, all held together by a rubbery, spongelike fungus of some sort that had grown up through the trash to make a solid, resilient mat. Clay tried to pinch a piece of the substance loose between his thumb and forefinger and found it to be tough as leather, impossible to pull loose with just his bare hands.

He stepped gingerly out onto the flat reddish-gray mass and felt his foot sink only a few centimeters into the strange mold. He walked across, the springy surface absorbing his tracks, re-

bounding slowly back as he lifted his feet. After a moment the
tracks disappeared as if he had never walked there at all.

Very interesting, possibly very useful, he thought. He stored
the fact for future reference.

On the far side of the hollow, he looked back and could see
no trace of his passage across. He scouted around until he once
again picked up the trail.

A hundred meters beyond the second such hollow the trail
dipped downward into a place where the undergrowth once again
grew viny and jungle-thick. A few meters beyond that it widened and came out upon a pool of water cradled in a wide rock
basin.

As Clay came up to the pool, something small spooked from
the water's edge and crashed into the cover of the tall weeds that
grew a short space back from the basin.

He grinned to himself. Things were looking up. He knelt on
the flat rock at the edge and drank deeply of the cool, clean-
tasting artesian water.

When he had taken his fill, he leaned into the pool, im-
mersing his head and face, letting the cold of the water shock
and refresh him. He wiped the water from his eyes with one
hand, steadied himself with the other.

Under the palm of his hand he felt a strange shape in the rock.
He leaned closer to look at the flat stone he had stretched out
on to drink and discovered that it was virtually covered with
carved shapes, starting at the water's edge and disappearing under the dirt and grass that covered the stone's far end.

Clay stared at the runes or ideographs, chiseled into the stone
with profound surprise. The stone edges of the cut figures were
rounded with age, much more so than would have been possible
if the runes had been cut in the hundred or so years colonists
had been on Ithavoll.

He looked up, studying the pool from which he had drunk,
and realized with a start that the entire basin was artificially
regular, a wide oval that showed the symmetry of intentional
design. Someone, sometime, had *built* the pool out in the heart
of Ithavoll's unexplored jungle.

Stunned, he sat back on his haunches and tried to think
through what he had found. The runes and the basin were clearly
evidence of some sort of alien culture, one capable of a language

or at least of signs, which had existed, perhaps even thrived, some time long before the Terran colonization of Ithavoll.

The thought was shocking, unbelievable.

Men had searched for some sign, some small evidence of another intelligent race, ever since humans had taken to space at the end of the second millennium. They had searched, hoping to discover that they were not alone in the universe, that others, too, had looked upon the eternal stars and longed for what they promised.

He touched the runes and felt the strange shapes cut into the smooth stone. Now, alone, deep in the malignant heart of the jungle of a planet that had been settled by men for a hundred years, he had found what explorers and archaeologists by the untold thousands had been searching for. The wild improbability of it was enough to make his head spin.

Clay followed one complex rune with a fingertip. He had never heard of relics of any sort being found on Ithavoll, though chipped stones and bits of bone had been brought forth in the past as supposed evidence of very rudimentary indigenous cultures on other colonized worlds.

But nothing like this.

The words, phrases, ideas, whatever they were, meant nothing to him, yet the runes possessed a certain symmetrical grace that he found pleasing. They were as enigmatic as the mountaintop ruins of Machu Picchu in Old Peru, back on Terra, and as saddening. Here, at one time, had existed a culture that was doubtless as full and varied as that of the long-dead Incas, he reflected with wonder, or as that of his own various Indian ancestors.

The runes had once had some meaning to some forgotten people, religious, perhaps, or perfectly mundane, but important enough for someone to have taken the trouble to chisel them into stone. Now the people, culture, and meaning were all for some unknowable reason gone.

That thought left him with an indescribable feeling of loss. To have known those people—what that might have meant to his race, to the peoples of Terra. It was a feeling of intense and unreasoning loneliness, the feeling of absolute isolation in the wide, empty expanse of the universe.

Like this people, he suddenly felt, his own people—or at least his grandmother's—were gone, and suddenly he deeply felt that loss, too. Though in a way that people lived on, inside of him— a heritage as deep and as mixed, he realized, as that of the new people of this planet, the new Ithavollans.

Even the *yamabushi*, perhaps especially the *yamabushi*, shared in the inheritance of ancient cultures, both Asian and Western. Looking at the runes carved by some long-dead alien hand, Clay felt for an instant a certain strange kinship with the man he had vowed to kill.

He shook the feeling off. There were more important concerns, matters of the here and now, of survival, he had to attend to. He had no time for sentiment.

The important question was, how could Tind's people have lived on the planet for as long as they had and not have discovered what he had found, here in the open, by sheerest accident?

The simplest answer was that they hadn't.

The Ithavollans must have known about artifacts like the runes Clay had found for at least a good part of the century since they had begun to settle the planet. Which meant that they had kept, and continued to keep, the knowledge of a forerunner civilization from all outworlders.

Why?

There was no obvious answer. The only thing he could know for sure was that since no other survey team had reported similar artifacts, either it had to be a purely local phenomenon or, possibly, the Ithavollans must have gone to great pains to keep such things from being discovered in the past. Or perhaps both.

After all, he and Rankin were already far outside the area they had been authorized to survey by Qianzhi, the emperor's *shikken*.

And if artifacts such as the one he had found—he traced another of the runes with a fingertip—were to be found only in this one area, did they have something to do with the strange new weapon that was turning Shotoku's enemies into so much fine, dry powder?

He pressed his thumb into one of the strange, carved shapes, as if the mirror image it left in the pad of his thumb could somehow tell him something, could somehow explain the why and the how of the ancient and enigmatic signs.

But it could tell him nothing. He stared for a long while at the runes, feeling the alienness in their mute indecipherability. He felt awed and intrigued and suddenly very much alone.

When he had drunk again from the spring, he stood and surveyed the area about the pool, then selected a place that seemed likely and pushed into the weeds and waxy-leafed tropical plants that stood near the water.

He squatted down comfortably on a cushion of weeds and arranged the plants before him so that he had a more or less unobstructed view of the trail where it widened out at the water's edge.

Then he waited.

Within ten minutes he heard the light rattle of hooves on the clay of the trail. He set the rifle aside on a cushion of pushed-down weeds and pulled the knife from his boot top; he had few enough shells left, only what were in the rifle itself and one spare clip that sat heavy in the thigh pocket of his fatigue pants. He weighed the boot knife in his hand, blade toward his wrist.

When the animal came into sight, Clay hesitated. It was not large, about the size of an average Terran dog, but it seemed to be armored—bony plates were arranged in two symmetrical rows on its humped back. Clay had no idea what the beast might be called or even its approximate physiology, but he knew it was a good bet that any vital organs the thing had were covered by the protective plating.

The thing snorted, edging warily up to the water.

Smells me, Clay thought, and doesn't quite know what to make of it.

After testing the air for another few moments, it nuzzled into the water and drank. Clay rose a bit, waiting for the animal to become fully engrossed in its drinking.

He counted ten under his breath, then cocked his hand up beside his cheek and threw the knife with a deft flick forward of hand and wrist. The blade arced out and drove home in the flesh above the animal's near shoulder.

The animal squealed in pain and tried to draw its head back into the armor plating, but the knife's haft was in the way, the blade having driven itself half its length into the gap between the armor and its neck.

It wheeled and took a half dozen steps toward the forest before its scaled legs gave way and it collapsed. Clay rushed clumsily out from his blind in the weeds, pulled the knife free, and cut the beast's throat, letting the blood run freely onto the clay, and trickle down to the water. It was red, like the blood of a Terran animal. Clay dipped a finger into it and tasted it; it was salty and slightly pungent.

He skinned it quickly, careful not to pierce the scaled hide. What he had thought to be chitinous plates were in fact simply places were the hide was especially thick and mottled a darker color. The leathery plates were as effective as armor, though, hard and tough enough to turn a knife blade or, in the case of its natural enemies, tooth and claw.

With the edge of the knife he scraped away all traces of flesh and fat from the hide, using a smoothly rounded boulder as a backing as he worked. He sacrificed a short length of one of his boot laces to sew up the open end of the skin, looping the lace at either end so that he could attach the sling from the rifle. Then he held the finished water bag under the water's surface and let it fill.

When he pulled it from the water, it leaked a bit, but he knew that shortly the hide would swell from the water and seal the part of the seam that needed to be watertight. The skin was green, and he knew the water would taste rank, but he had drunk worse many times in the past. Anything that didn't kill him he could endure.

He slung the water bag over his shoulder and retrieved his rifle.

He regretted wasting the animal's carcass, but though the hunger had begun to gnaw at him, he felt the need to move on, and building a fire would take more time than he could spare. The hunger hadn't reached the stage yet where he was willing to eat strange meat raw.

And he had seen enough of Ithavoll to know that little on the planet went to waste; the carrion eaters would find the carcass soon enough.

CHAPTER SIXTEEN

It was almost nightfall when Clay found signs of Rankin. He found spent casings scattered on the trail as it approached an outcropping of veined, marblelike stone that stood in a small butte beside the trail as it marched north. Clay retrieved one of the casings and sniffed at its open end, the odor of cordite strong in his nose.

Clay scouted around the spot and determined two things: first, that Rankin had encountered the *yamabushi* since the last rain— the shells had all been lying in the depression of the path and would have been immersed enough to rinse out most of the burned powder.

And second, that Rankin had probably come out of the encounter more or less intact—there was no blood, no sign even of a struggle beyond the shell casings. Clay guessed that an ambush had been attempted and that Rankin had been wary enough to have anticipated and countered it.

The rock outcropping was scarred from Rankin's shots with streaks of white near its summit. The Ithavollan warrior appeared to prefer ambuscade from heights; a good bet, Clay mused. He knew from the past that men were much like most animals in having a blind spot for danger from above.

But the bastard had found out that Rankin wasn't the average colonial, easy prey to simple ambush.

Good, Clay thought. I hope it gives him nightmares.

He traveled at a trot for another few kilometers but saw no further sign of Rankin or the *yamabushi*. The day gave out into the purpling of dusk, and Clay beat his way back into the bush to find a good tree to build a quick lean-to against. He considered traveling on through the night, but the appearance each night of Ithavoll's moon was becoming more brief, the tiny slice becoming thinner and more dim, and he didn't want to chance walking into the gorge or one of the pig-beasts in the thick darkness.

And he didn't care for the thought of walking blindly into the *yamabushi*.

In the morning Clay made a faster's breakfast of the last of the water in the skin. The hunger had begun to swell in his midsection, and he knew he would have to eat soon or risk the lethargy and exhaustion that came with fasting. A man could live for a month or more without food, given an adequate supply of water, but it didn't take long for the lack to dull his senses and weaken his defenses.

But he felt the goad of the need to catch up with Rankin and give him support against the common enemy. From appearances, the attack on the trail hadn't even been a near thing, but no one could stay ever-vigilant, and it would take only a moment's relaxation to kill him. Once he found Rankin, they could watch each other's backs.

He jogged sluggishly up the trail, which had leveled out for the most part, a thousand meters or more above what Clay guessed to be the planet's mean sea level.

The going was not particularly hard, and after a while he felt better and picked up his pace. He kept his eyes on the forest and watched especially for anything that rose above or extended over the path, providing a ready opportunity for ambuscade.

After what he guessed to be roughly four kilometers, he came to a place where the trail forked. Until then the trail had run more or less due north, following closely the rim of the river gorge, and the wider part of the trail still continued northward with the river. But a smaller, though clearly man-made, trail ran to the west at almost right angles to the original. There was a scrubby evergreen growing haphazardly from a wide crack in the rock at the intersection of the two paths. Someone—Clay assumed Rankin—had broken back one of the branches so that it pointed west, down the side path.

Clay touched the raw wood where the branch had been broken

and found that the milky-gray sap was still wet and thin, only a few hours exposed.

He shrugged inwardly and turned onto the new path. He had seen no one since leaving the squatter's camp. If Rankin hadn't marked the trail, his attacker had, and Clay was in a mood for confrontation.

As he jogged, Clay noticed the forest on either side of the narrow path begin to change, the trees becoming gradually smaller and of a different, narrower-leafed type than the evergreens he had become accustomed to. And the undergrowth was thinner.

A result of the rocky terrain, he thought, and the altitude. For the moment he appreciated the change, if for no other reason than that there was less that could cover ambush.

Before, he had been accompanied by the constant sussurus of the noise of the river rising from the gorge; with more elevation, he heard only his own footsteps on the clay and the buzz of insects. It was pleasant in a way, and Clay felt a small part of himself relax, though only to a degree.

Then, as he watched the trail ahead, a flock of raven-sized animals—he hesitated to call them birds; they seemed much closer, he thought, to Terran bats, featherless and furred—broke from the trees a hundred meters up the trail. Clay stopped and watched them fly frantically across the trail, a hundred or more strong.

There was a possibility he himself had spooked them, he thought, though he had been moving quietly and hadn't really come very close. Or the animals might simply have spontaneously decided to move at that moment.

Or someone moving through the brush up the trail could have frightened them into leaving their perches. Clay weighed the possibilities for a split second, then dodged off the trail into the underbrush on the side from which the bat-birds had flown.

He moved quickly, ignoring the rustle of dead leaves and twigs under his feet. He had to work under the assumption that the *yamabushi* had seen him first, that the movement that had spooked the bat-birds was a movement from point of observation to point of ambush.

He reached a place above and to the right of the spot from which the birds had flown. He brought the rifle to his shoulder and scanned the area before the trail through the range finder, looking out over the rifle's muzzle into the dappled shadows of the forest.

For a long moment there was nothing, then something separated itself from the shadow of a tree twenty meters downrange.

Clay instantly recognized the thick-furred silhouette and fired once as the scope's crosshairs crossed the figure, then a full burst as his target dived and rolled. The big explosive rounds tore up divots of leaf humus a scant instant behind the rolling form, then knocked fist-sized craters in the solid trunk of the tree behind which the *yamabushi* had taken cover.

The rifle snapped on an empty chamber, and he hastily ejected the empty clip and dug in his thigh pocket for the spare. Orienting it by touch, he slammed it home into the receiver, then looked up quickly to see the figure of his enemy loom suddenly above him.

Clay lunged desperately to his right and came up hard against a tree. His assailant followed, chopping down with the long-knife.

Clay blocked the blade with the rifle, but only barely, the blade skidding along the weapon's stock and cutting across his knuckles. The *yamabushi* recovered, raising the long-knife again, and Clay jammed the muzzle of the silencer into his midsection with all the force he could muster.

The man staggered back, and Clay scrambled to his feet, working the rifle's action.

Before he could bring the weapon to bear, the warrior was on him once again, shoving the rifle aside and slashing in with the knife. Clay flinched away, losing his grip on the rifle, the force of the thrust throwing him back, but the knife itself slid harmlessly off his vest.

Clay realized two things: His opponent was incredibly powerful, more powerful than he would have believed from his size and build, and he was not some unskilled, untrained back-world rube—the *yamabushi* was an infighter to be reckoned with.

The warrior followed, slashing with the knife. Clay saw a slight opening and kicked suddenly out under the man's knife hand, striking him hard in the solar plexus with the edge of his boot.

The *yamabushi* fell back with a surprised grunt, and Clay

grappled for the pistol in the shoulder holster under his arm. But the man was too fast. He recovered instantly, and his free hand whipped up and grasped Clay's wrist and twisted. The handgun flew harmlessly into the brush.

Clay kicked again, a glancing blow but enough to loosen the warrior's grip on his wrist, then turned and ran into the forest, sprinting as hard and as fast as the undergrowth would allow.

After a hundred meters or so he stopped, winded, his arms and face bleeding from the scratches inflicted by the brush he had charged through. The path he had left through the trees was obvious and easy to follow, for the most part just a hole he had punched through the underbrush.

Good, he thought. Let the bastard follow.

He picked a tree in line with the trail he had left and climbed it, shinnying into the lower branches, then pulling himself up. His wounded hand burned with the exertion, but he ignored it.

He pulled the combat knife from his boot top, then inched out on a limb, directly over the path he would have taken if he'd continued to flee deeper into the forest, and squatted there, waiting.

Frustration welled in him over the loss of the rifle, but he subliminated it into the fine hate that worked for him, honing his battle readiness. He willed the *yamabushi* to follow the trail he had left.

Come ahead, he thought. Come ahead.

The warrior came into sight ten meters down Clay's path, moving quickly but with care, studying the trail and the brush as he moved.

He doesn't underestimate me, Clay thought, noting his enemy's caution. Fine. That just makes it all the more interesting.

He held very still, counting on the chance that the *yamabushi* wouldn't be alert to his own favored tactics. Clay watched the man work toward him and noticed for the first time the gray hair, the mapping of age lines in the weathered Oriental face.

He was only mildly surprised; if the man had been younger, his reactions a shade finer, Clay wouldn't have survived their first encounter back by the trail—and Clay knew he should have died.

In the heat of battle he hadn't had time to consider it and had attributed his survival to rank luck. Now he knew better.

As if compelled, the *yamabushi* walked without hesitation toward the tree where Clay waited.

Clay steadied himself. His enemy moved underneath the tree.

Then, as if a voice inside his head told him to look up, the old warrior's face turned up, and Clay stared for a long instant into wide, maddened eyes. For that same instant he felt again the swirling nausea, the presence of another being he had felt in the street with the boy he had killed, touch him in a way that made him feel momentarily possessed by something alien and impossible.

Then, as suddenly as it had come, the presence was gone, and as if he had been released from some puppeteer's hand, he dropped from the limb onto the warrior's broad back, the knife held high for a killing stroke.

He rode the *yamabushi* down as his weight pushed the warrior to his knees and brought the knife down hard, stabbing into the man's chest. The knife jarred against his hand as it struck, and Clay felt the stubborn resistance of the bearskin over the man's heart as the knife pierced through. He knew with a sickening certainty that he had chosen the wrong stroke.

The blade buried itself into the flesh between the ribs but stopped, held fast by the thick hide, before it reached the heart. The warrior jerked up powerfully with an inarticulate roar.

He grasped the arm that held the knife and threw Clay over his shoulder as if he weighed no more than a child, slamming him hard through brush to the ground.

Clay managed to keep his grip on the knife and pulled it free as he flew over the warrior's shoulder. He landed and rolled, the pain sharp in the shoulder of the arm his opponent had wrenched.

The *yamabushi* followed, pressing the attack, but staggered before he reached Clay. Clay scrambled away.

"Fight!"

The warrior stood holding a hand against the wound Clay had made. Blood matted the thick fur over the hole and flowed down across his belly. He swayed, then steadied himself and pointed the long-knife at Clay. He repeated his demand, his voice harsh and accented.

"Fight me."

Clay balanced his knife in his hand and considered throwing it. It was his only weapon, though, and if he missed the kill, he would have to face the *yamabushi* bare-handed. And even wounded, the old warrior had the advantage—his weapon was more a sword than a knife, more than a half meter long. Clay was a bit shaken by his underestimation of the man. He needed time to recoup and rethink.

Another time, he thought, on ground of my own choosing.

Clay turned and pushed violently into the brush, heading back the way he had come, running full-tilt. He knew the *yamabushi* would follow, but the wound he had made was bleeding well; Tind would have to stop and dress it, and the blood he had already lost would weaken him, slow him enough that Clay could put some distance between them.

He reached the spot where he had first fought the *yamabushi* and searched the area for the rifle. He found it where the *yamabushi* had thrown it into a deadfall.

The clip was missing.

Clay worked the action, and the shell that had been in the chamber was gone, too. He searched around in the deadfall for a minute with no success. He cursed and threw the rifle back into the deadfall.

Without the shells it was dead weight, not even an efficient club. The pistol, too, was gone, and he had no time to search for it.

Again he channeled the anger. The time would come, soon enough.

First he had to find Rankin. If Rankin was still alive.

He found the water bag where he had left it, at the place where he had spotted the *yamabushi*. He looped it over his shoulder, trotted down to the trail, and headed westward at a quick jog.

CHAPTER SEVENTEEN

Clay was forced to rest after only four or five kilometers, the adrenaline fading from his system and taking with it the already depleted reserve of strength that the lack of food had left him.

As he rested in the shadow of the undergrowth beside the trail, he took stock. The need to find Rankin quickly was now paramount.

He was forced by events to shift the likelihood that the colonel was still alive from a probability to an unknown quantity. The fact that the *yamabushi* had come for him, had been lying in ambush for him, spoke persuasively for the possibility that Rankin was in fact dead.

If that was the case, it left Clay a free agent. But while duty was not particularly strong in him, personal loyalty was; he had to be certain.

When his breathing slowed from the ragged heaves for air that had forced him to stop, he levered himself up, fighting the numbness in his muscles and the spinning nausea in his head. The wounded hand was a fierce pain that he was finding hard to ignore.

The gash was relatively superficial, but the bones of his knuckles had been exposed by the glancing blow from the *yamabushi*'s blade, and he worried about infection—a man with one hand was very nearly useless in any sort of infighting. He bound it as best he could with a strip torn from a pants leg and moved on.

As he traveled, he searched the trail and the underbrush for signs of Rankin's passage. Occasionally he found a bootprint, a scuff in the dirt, careless indications of Rankin's movement down the trail.

It became obvious to Clay that Rankin had made no real attempt to cover his tracks, had even gone out of his way to make his trail easy to follow. The old man had wanted a confrontation as much as Clay had.

Though, after one such confrontation with the warrior, Clay was not sure he wanted a second. Or rather, he wanted to be a damn sight more prepared for it when it happened. He knew now what to expect.

His need for care in scrutinizing the trail ahead and to the sides made it difficult to spend time watching his back. Though he knew intellectually that the *yamabushi* would have to dress the stab wound in his chest and would travel slowly to keep from dying of blood loss before he had the chance to kill Clay, the paranoid itch between Clay's shoulder blades was almost unbearable, and he had to force himself to keep his eyes forward.

He had seen the sort of relentlessness the *yamabushi* had displayed before in other men, usually men he had fought with or against. More often than not they were men who died very young and very foolishly.

That the *yamabushi* had stayed alive long enough to acquire gray hairs spoke for more than simple monomania. He was a dangerous foe, and Clay preferred to keep such a man in range, where he could watch him.

And that contagious madness, the feeling of an *other* that lived in the man's eyes, touched him with something that neared terror. He didn't know what possessed the old warrior, but it frightened him.

He pushed it back; the old warrior was simply a man, nothing more.

The trail dipped into a wide, shallow ravine, and Clay followed it down, carefully watching his footing on the slick, rain-washed clay. At the bottom, as the trail crossed a wash and began to climb once more out of the ravine, Clay found further signs of Rankin's passage, this time more spent rifle casings, scattered like a fistful of gold pieces across the bottom of the wash.

He studied the marks in the dirt and the empty casings and turned away from the trail, following the northward turn of the ravine where the brush had been beaten down. On a stone not far from the trail he found blood and, farther up the ravine, more, spotting the rocky floor.

Clay grimaced. It didn't take much imagination to guess what had taken place.

Rankin had come into the ravine, concentrating on keeping his footing. The *yamabushi* had been waiting for him at the bottom, hidden in the brush that grew in a clump on an open patch of ground at the bottom of the ravine.

Obviously, Rankin had survived the first attack, but Clay had little doubt that as he climbed up the narrowing end of the ravine he would come across Rankin's slashed remains somewhere ahead.

Clay remembered suddenly that the *yamabushi* had been wounded—there had been a blood-caked bandage on one thigh. It was possible that Rankin had managed to hit him, though as he pictured the *yamabushi* in his mind, the bandaged wound looked old.

The walls of the small ravine grew steeper, becoming almost vertical as he moved away from the wider, shallower point at which the trail crossed. Soon Clay was forced to use his hands to help him climb, and a fresh jolt of pain shot like fire through his wounded hand each time he had to use it to balance himself or pull himself up over the broken rocks near the head of the ravine.

As he came near the top, it narrowed down to a little more than a meter in width, the rock walls rising almost sheer on either side. There was still a trail of blood to follow, occasionally drops and splatters on the rocks.

Something caught his eye, glinting dimly in the weak sunlight, and he reached down between two rocks and extracted a casing.

A few meters farther up he found another.

He examined the second casing and sniffed at it, noting the scent of the fresh cordite, then dropped it. It rattled against the rocks with a loud, tinny sound.

As he began to rise again to his feet, he heard a sound in the rocks above, and he dropped flat, the knife coming to his hand.

He waited for the sound to be repeated, but there was only silence.

It could have been anything; he couldn't begin to know all the native life-forms, but he was sure there was the equivalent of Terran lizards in the rocks, along with insects easily large enough to make the noise he had heard. Certain small life-forms were inherent to all ecologies.

He stood partially up and peered ahead over the rocks, and a bullet ricocheted off the boulder he had fallen behind, a half dozen centimeters from his head.

He dropped down again in a panic, the gun's muffled report echoing eerily between the rock walls. His cheek stung from rock splinters thrown up by the bullet; he touched his hand to his face, and a spot of blood came away on his fingertip.

But he knew the sound of that weapon.

"Rankin?" His voice sounded strangely loud in his ears as he spoke.

Silence.

He stood again slowly and crept gingerly forward through the rocks.

He heard a grunt of recognition, and a voice said, "I'll be damned."

Clay relaxed. "Rankin!"

"Up here." The voice was weak, tired. Clay scrabbled up through the rocks.

A few meters up, the ravine narrowed to barely wider than his shoulders and ended, a sheer rock face extending up to ground level, some thirty meters above. Rankin sat there, his back to the rock face, his carbine propped nearby up against a small boulder, its barrel wedged so that it was pointing down into the ravine toward Clay.

Rankin saw Clay as he came up and let the carbine slide off the rock and onto his leg. He grunted and let out his breath as if he had been holding it to make the shot, then to see if the face that arose from below was actually Clay's.

"Sorry for the lack of manners. Thought you were that bastard with the sword, and I figured I'd make him a warm welcome back."

Clay grinned despite himself. "Glad to see you. I'd about decided you had bought the farm back there. There's blood all over hell and gone."

Rankin nodded weakly, and Clay noted the hastily bandaged

wounds on his left forearm and on one leg. The arm wound looked minor, but both the bandage on the leg and what was left of the pants leg were soaked dark with blood. The leg was clearly badly damaged; without antibiotics, in a couple of days it would be gangrenous.

Rankin gestured to the leg. "He nicked me some, all right," he admitted. "I scrambled up here quick before I bled to death and made a stand. He managed to surprise me; I tossed a rock the size of your head into that clump of brush before I slung my rifle and climbed down into the ravine. He took it without a sound. Must've bounced off that thick goddamned Neanderthal skull."

He fingered the vest he was wearing. "This thing saved my carcass. He was all over me before I knew what was up, swinging with that long-bladed knife."

"Why didn't he finish the job?"

Rankin snorted. "You can bet he damned well tried. He came for me three times after I made it up here. I managed to spot him every one of 'em, but once it was close, very close. I guess he got tired of beating his head against a rather dangerous wall— I still had the carbine, and I came close enough a few times to rattle his cage. He hasn't tried for me for a day or more."

Clay showed his wounded hand. "He decided I was easier prey."

Rankin squinted at the hand and shook his head. "No, just that I wasn't going anywhere. He knew what shape I was in. Did you kill him?"

Clay shook his head and indicated a spot on his chest. "Cut him bad enough right about here to slow him down. Lost my rifle, though."

He picked up Rankin's carbine and worked the action. The chamber was empty.

"That shot I took at you was the last shell."

"Damn." He tossed the carbine down. "What now?"

Rankin shrugged. "We try to survive."

CHAPTER EIGHTEEN

Clay checked Rankin's wounds and saw that he could do nothing further to bind them or to make Rankin more comfortable. He let Rankin drink his fill from the almost depleted water skin, then pulled its strap over his shoulder and worked his way back down the ravine to the trail, crossed it, and continued down, following the wash.

As he had suspected, a few hundred meters beyond the trail the ravine bottomed out into a rocky pool. It was a damp climate. Low places were bound to collect water.

He submersed the water skin in the water and left it there to allow the seams to swell once again, wrapping the strap around a convenient rock.

They had water; now they would need food.

There was very little in the way of brush around the pond for the simple reason that there was little soil among the rocks, and he settled for squatting down behind a low boulder two or three meters from the pool to wait for whatever might decide to water at the tanque.

Nothing showed itself. He waited two hours until the daylight began to fade, then gave up and pulled the full skin from the water.

As he hiked wearily back up the ravine, he tried unsuccessfully to ignore the sour rumbling of hunger in his belly.

While he climbed, he picked up likely-looking sticks and twigs, and occasionally small twisted lengths that he pulled free from a dry woody plant that looked to be likely tinder, to add to the few pieces of deadwood he had noted before that had fallen from trees up above into the ravine near were Rankin had taken up position.

He kept alert for game of any sort as he walked, but again the local fauna seemed intent on frustrating his hunger. He saw nothing but the small, distant silhouettes of large birds wheeling in the otherwise empty sky.

More than once he had to resist trying berries or greens that looked invitingly similar to plants he knew to be edible on Terra and other planets where the majority of the flora had been imported from Earth; the chances were much too good that the similarity here, on Ithavoll, ended with appearance. Ithavoll had its own life; what man had imported struggled to flourish on the plowed and tamed lowlands. It hadn't yet—and no doubt never would, Clay thought sourly—made inroads into the planet's ecostructure.

There were plant toxins on all the outworld planets that no one, not even the colonists who had lived on those worlds for a hundred years or so, had discovered, much less developed antidotes for.

And even if he still had the medical kit, the chances were slim of finding an antitoxin that would work were he to poison himself, though the kit contained wide-spectrum drugs that would counter almost anything Terra could dish out. There were too many variables, too many possible toxins for even the most all-encompassing of drugs.

The only food that was more or less universally safe was fresh meat. Almost anything that walked, crawled, or flew would be nutritious, including the majority of insects, as long as one stayed away from the organ meats—he had lost a good friend, long ago on a planet called Montreal, when the man had eaten from the liver of a Terran polar bear, one of a group that had been genetically modified for size (they stood nearly two meters at the shoulder, on all fours) and imported to Montreal to help control some local seagoing pests and had bred to the point where they were used as a food source themselves.

None of the members of the hunting party had known what the youngest Montreal child knew, that at certain times of the year the bear's liver contained toxic concentrations of retinoic acid—simple vitamin A.

The man had tracked and killed the bear on a bet while they

were in the field, and at the celebration that ensued he had roasted the beast's huge liver and eaten chunks of it with unmitigated relish. He had died in agony a few hours later.

Ignorance had killed him just as surely as a bullet.

By the time Clay got back to Rankin, night had settled solidly in. Rankin muttered a greeting as he walked up, the harsh voice emerging eerily from the dark split in the rock where he waited.

Clay dropped his load of tinder and unshouldered the water bag, handing it to the lighter shadow that was Rankin. He heard the water slosh in the bulging skin as Rankin lifted it up to drink.

"I'm going to build a fire. I don't suppose you managed to save any of the starter tabs."

Clay could imagine Rankin shaking his head, though he couldn't see it. "At the bottom of the gorge, with everything else."

"It's okay, I think. Give me a few minutes and I'm pretty sure I can get something going."

Clay searched the area around Rankin patiently with his fingertips, wishing he'd thought to look while it was still light, until he found the stone chips he'd remembered seeing earlier in the day.

He pressed one of the chips against Rankin's hand to show him what he had. "It's not flint, but I think it will do the trick."

He then built up a small pile of dry tinder near where Rankin sat and held a flat piece of the quartzlike crystal tightly with one hand while he struck it with the back of his knife blade. Each stroke threw a small spray of weak sparks into the tinder.

The fire proved elusive, the sparks dying out almost instantly as they fell on the tinder. He kept at it patiently, changing the striking stone from one hand to the other when his arm tired.

After a time the tender smoldered and caught, and he blew gently on it until a flame rose up through the pile of twigs and dry grass. Then he fed it sticks until the fire crackled and climbed, flickering in the rocky crevice.

"Keep it low."

Clay looked up and was surprised by Rankin's countenance in the light of the flames. His eyes were sunken deeply into the sockets, the shuddering light of the fire making him look almost macabre.

"He knows where we are," Clay said. "Besides, the walls of the ravine hide the light."

Rankin shrugged, and the movement heightened the strange effect of the firelight, making long shadows under his eyes and across his face. "It's not the *bushi* I'm worried about this time. I saw a government hopper earlier today. A small one, scout size."

He gestured up weakly toward the sky, moving only his hand. "Flew right overhead."

Clay pondered for a moment. "This far out, it means a base close by."

Rankin said nothing.

"Which means we're close," Clay continued. "This thing is somewhere near here, probably no more than five or six kilometers."

Rankin nodded. "A little to the northwest, I think. That hopper was moving too quickly for surveillance. He was either headed out or home. I think home."

It was Clay's turn for silence. After a minute Rankin shifted with a groan.

"Which means you have to leave me here and get the hell out. I'm no longer mobile. Someone has to get back to the Terran survey center with the location of that bastard so they can send someone else to blow up the damned thing. I can't do it, so the responsibility falls to you."

"I don't think your *yamabushi* has any intention of letting either of us get out. We've got to kill him or he'll hound our heels the whole way back and probably end up taking us both." Clay counted in his head. "We've still more than a week before pickup. That's too much time, too many opportunities. We'll be walking targets . . ."

"You're not listening. I said nothing about 'we.' Alone, you can make it back. Once in the village you can arm yourself, even if it's just with an antique blunderbuss."

Clay shook his head. "No."

Rankin raised an eyebrow, the expression strange on his sunken face. "Sorry I gave you the impression you had a vote. This is Combined Forces business. I'm not asking; it's an order."

Clay nudged the empty carbine with his foot. "I don't think

you're equipped to enforce orders any longer. Besides, it's standard operating procedure that in the field when an officer is
wounded badly enough to be incapacitated, as you clearly are,
his second in command takes over. Since there's just the two of
us, that would be me. I like my way better. So that's how we do
it.''

Rankin glowered but said nothing.

Clay settled back on his heels and looked out into the night.
He saw something flash for an instant in the darkness at the edge
of the firelight. He pulled the knife from his boot top with a
minimum of motion.

It flashed again, this time in two distinct points—an animal's
eyes. He weighed the knife in his hand and held a finger to his
lips to hold Rankin quiet.

The animal edged closer, attracted by the fire. It was small—
Clay guessed about five or six kilos—and vaguely ratlike.

Move slowly, Clay thought. Don't alarm it.

He raised the knife gently, slowly, until it was even with his
cheek, then threw, striking the animal behind a foreleg and
knocking it down.

Clay was up instantly. He grasped the dying animal roughly
by the neck. It struggled weakly, and he twisted until the bones
of its neck ruptured with a snap.

He gutted and skinned it, then cut the meat into chunks and
spitted them on a finger-thick twig. He roasted them over the
little fire, the dripping grease making the flames sputter and
leap.

He left the meat over the fire until it was cooked through; rare
meat was the luxury of those who ate food that had been nurtured in the sterile hothouse farms of Terra. Wild game carried
parasites.

When it was roasted to his satisfaction, he gave a large piece
to Rankin, speared on the knife. The cooked meat was gamy
and vaguely bitter, but Clay ate it with the relish of true hunger.

When he had eaten his fill, he stretched and scraped the hide
in the same way he had with the water skin, careful not to pierce
it.

If he was lucky enough to kill another, he would drain its
blood into the new skin, and they would drink that in lieu of the

water. There was little that was more nourishing than raw, fresh blood.

He felt invigorated, the full belly making him feel warmly satiated though somewhat uncomfortable. Still, he was cheered. A good deal of optimism could be generated by a solid meal.

He rubbed his hands and arms with sand grubbed up from between the rocks. There was water, a good six liters or more, he guessed, but he doubted he would get the chance to make another unharassed trip to the pool. Even wounded, the *bushi* warrior would come soon.

The sand didn't have much effect on the clotted blood and excreta that matted the hair on his arms. He became suddenly aware of his own odor; the smell of death on his body had soaked into his tattered fatigue pants.

Rankin finished his meal and tossed a bone into the fire, sending up a rush of sparks.

"Are you enjoying your tour of duty?" There was no humor in the question. He watched Clay narrowly.

Clay returned his gaze. "I'm not sure I know what you're asking."

"Simple question. Are you enjoying yourself? I rather think you are. I've worked with men like you all my adult life—a considerable amount of time. I've yet to meet the professional soldier of fortune who fought only for the money. The percentages are too much against living long enough to spend what you make on a consistent basis."

Clay shrugged. "I've lived this long."

"Doesn't answer the question."

"Okay, okay. No, not particularly. I'd rather be back in Miami, mindlessly watching vid with the rest of the unwashed multitude."

"Why aren't you, then?"

Clay gritted his teeth. It was an argument he'd had with himself more than once. "Because I've lived this long."

"I don't follow."

"It's what I do. I'm good at it. And it hasn't killed me yet. Like everyone else, I can't really believe I'm ever going to buy it. Soldiers are optimists; you of all people should know that."

Rankin shook his head. "No, not really. When things look bad, I've seen too many get religion. 'Foxhole Christians'—or

Buddhists, or whatever. Someone who believes he isn't going to die doesn't need God. No, most fight because they need the shock, the adrenaline kick.''

"Is that why you do it?''

"Let me amend that—most fight either for thrills, or they fight because they believe in something. I'm too old to run around tangling with the likes of our friend with the knife for the fun of it. I'm not naive enough to think that anything I've done or will do is going to make great changes, but the C.F. is all that's holding this ball of wax together, and I do what they ask me to.''

Clay snorted. "The Combined Forces exists to perpetuate itself. Nothing more, nothing less.''

Rankin shifted again with a groan. "Look, you've had some bad times with the C.F. Like any organization grown large and unwieldy, there are parts that need to be excised. You did just that yourself, and if you hadn't done it in an embarrassing way, they would have clapped you on the back—in an unpublic way— for doing the Forces a service. You can't simply shoot a superior officer in the field, not when the known universe might hear about it on the vid.

"Still, chaos is much worse than the Forces could ever be, and that's what we'd have without the C.F. and adjustments of the sort we attempted here. More people died during the twenty years of the Luna wars than in any time in human history, and only a fraction of them in battle. Most died on the colony worlds in the anarchy that came about when the Combined Forces pulled out and left them to their own devices. It's the nature of the beast—they need a strong hand.

"Which still leaves you as an unknown quantity. It's not for the love of it or the money. So why?''

"I don't really know,'' Clay admitted. "Like I said, I suppose because it is the one thing I do well.''

He pushed a stick into the fire and watched the flames touch it and take hold. "That's the best reason I can come up with, anyhow.''

Rankin grinned suddenly, the expression macabre on his sunken face. "It's the best reason there is. The gods frown on wasted talent.''

Clay felt pain swell again in his heart, remembering that

Greene had said something similar to him when they had swum together in the river near the squatter's village. That moment, only a couple days gone, seemed somehow part of a distant and lost past. He stifled the emotion before it could show on his face.

"The gods? Whose gods?"

"Maybe his." Rankin pointed out beyond the fire into the night. "And I don't want to meet them tonight. I'd appreciate it if you could keep a weather eye out while I get a few hours sleep. It's rough trying to sleep without someone to watch your back. Wake me up later and I'll spell you."

Clay nodded. "Be happy to oblige."

Rankin settled back and in a few minutes was asleep, his breathing heavy and rhythmic.

Clay watched the edge of the firelight for a while, but nothing else was drawn to the flames. He let the fire die down to embers and listened in the darkness for any sound that didn't belong to the alien night, but there was no sound at all beyond the rustle of the wind.

CHAPTER NINETEEN

Clay shook Rankin awake a few hours later. He handed over his knife, settled down as comfortably as he could among the rocks, and tried to sleep. Though he was bone-tired, his waking mind refused to give way.

"I would have thought he would have shown up by now," he said after a time, breaking the night's silence.

Rankin cleared his throat. "Perhaps you wounded him worse than you thought."

Clay shook his head, then realized that Rankin couldn't see the gesture. "I don't think so. Bad enough to bleed him some, yes. But not enough to kill him or to stop him for any longer than it would take to plug the wound up with something. Given that he took it slow, favoring the wound to keep from bleeding to death, I still expected him to come charging up these rocks sometime after sunset."

"He's smarter than that. An old fox."

"Yes, old. Still strong as hell, though. Too strong. They've done something to him, maybe. Mind-wash or drugs. I felt the same thing from him I felt in that boy in the city. It's strange, really strange. Maybe something esper. Whatever was working on them worked on *me*, just for an instant."

"Perhaps. Regardless, my money says he's waiting somewhere below for one or the both of us to try and leave. That's his safest bet—he has time and the water supply on his side. Don't underestimate experience, son. That bastard's killed more than one young turk, and he knows better than to charge blindly up here after you. He'll just bide his time until we have no choice but to face him on his own ground."

Clay nodded to himself. He had no doubt that Rankin was right. And he had no intention of sitting in those rocks until thirst and hunger drove him to face the *yamabushi* after the lack of nourishment had weakened him.

"When the day breaks, I'll head out. If he's waiting out there for me, I'll kill him. If not, I'll leave enough sign so that he'll more than likely follow my track and leave you be. When I get back to the village, I'll radio the consulate to send a team, and we'll come back for you."

"And if he comes for me instead?"

"He won't. He still thinks you're armed."

"You've been with me. He'll figure you're armed again now, too."

Clay shook his head impatiently, forgetting that Rankin couldn't see it. "You're immobile. He'll know that for certain when I leave here alone, if he doesn't already. He'll know he can take you at his leisure, after you pass out from hunger or fever, if he can kill me first, before I can get to a transmitter. He won't care if I'm armed—he damned sure hasn't yet."

Rankin grunted acquiescence. "I see your point. I reckon I'll go along with it."

"Good," Clay said simply. He was glad Rankin wasn't the sort to argue rank against reason. But then, he reflected, he hadn't much choice.

He settled back again and forced himself to relax, chanting his mantra, and soon drifted off into a restless and dream-filled sleep.

He woke just as the sky was growing pink with morning and shook his head to clear away the residue of a dream that had followed him up from the depths of sleep. The dreams troubled him somewhat; he had always slept dreamlessly, or at the least he had always forgotten whatever he dreamed. But these dreams stayed with him, leaving an unpleasant feeling of unease, a nervous anticipation. It was as if something unwelcome had visited his sleeping mind and left it tainted and sullied.

He readied himself quickly, retrieving his knife from Rankin and taking a long swallow from the water bag. He poured about a liter into the new, smaller skin.

"I'll leave this with you." He set the large water skin beside Rankin's near leg. "There's plenty on the way out of here."

Rankin glanced up. "Fine. Just don't get yourself killed. Or at least take that bastard with you so I don't have to deal with him."

Clay grinned idiotically. "I'll do my best."

He started down the ravine, then stopped.

"Did you dream anything last night?"

Rankin shrugged weakly. The effort he put into the movement spoke volumes to Clay. He would have to be quick; Rankin would not last much longer.

"Strange you should ask. I always dream here. It's funny, but since the first day I stepped on this forsaken ball of dirt, I've dreamed the damnedest dreams, and I don't know why. I've heard tell that certain of the locals say there's native life we haven't discovered yet hiding in the forests and hills. They call them *kami*—that's Japanese for fairies, pixies, and the like. They say the *kami* sleep in your head and give you dreams. But then again, who knows what's in the local water that might mess with your head, stuff that all the testing in the world might not pick up. Or maybe in the food, some local hallucinogen they inadvertently use as a spice."

He smiled. "Makes you think, anyway."

Clay nodded. "It does that."

There was a moment's awkward silence, which Clay broke by rising.

"Good luck," Rankin said quietly.

"Thanks," Clay slapped his shoulder and started out away from the little camp, picking his way down through the rocks, careful to avoid knocking loose any stones that might betray him to an ambusher.

He made the journey down the bottom of the ravine warily, stopping every few paces to listen for movement. To his great surprise, he made it out to the place where the trail he had followed the day before dipped into the ravine without confrontation.

He watched the trail from cover for several minutes but could see no way in which the *bushi* warrior could have concealed himself well enough to escape observation. The trail was flanked only by thin scrub, except at the point at which Clay himself stood, the first place from which the *yamabushi* had doubtless ambushed Rankin the first time.

When he was satisfied, he pushed out onto the trail and climbed up the way he had come, making it clear in the signs he left that not only had he come into the ravine, he had left it as well.

Then he set off at an easy lope down the empty trail.

The sound of the Terran's passage had wakened Tind from his own troubled sleep. He shifted carefully in his vantage among the rocks that were piled high along the side of the ravine and watched his enemy pass by.

He made no effort to stop him. The wound in his chest would need at least another day or it would bleed in battle until he was helpless. The Terran's knife had struck deeply, very near the heart. The fact that he had even survived was an omen in his favor.

He had no choice but to wait, then follow behind, taking the Terran somewhere below, before he could reach help. He tightly held the pouch, stained with his own blood, that hung from the string around his neck.

From within the leather he felt the presence of his lord flow up through his hands, through his wrists and arms to his heart. He could feel the muscle of his heart swell painfully as if his blood were growing suddenly vicous and thick. His head swam and his blood burned, and he could taste the bitter smoke of the *maki* on his tongue. The leather bag seemed to swell in his hand, to burn blood-warm, to beat in time with his heart.

After a moment he could feel his waning strength begin to return, the ache dissolve from his wounds, the pain leave his aging knees.

His mind left him, and he felt the mind of *Hachiman* fill him until there was nothing else but the power of the gods. *Serve me,* the god ordered, and Tind ached to do so. *Worship me. Protect me. Kill for me.*

Long after the Terran had passed, Tind's own mind returned, and when the dizziness ended, he stood carefully from the bed he had made among the rocks and set out through the forest, forcing his way through the underbrush and trees in a direction that would allow him to intercept the trail ahead somewhere close behind his quarry

The passage through the dense growth took most of his concentration, but a small part of his mind dwelled on the portent of the recurring dream, the one that had savaged his sleep by the ravine. His god was warning him. Or taunting him with his own defeat.

Either way, he had no choice but to pursue and do battle with the Terran.

If he were destined to die at the Terran's hand, then so be it. He would die with glory, a battle cry on his lips, his knife soaked in the Terran's blood for his ancestors to see as they welcomed him to heaven.

He *would* kill him!

CHAPTER
TWENTY

Clay slowed to a walk after a few kilometers, fatigue making his legs rubbery. The lack of sleep was telling, and he could feel the rumbling in his intestines that warned of the beginnings of dysentery, a product of the strange food and the bacteria he had taken in with the water.

He kept moving, making slow progress down the trail, but now he had to stop frequently to let his body spasm and purge itself and to rest, the sickness draining away his small reserve of strength.

Ithavoll's sun was, as ever, dissipated and relatively dim, but he began to wish he had a hat of some sort; his fatigue cap was long gone, though he couldn't remember exactly when he had lost it. Somewhere in the blur of events of the last two days. He felt somewhat delirious.

He hunkered for a time in the cool shade of a tree and waited for the sickness to pass.

When it did, he continued on, sheer will at times all that kept him on his feet. The need to cover distance was uppermost— he couldn't risk traveling far in the almost absolute darkness of the planet's night; a broken leg or a fall into a ravine or into the river gorge might be the result—and he needed to put as much distance between himself and his enemy as possible.

He wasn't sure the *yamabushi* would have any such compunction; the man was just insane enough, Clay thought, to travel blindly through the broken terrain, risking a bone-breaking, maybe fatal spill. Besides, it was his country, and he might well be familiar enough with the area to travel sight-less.

The thought drifted away from him, and he lapsed for a time into an exhausted fog, his mind jumping erratically from image to image. He concentrated on placing one foot before the other, then on keeping on his feet at all as he found himself swaying drunkenly from one side of the trail to the other.

He rested for a minute, shook his head hard, and continued on.

The walking gradually became easier, and a certain amount of his strength returned, but he still felt childishly weak. He knew with a cold certainty that if Tind came upon him now, wounded or not, he would die helplessly, impaled on the blade of the old warrior's long-knife.

He had made another kilometer or so since resting when something beside the trail caught his eye.

In a low place beside the path, in a pool of standing, stagnant water was a thick knot of tall slender trees bunched together like a canebrake.

Clay eased himself down the shallow bank to the plants and looked them over. The trunks were smooth and seemingly bark-less, slightly damp and slick to the touch.

The trunks all seemed to grow from one standing root, each thin and branchless, clothed only by a tuft of foliage at the top. Several of the trunks had broken from the main root and lay scattered about in the depression.

These, the dead, broken trunks, were what had initially caught Clay's attention. Whereas the living trunks were a vague green, the broken ones were weathered in a smooth obsidian black, each roughly two meters long and straight as a rule. Clay knelt and picked up one of the trunks; it was light, surprisingly so, and as hard as stone.

He weighed it in his hand, then took the boot knife and struck at the withered foliage at the top of the broken-off branch. The back of the knife glanced off just below the tuft, chipping off a piece of the material. He hit it again, and the trunk broke cleanly. He then chipped away at the other end until he had a satisfactory point. When he had finished, he possessed a strong, resilient pike almost two meters long.

Come on, now, you bastard. He hefted the pike; it felt good in his hand, solid. It also gave him a meter and a half's reach on the *yamabushi*.

Come on, now.

Tind followed, walking stiffly, carefully, to favor the wound. He saw the signs of the Terran's sickness and thought grimly that if the gods were not with him, they did not walk at the Terran's side, either.

He touched a hand to the wound in his chest as he walked, pressing against the poultice of leaves and roots he had pounded into a paste with a stone and bound against the wound. There was some pain, a small burning in his chest as he pressed, but no new blood.

Another twelve hours, he thought, perhaps a day. Soon, though the wound would not be wholly healed, the scabbing would be solid enough that he could fight at least long enough to kill the Terran. Whether he died soon afterward was irrelevant. If the Terran died first, then all was well.

When the sun started down, he made a decision and left the trail, cutting southward into the thick forest.

He was confident the Terran would sleep through the darkness. With luck and the favor of *Hachiman*, he would march through the night through the forest, circumventing the Terran, and come out ahead of him on the main trail into the highlands with enough time to arrange a welcome.

He thrust through the brush a bit more quickly. The thought pleased him.

Clay reached the intersection of the two trails before nightfall and turned southward, following the new trail down, retracing the footsteps he had made, it seemed, an eternity before. The sound of the distant roar of the river in the gorge reassured him curiously, like the company of an old friend, a known quantity.

He traveled as swiftly as he could, trotting loosely until all the light had leached away and the only way he could keep to the trail was by the faint sound of the river in the gorge to his left. He went another kilometer in that fashion, then stopped in frustration, the darkness around him inky and impenetrable.

Ithavoll's nighttime moon had turned fully into the shadowed portion of its cycle. Without even the scant light from the thin sliver of moon that had guided him before, if he moved on, there was a good chance he would eventually walk right off the twisting path as it followed the cliff's edge and into the river gorge.

An outcropping of black rock loomed a few meters down the trail, a darker shadow in the general darkness. He shuffled carefully to it and settled down, his back against the cool stone.

He strained to listen for any sound of movement, but gradually, as the thickest part of the night settled in, each of the myriad small forms of life that thrived in the forest undergrowth wakened and added its voice to a growing cacophony. The sounds of the night blended in with the sussurus of the distant river to make a dull roar in his ears.

The steady noise and the pure blindness of the dark began to work on him. More than once he started at a sound and then was unsure he had ever heard it.

Late in the night he was jolted into awareness from a light doze by the sensation of unseen things crawling on him, and he brushed at his arms to find nothing there.

Just like a great smothering sensory-deprivation tank, he thought. Deprive a man of enough sensory imput, and imagination takes over. He starts to hear things, feel things that aren't there.

It was maddening. He clenched his teeth and tried to blot it all out, forcing his muscles to relax. He tried to focus within himself, to lapse into meditation.

Then he heard another noise. He almost dismissed it, then sat stiffly alert as a large, vague form emerged suddenly from the general darkness a short meter and a half from where he sat against the stone. It passed slowly by him, snuffling at the damp ground.

Clay recognized the humped shadow-shape as one of the giant pig-beasts. It moved on into the darkness, but he could hear it grunting nearby, digging in the leaf mold with its tusks, for nearly a half hour.

There was only the sound of the night for a while, then Clay started at the terrified squeal of some small animal as the boar succeeded in its rooting hunt.

He tried to relax enough to sleep, using his mantra, letting it coax his mind to focus and then empty. It was a good trick, one of the many things he'd learned, compliments of the C.F. drill instructors, while he was in basic training. No concern for his comfort there—fatigue lowered morale, and low morale affected combat efficiency. Simple behavioral statistics.

The generals of every army and every war throughout any history he had ever read had always given much more weight to numbers than to men. It was the nature of the bureaucratic beast.

After a while he dozed a bit, but total immersion eluded him. He slept in a sense, but his overburdened mind wasn't able to let go, to allow him the deep sleep he really needed to take away the fatigue that had burrowed itself deep into his muscles, into his spine. He woke long before dawn and decided to take his chances in the dark.

He moved carefully along the trail—occasionally, when his confidence wavered, on his hands and knees, feeling along for the cliff edge that he feared might open up under his feet into the abyss. He could see large shapes—trees and boulders—as shades of black, but the ground he walked on was shrouded completely in the featureless darkness.

The thirst burned in his throat, and he finished the few swallows of water that sloshed in the small skin. When the thirst returned a short while later, he searched around, brushing the ground with his fingertips, and found a small round pebble. He brushed it clean on his fatigue pants and placed it under his tongue, rolling it gently around to stimulate his salivary glands.

His progress forward was painfully slow, impossible to measure without reference points. He imagined he had crawled and walked two, maybe three kilometers.

He wondered how much darkness remained. One hour? Two? The night seemed interminable.

After an eternity the western sky began to lighten, and slowly, by degrees, he began to be able to make out his footing. He increased his pace until he was trotting along the narrow trail.

The dawn broke pearlescent above the trees. He felt his confidence grow with the morning light.

Late in the morning he came once again to the place where the *yamabushi* had killed Fitzgerald, and again he was tempted to try climbing down into the gorge for the packs. The pike and combat knife seemed puny and ineffectual in comparison to the explosives and automatic rifles that the *yamabushi* had tossed over the cliffs into the river gorge with the rest of the supplies.

He looked quickly once again over the cliff's edge into the

river mist below, then turned away, shaking his head. Too much risk, not enough time.

As he turned, he saw something move on the path, a hundred meters down-trail. He crouched and shaded his eyes, squinting at the irregularities of the path.

A figure rose from where it had been lying in the dust of the trail and resolved itself into a man.

It was the warrior.

Clay dived instinctively for the undergrowth at the side of the trail.

He landed hard, breaking through the thick brush, and something sharp pierced through his side and leg. He bit back a scream and tried to jerk himself free, the stakes he had fallen on holding him deeply, burrowed in his flesh.

He blacked out for a second, awoke almost immediately, and pulled again against the stakes. One, in his side just below the ribs, pulled free. Twisting, he yanked at the other, ignoring the agony, until it pulled out of the ground, still buried for a third of its length in his thigh.

He pushed himself upright, tried to stand, and felt the blackness begin to close around him once again. He managed to sit up, roll awkwardly to his knees, then rise to his feet.

A few meters away he could hear the *yamabushi* crash into the brush down the trail, moving out into the forest instead of directly for Clay.

Coming around from behind, Clay thought. Doesn't want to get fouled in his own trap.

He looked quickly around. For about three square meters the ground sprouted thickly with sharpened stakes. The warrior had sprung his trap an instant too soon, and Clay had fallen at the edge of the bed of spikes.

Dragging the pike, Clay limped deeper into the woods, away from the *yamabushi*'s approach through the brush. He used his free hand to press the material of the vest against the wound at his left side.

He would have to dress that, he thought absently, before the blood loss was too severe. It occurred to him that the vest had failed him in the same way it had failed Greene, riding up as he dived into the brush and exposing his side to the stake that had punched into him.

He pushed through a thicket of briery brush, holding his forearm across his eyes, the thorns tearing at his skin and pulling agonizingly at the stake that jutted like a handle from his thigh. He could hear the old warrior behind him, still crashing through the brush like some large animal rampaging through the forest.

When he had cleared the briers, he stopped and grasped the stake as well as he could with both hands. He took a deep breath, held it, then pulled.

It resisted, then gave with a moist drawing sound. He dropped it and pulled the combat knife from his boot with his right hand and held the pike and his side as best he could with his left.

The brier bushes shuddered as Tind pushed into them, following Clay's spoor.

Blood made the knife slippery in Clay's hand. He balanced it in his slick palm and waited. He saw a sudden flash of black fur through an opening and threw, whipping the knife into the gap in the brush with all his might.

He heard a grunt as the blade stuck home. Then he turned and ran, dragging his injured leg, holding the wound in his side with one hand and the makeshift pike in the other with a tenacity born of pure desperation.

The thick brush gave way quickly to a more open but still lush undergrowth beneath the giant broad-leafed trees. Clay stopped, choking for breath, against one of the thick-barked trunks and listened.

After a moment he heard the sound of the warrior's pursuit. The noise of his movement was intermittent but not far behind. Tind followed only a little slower, reading Clay's escape in the broken brush and blood spoor he had left behind.

He had had little hope that the thrown knife would actually kill the *yamabushi*. Too much that was vital was protected by the tough hide of the bearskin Tind wore. But the chances were strong that he had wounded him seriously enough that the blood loss would make him less of a foe when Clay finally had to face him. That was all he could hope for.

He limped away from the tree into the depths of the forest, putting ground between himself and his pursuer.

CHAPTER
TWENTY-ONE

Tind braced himself and pulled the Terran's knife from his gut. The blade pulled free easily, sliding through the muscle, leaving a thin, inch-wide puncture from which a dark red stream of blood flowed.

He studied the blade for a long moment, turning it in his hand, then threw it from him into the forest. There had been blood on the hilt, not his own.

It is good, Terran. Our blood mingles; we are one. When I die, you will serve me in the afterlife; you will sit at my feet, and I will say to my honored ancestors, "Here is one I have slain whose very blood I share." He gritted his teeth. *Even those of purer blood than my own will give me homage for killing such a warrior, even though you be a godless Terran.*

He followed the clear trail the Terran had left through the brush to a tree where he had stopped. Blood stained a darker spot on the red of the bark and pooled in the clay between the roots.

He followed the scattered spots of blood away from the tree into the deeper forest. He came to the place where the Terran had stopped again and bound his wounds. The blood spoor ended, but he had no trouble finding the trail, reading easily the scuffs in the dirt, the slight bend of a weed brushed by the Terran's passage.

After a time he came to the place where the Terran had crossed one of the wide leaf mold–filled hollows that pocked the forest. The trail ended at the edge of its resilient surface. He bit back frustration and followed the edge of the depression until he found where the Terran had left it, at an angle out the right side.

He followed this, and soon the trail came to another hollow, wide, featureless, and unmarked. He cursed, slamming his fist hard against a tree trunk, and bellowed his burning rage to the gods.

Clay found and crossed a half dozen of the track-absorbing hollows before he came to a game trail that cut through the thick forest growth.

Countless years of the passage of animals down the trail had beaten and packed the earth into a hard clay rut. He debated with himself for a time as to which direction to take, but in the end it didn't matter, and he took the one that meandered generally south.

The important thing was that the hard, hoof-packed clay would hide his tracks much better than the open forest floor, perhaps well enough that his pursuer would choose the wrong direction.

He moved very carefully down the trail for the first few hundred meters, taking pains to avoid disturbing the clay or the growth on the flanks of the trail. Then he moved on with more dispatch, favoring his leg but making good time.

He had been forced to staunch the flow of blood from his side and leg with more strips torn from his ravaged fatigue pants. The wound in his side had bled heavily, but it wasn't particularly deep, as the stake had skittered across his lower ribs before piercing his side. The blood loss had weakened him, but the flow of blood had probably helped to clean the wound somewhat of dirt and whatever else might have been on the sharpened stakes in the warrior Tind's trap.

He worried about the filth on the cloth itself, but there was nothing for it—the blood had to be stopped or he wasn't going to survive long enough to do anyone any good. And Clay wasn't the type to roll over and give up. The inevitable infections and blood poisoning he would have to worry about later, if he lived long enough.

The animal trail began to climb, switchbacking up the shoulder of a hill, and walking became an exercise in slow torture. He could use the injured leg—the wound was deep but narrow and fairly clean—but only with extreme care, and the jagged puncture in his side made it incredibly painful to breathe.

After a few hundred meters of slow climbing, his breath came in ragged gasps and his side was a searing mass of pain from the labored heaving for air.

He stopped and sat in the center of the trail until his head ceased spinning and his breathing became more even. He looked up into the brightness that was the sun, a mere blur in the sky, small and far away, only the opaqueness of the atmosphere keeping up the planet's muggy heat.

The growth was thinner there, and a breeze reached him. It was cool, smelling faintly of salt water. He breathed deeply of it and was surprised to realize how much he had become unconscious of the musk and mildew odor of the forest. The sea smell awakened a longing in him. If I survive this, he thought, I'll build a beach comber's shack on some peaceful half-civilized planet and spend what's left of my life picking through the surf for shells and sea wrack.

Blood had begun to seep through the makeshift bandage at his side, and he rebound it, using a folded piece of his pants leg for a pad. The blood loss and the exertion had made him lightheaded, and the dizziness forced him to lay back when he had finished.

At this rate, he thought, I won't be much of a challenge when that son of a bitch catches up with me. But then again, neither will he. The ludicrous image of two crippled old men fighting with canes came to him suddenly.

But he remembered the *yamabushi* charging up on him through the briers, a wound in his thigh and another deep stab wound in his chest. The man had seemed neither old nor crippled. Clay felt suddenly a certain sense of awe and, not for the first time, a small rise of pure fear.

He levered himself painfully up to his feet, supporting himself on the pike, and started once more up the game trail. He judged from the position of the sun that the trail, which had led generally south when he had discovered it, now worked its way eastward into a series of foothills beyond which were high, jagged peaks.

He shrugged inwardly and kept walking. He couldn't go back, and he had no confidence that he would get very far if he set out across country—the terrain was too rugged, too thickly over-grown.

The game trail split a little farther on and again a few meters beyond that, the main trail becoming narrower at each tributary. A kilometer farther, the main game trail he had been following petered out into dozens of small runs that meandered aimlessly through the field of thick grass on the shoulder of the hill.

He had chosen the wrong direction.

He looked back the way he had come. Somewhere below was a major source of water or forage that had attracted the animals that had made the trail, drawing them out of the foothills and into the forest.

And now he found himself at that trail's beginnings instead of at its destination, a lake or a salt lick from which there were doubtless myriad paths and game trails that led out of the wilderness.

He walked in a small circle to make a pocket in the heavy grass and sat, making himself as comfortable as possible. He considered his options.

There were three: He could follow the trail back and almost certainly run headlong into the *yamabushi* or, worse—into an ambush if the man knew that the trail he had followed led no-where. He could set out into the wilderness and hope to beat his way through the dense forest to a place where he could find a radio or steal a copter.

Or he could wait for Tind to find him.

At least then, Clay thought, I can fight him on terms of my choosing.

And he had tired of running. The confrontation seemed finally inevitable; if he must fight, he would at least decide on the battlefield.

When he had rested, he scouted the area on the side of the hill until he found a spot to his liking, a large boulder jutting like a cracked tooth from the side of a hill. One side of the stone had been split away, and it offered a shallow concave depression facing downhill toward the direction from which the warrior would come, following Clay's trail.

Clay inspected the depression in the boulder. It was roughly oval and deep enough for him to fit himself completely inside.

He ran his hand along the shadowed back of the depression and felt a roughness that was familiar and not part of the natural stone.

He followed the roughness with his fingertips and made out the odd twisted shape of the carved runes he had found cut in the stone by the spring.

Yes, Clay thought. This is the place. Destiny. His own heritage seemed to proclaim it, the edict etched in the very stone before him.

He settled there, his back against the wall of stone, to wait for his enemy.

The late afternoon sun crawled toward the eastern horizon, and Clay's mind wandered feverishly. He turned his cheek against the cool rock of the boulder's face, the solidity of the stone an anchor against the drifting delirium.

Standing in the depression in the side of the boulder, he was protected from attack above; Tind—again, the old warrior's name seemed strange and alien as he formed it in his mind—could come for him from one direction only: head on.

He felt protected there; the hollow was almost womblike. His grandmother, a woman born in a city but nevertheless almost full-blooded Oglala Dakota Sioux, had taught him when he was young that all stone was sacred—*Inyan*, she had called it, the rock that was god. The stuff of creation, the least variable of all things. A boulder—his boulder—was a god unto itself, protective.

He pressed against it, feeling irrationally strengthened by the contact.

That's how it's going to be, he thought, my strength and my gods against his. *Except I have no real gods. My grandmother's people are gone, killed off, absorbed into the cultural homogeneity of an overpopulated, overcivilized world, a world that doesn't need gods. The Dakota's gods died with the Dakota. And that evil son of a bitch not only has gods but a warrior heaven to go to when he dies.*

But the *yamabushi* wasn't evil; evil was a null concept, a fallacy. Long experience had taught him there was no such entity as evil; there were only causes, points of view. One fought honorably and well, and that was all.

As cliched as it sounded even in his own mind, he had fought the good fight. He felt suddenly relaxed, the tension draining away. He had no claim to right, no ideological advantage over the man who called himself Tind, no battle cry to herald a cause. They were simply two men, two warriors who fought because that was what they did, what they had to do.

He had been wrong in what he had told Rankin and Greene. He was not a soldier only because he had some special talent for it or even because he believed in something.

He fought because he had to fight. He fought for honor, for his own soul.

Rankin, he suspected, would call it mysticism, the Indian in him counting coup. Or the Oriental finding salvation in dying honorably.

Perhaps so, he thought. And perhaps a warrior was truly born and not made.

It was something he felt his grandmother's people would have believed, and he embraced it as a certainty.

The thought drifted away from him, and for a time he slept.

He awoke with a start. The afternoon had given way to evening, and the stone at his back was cold, sending a shiver through him.

He stood stiffly, the effort making him dizzy, walked out a few paces from the boulder, and looked around. There was no sign of the *yamabushi*.

The general area around the boulder was open, knee-high grass seeming to flow riverlike toward him in the steady breeze, breaking here and there around rocks and smaller boulders and an occasional stunted and scrubby chest-high tree.

His field of view was good; he could see for a hundred meters down the steep hillside to where a rock outcropping obscured his view of the forest at the immediate foot of the hill.

He inspected the nearest scrub tree and found a branch that suited his purposes, wrist-thick and about a meter long, with a fist-sized knotted growth toward one end. The wood was gnarled and blue-tinted, and when he touched it, his hands came away dusted blue.

He gripped the branch near its end and bent it back until the wood began to give, then leaned his weight into it. It gave way suddenly with a snap, and he nearly fell, pain shooting up his leg and side.

A strip of the branch's tough bark held on tenaciously to the tree at the break, and he twisted hard one way and then the other, wishing heartily for his knife. Finally, fatigue set into the stringy wood fibers, and it gave way with one last tug, coming loose in his hands.

He twisted off the few small twigs that clung to it and balanced the result in his hand. He swung it across and back easily a few times.

It made an acceptable club, though he had no intention of using it as such. It was a prop, one he hoped would be convincing.

When he had finished, he returned to the cavity in the face of the boulder. His thirst had returned with a vengeance, but there was nothing in the immediate vicinity of the position he had taken that held any promise of water.

He searched again until he found a tiny round pebble and put it in his mouth, rolling it around under his tongue. That at least would keep the membranes temporarily moist, and the dry ache wouldn't torture him as much, though the relief was in a large part illusory. He would become dehydrated soon, the water loss accentuated by his loss of blood, and even the salivary glands would dry up until he could no longer even speak or swallow.

The murky sky began to purple with dusk. Clay cupped his hands around his ears and wished irritably that the constant breeze he had found so welcome at first when he had climbed the hill would stop. It made a steady rustling in the grass and whistled between his boulder and the forest. He would have to see the warrior coming—he certainly wouldn't hear him.

The sound of the wind, the tiny voices it made in his ear, brought him back to thoughts of his grandmother and her people, *his* people.

Raised places—hills and mountains—were also sacred to them, the homes of the spirits. The Dakota Indians back on Terra had considered the Black Hills of North Dakota the most holy of grounds.

It was strange to think of those beliefs, the aboriginal superstitions of a tribe that for all intents had died out, assimilated into the general culture many years before on a planet so far away that its sun wouldn't even be a speck on the night sky even if Ithavoll's skies were clear enough for the stars to shine through.

He stood in the rock depression and watched the open stretch of grass. There was still enough light so that he could see as far as the rocks below, but the forest had become a shadowed blur in which it was impossible to make out detail.

He stared so intently at the rock outcropping, trying to make out its irregularities as the failing light blended its crevices and passes together, that he thought at first the movement was a trick of his eyes.

He looked away, rubbed his eyes hard, then looked back again.

A dot moved against the shadows of the rocks, resolving itself into a head and then the figure of a man as it came into the sloping field of grass.

The old warrior climbed without hesitation straight toward Clay, the knife in his hand held low, brushing across the tops of the grasses.

"Son of a bitch," Clay murmured.

He slowly picked up his homemade club. He watched the *yamabushi* for a moment, then stepped back against the depression in the rock. He searched out the design carved into the stone and traced it with his fingers. A talisman. A link to his own gods.

He stood erect against the boulder and waited, the club held loosely in his suddenly sweat-slick hand.

CHAPTER TWENTY-TWO

Clay waited, swinging the club slowly in front of him, for Tind to charge up the hill, but the old warrior simply plodded up at the same slow-steady pace he had been making when he had first come around the rock outcropping, the long-knife held low in one hand.

Halfway through the field of grass, he stopped and looked up unblinking at Clay.

Clay felt the battle adrenaline rising in him, and his fatigue eased, the pain dropping away. He felt tensely ready to fight the *yamabushi*, to end it. The wind whispering in his ears was no longer irritating; it seemed right, the grassy stretch between them flowing in smooth graceful waves.

Clay met the warrior's eyes. There was no hate there. They met as equals in simple combat. Clay gestured with the club.

"Come ahead!" His voice was surprisingly loud, echoing faintly against the rocks.

The warrior didn't move. Clay saw that his chest was heaving from the exertion of the climb he had already made. He noted the still-bleeding wound in the man's belly with a twinge of satisfaction.

The sky darkened another shade, and Clay knew that the moment had come. He could not afford to wait for complete darkness. But in the twilight what he had planned had its best chance of succeeding.

"You—" His throat constricted with dryness, and he swallowed hard to clear it. "Fight me! Now!"

The warrior pulled something from around his neck, held it

to his forehead, then touched it to his lips. Clay watched him closely. After a moment the warrior seemed to gather himself and stood jerkily erect, shaking his head wildly from side to side. A drug, Clay thought. Some incredibly potent stimulant. That's what's kept him going. There was nothing else it could be.

But still he doubted.

Once again the *yamabushi* began to climb. Clay could hear him grunt with exertion above the sound of the wind, but he came on strongly, without hesitation.

It took almost a full minute for the warrior to reach the place at which the field leveled somewhat before the boulder, twenty meters from where Clay stood with his back against the rock. He stopped again when he reached that point and stood, panting, a tall, imposing silhouette set against the darkening sky.

Clay watched the contorted face. Even in the dim light he could see the crazed wildness in the warrior's eyes, the twisted expression of rage.

Clay held the rough club before him, the knotted tip extended toward the *yamabushi*. The man's chest heaved, his breath coming in labored pants that Clay could hear clearly.

Suddenly, as if someone had spoken a command that Clay could not hear, the Warrior's face screwed up in a mask of complete rage, and he charged at Clay with a roar, swinging the long-knife over his head.

Clay's stomach clenched in something very like terror. He held his place, the club a heavy, dead weight in his hands, until the *yamabushi* had covered ten of the fifteen or so meters between them.

With another stride the warrior crossed an invisible point that Clay had marked in his mind.

Now!

Clay dropped the club and knelt suddenly, grasping in one hand the wooden pike he had hidden in the knee-high grass before the boulder. In one quick motion he jerked the point up, bracing the shaft with his other hand and shoving backward to bury the butt end in the soil at the base of the rock.

The *yamabushi* didn't even try to stop. Clay doubted he ever even saw the pike through the blindness of his rage. He struck the pike's sharpened tip with a force that knocked Clay back, the butt of the pike burrowing deeper into the soil until it stopped against the buried side of the boulder.

The end pierced through Tind's chest below the sternum, then drove through his arched back as the butt struck stone.

The warrior screamed in rage and pain and lunged forward, a half meter more of the pike's shaft burrowing through him, slashing at Clay and then at the pike itself with the long-knife, the blade singing on the hard black wood.

Clay backed away a step into the depression in the rock, holding the pike erect with all his dwindling strength, struggling to keep the remaining two meters of the pike shaft between himself and the warrior's blade.

With his off hand, the warrior grasped at the smooth shaft of the pike and dragged himself forward, the black wood sliding wetly through him.

He stopped and staggered as his legs began to give way. Clay saw the light in his eyes dim and knew the man was dying. Then, again as if someone had spoken to him, ordering him up, the warrior gathered himself and slashed out again with the knife, cutting a shallow slice in Clay's forearm.

With a strength of will that was terrible and terrifying, the *yamabushi* again began to pull himself down the rough shaft.

For the third time in as many days Clay looked into another being's eyes and felt a presence touch his mind, staining his soul the way a flame soots a lamp's chimney. He struggled against it, thrust it forth. Tind pulled forward another few inches and raised the long-knife for a blow.

Clay wrenched the pike with all his might to one side, then the other.

Die, goddamn you!

Tind shouted in agony and lost his grip on the knife, dropping it into the grass at Clay's feet. He reached for it, then stared dumbly for a moment at the shaft through his body that held him in place and prevented him from reaching it. His legs gave way suddenly, and he fell to his knees.

Clay held firm. The *yamabushi* coughed wrackingly, vomiting up blood, then tottered and collapsed to one side, dragging the pike from Clay's hands.

Clay pinned the pike under his boot and stood panting above the fallen warrior.

The twisted mask of rage was gone from the old warrior's face. In its place he saw only the weathered and sallow face of an old man.

The old warrior retched, bringing up more blood to pool in the dirt under his head. He still lived, though barely. Every breath rattled with the nearness of death.

Clay retrieved the warrior's knife. He leaned over the dying man and grasped him by his graying, coarse-cut hair and gave him warrior's grace, cutting his throat in one deft movement. The *yamabushi*'s lifeblood flowed out. He spasmed and died.

As the life left the old man's body, Clay saw a bluish spark leap out from the pouch hanging from the warrior's neck. The light was intense and lasted only a fraction of an instant, as if the tiniest of lightnings had leapt suddenly up from the dead man's body and disappeared.

If not for the deepening evening, he would not, he thought, even have seen the spark. As it was, he was not sure it wasn't simply a product of his fatigue or imagination. He stared for a second at the pouch where it lay across Tind's chest but saw nothing but a stained leather bag held by a thong.

Clay let the bloodstained long-knife drop from his hand into the grass. He knelt unsteadily and yanked at the pouch until the thong broke.

When he pulled it open, there was nothing inside but a fistful of crumbling soil, simple dirt.

He dropped the pouch, stumbled away from his enemy's corpse into the clean, empty field, and collapsed, letting the thick bed of grass embrace him.

The wind rushed through the grasses as he lay there, taking deep, cleansing breaths of the cool, alien air. The thick blackness of night closed in, and he fell into the dreamless sleep of the battle-weary.

CHAPTER TWENTY-THREE

Clay woke with the sun already high, amazed at how soundly he had slept. The wind still murmured through the grass, though with a higher note, whipping at the dry field.

Lying on his back, he watched as the murky sky grew darker and more opaque, storm clouds blowing up and building.

He pushed himself awkwardly up. The wounded leg had stiffened in the night, and his side was a continuous dull ache, but he could walk after a fashion, and he hobbled back to where the old warrior lay sprawled in the grass, propped on his side, the tree-trunk pike still run through his body.

Clay grasped the butt end of the pike and pulled; the shaft resisted for a moment, then pulled free. He threw the pike away, down the hillside.

The *yamabushi* lay on his back, mouth and eyes open, gaping blindly up into the darkening sky.

A man, like me, nothing more. A man who had been used, as were all soldiers, for purposes not his own, for men who considered themselves his betters because his blood was less pure. But he had died with honor, and that was enough.

Clay pulled off his vest and covered the withered face, then stood and scanned the area around the hill, squinting against the gusting wind.

Higher up the hill, twenty meters or so above the boulder, the terrain became more broken, scattered with smaller boulders and rubble. Clay climbed upward, pulling himself along with his hands when the slope became steep enough to threaten his precarious balance.

He made a dozen trips, climbing painfully up and back down the hillside, before he was satisfied he had enough stones. Each time he came down, he added another armload of fist-sized stones to the growing pile he had begun at the base of the boulder.

When the pile was large enough, he pulled the warrior's stiffened corpse into the lee of the stone at the base of the depression that had been his sanctuary. With steady intent, he paced back and forth between the pile he had made and the *yamabushi*, building a sturdy cairn of stones up around the dead warrior.

It was heavy work; twice he stopped and rested. Thunder rumbled soddenly in the near distance.

Before he finished, the rain began in earnest. He placed the last stone on the makeshift grave and stood silently in the downpour. After a time he retrieved the long-knife from where he had dropped it in the grass the night before and wedged it upright, blade down, in the stones at the head of the grave.

As he stood, the wind whipped the rain against his bare back, and he shivered.

There was nothing he could say over the old warrior's grave. The man had been his enemy; a warrior is not mourned. The talisman rune that stood over him was sufficient.

Lightning flickered suddenly close by, and a thunderclap split the air. He walked away, hobbling down the hillside, feeling a strange, unbidden sorrow.

He followed the game trail once again, moving away from the hillside, until he was well within the shadows of the trees. Then he cut into the forest and found a place where it would be easy to build a lean-to against the sprawling roots of a tree that had been recently blown down.

He worked quickly, the cold rain beating against his back as he leaned deadwood against the roots and covered the framework with fronds and wide leaves. By the time he had finished, he was shaking miserably with the chill.

He had no way to make a fire and no food, but, pressed comfortably against the dry soil around the tree's upturned roots, he felt more content than he could remember feeling in what seemed a great while. The cavern formed by the roots and the thrown-together lean-to was dim and musty with the clean smell of dirt.

He took off his battered jump-boots and rubbed his feet vigorously with the dry leaves that had gathered in the hollow beneath the tree. Then he relaxed back against the roots and dozed.

The storm died suddenly, the wind and rain stopping, leaving only the heavy slap of the drops falling from the trees to the spongy humus of the forest's floor to break the abrupt silence. Clay climbed up from the lean-to and stretched, favoring the tightness around the wound in his side.

He felt remarkably refreshed. Hunger rumbled in his belly, and he thought of the last meal he had eaten. It seemed long ago that he had shared with Rankin the animal he had killed in the ravine.

Thirst burned in his throat, and he searched for a few minutes until he found a place where the new rain had been caught in the hollow of a leafy, cup-shaped plant. He drank his fill of the fresh sweet water.

He then pushed his way through the brush back to the path and followed it eastward at a good pace, the fresh layer of mud pulling like hands at his boots as he walked. The day grew warmer, the sun shining with a diffused brightness in the early afternoon sky.

The trail wound generally eastward for another four or five kilometers through mostly even terrain. Clay was grateful for the easy walking.

He spooked several small animals that had chosen to use the same trail and watched them bound panic-stricken into the cover of the forest. But since he had lost the knife and left the *yamabushi*'s blade behind, he was probably of less danger to them than they were to him.

He thought suddenly of the boar he had killed and hoped fiercely that the relatives of that worthy would chose another pathway, at least for this one day.

Eventually the game trail widened and ended at another pond, this one larger than the first one he had found, spreading out several hundred meters square, making a wide opening in the forest.

The water was fresh and clear, probably spring-fed, Clay

thought. He bathed in it, letting the water soak loose the caked bandages on his leg and side, washing the strips of cloth clean of the clotted blood as best he could.

There was some reddening in the skin around the wound on his leg, and it had begun to swell somewhat, sure signs of the beginning of infection. He scrubbed the open, thumbnail-sized puncture in the flesh of his thigh as gently as he could with the rinsed-out cloth, and still the pain shot through him, hot and blinding.

When he had cleaned the wound to the best of his ability, he rinsed out the strips of cloth once again and rebound it, then performed the same operation on his side.

I'll need antibiotics soon, he thought, or I will lose that leg.

Another voice, inside his mind, reminded him that if the infection truly set in before he could get the drugs he needed, the leg would be irrelevant. He would die slowly, the wounds purulent and gangrenous, the fever burning through him like flame through tinder.

When he had finished with the torturous ritual of cleansing the puncture in his side, he set out into the brush, following the northern edge of the pond. He ran across one game trail that led away from the pond, crossed it and found another that ran more or less toward the northeast, and started down it, moving as quickly as possible.

The trail was narrow but beaten smooth, and Clay made good time. For most of the afternoon it headed arrow-straight in the direction he desired.

The trail came to a shallow, wide creek bed that ran roughly southeast and northwest, and then it turned to the west, following the bank of the creek. Clay stared blankly at the onyx-black sand of the creek bed, at the trickle of silver water running through the center of the black slash across the body of the forest.

He stood at the point where the game trail angled away westward and tried to orient himself. The direction he needed to travel was a great deal north and east of the course the game trail now took, he was sure.

He could continue to follow the trail, hoping it would once again angle eastward, or he could leave it and try to beat his way through the thick forest growth. He looked at the wall of green on the far bank of the creek and quailed at the thought of fighting through it for any distance.

But then, the game trail could travel west for dozens of kilometers, perhaps even eventually turning southward again. He licked his cracked lips, feeling weak and feverish.

He couldn't take the risk; there wasn't time.

He eased himself down the sandy bank into the creek bed and walked across, wading through the thin strip of creek in the center, the water slipping cold and alive around his calves, sinking into his boots.

CHAPTER TWENTY-FOUR

Once into the openness of the creek bed, Clay could see for a good distance, a half kilometer or more, in either direction along the thread of water, the creek running arrow-straight between the trees. He stopped midstream and studied the banks of the creek upstream to the northwest, then downstream to the southeast.

Somewhere below, in the southeast, the creek emptied into the river, perhaps below the gorge. If he followed the creek itself downstream, he would eventually come out onto the river but hopelessly far from where he wanted to be. It was a temptingly easy way out. Rankin was probably already dead, and there was a chance he could reach help in time to save his own skin.

But he might well find that wherever he went on Ithavoll, to the squatter's settlement or to the rendezvous village, he would be taken as a spy and—albeit failed—saboteur and summarily executed. As it was, he was in no shape to defend himself. He was also in no shape to challenge the tangled rigors of the forest.

There was a chance that he could find easier going than simply thrusting himself into the density of the woods, but it was slim. The creek was small, which would suggest that it probably didn't have any significant feeder streams that supplied it upstream. He couldn't see anything for the half-kilometer distance downstream, such as a widening in the main creek or a break in the trees, that would indicate another stream emptying into it.

He faced the forest that rose above the creek across from the game trail. He had the feeling that the wall of green would resist him like an animate thing were he to try to push into it; the brush and hanging tree limbs were tangled with vines, intertwined like arms, tied into place.

Exhaustion weighed down his limbs and made lead of his soaked boots.

No, the forest was too much. He had defeated the *yamabushi*, but he hadn't the strength to pit himself against the congealed might of Ithavoll's woods.

He stepped up from the water on the far bank and plodded on through the loose sand and pebbles, walking downstream along the creek bed.

He covered the half kilometer in a few minutes of steady walking. Ahead, he saw a bend in the creek bed, bringing it more to the east. His heart rose, then fell again when he rounded the bend and the creek immediately shifted southward once again, curving around in an elongated S.

He followed the bend southward, feeling disgusted and helpless.

He kept on for another kilometer, stumbling, lurching forward, the sand dragging at his boots. He rested, then continued.

Two hundred meters farther down, the creek widened and swelled into a pool, filling the black creek bed to the banks. He splashed into the deeper water, almost falling as water-rounded black stones rolled under his feet. The pool was deep, the water rising to his chest, a new current pushing out around his arms. Surprised, he followed the new urgency that pushed the water against him to its source and found the opening, hidden by a thick canopy of overhanging branches.

Flowing out from the choked darkness under the trees that brushed the water's surface, a stream ran from the north, merging into the creek.

He ducked into the water until it lapped under his chin and pulled himself up the tongue of dark sand that projected into the pool from the shallower side stream, allowing the water to support his weight. It was an almost luxurious sensation despite the uncomfortable tugging of the current at the waterlogged bandage on his side.

He traveled that way for a good distance, pulling himself leisurely along in the knee-deep water, letting it take the burden of his weight while he tugged at the bottom with his hands and pushed forward with his knees. The stream's bottom sand soon gave way to pebbles; the stream was traveling, he guessed, mostly northward and a little to the east.

The trees, brush, and vines wove together over the stream, making a deep, turquoise-blue tunnel through which he moved, sliding through the water like a snake, only his head just above the flowing water, the green roof of this new, dark world coming together thick and impenetrable only inches above his face when he looked up.

He felt elated by his luck. The cold water eased the pain in his side and leg, the relatively slight exercise of his movement keeping the leg from stiffening. For the first time in the last few days he felt something akin to serenity. It was good. Things were finally going well.

The ordeal that was ahead he put from his mind.

He moved through the endless green tunnel of leaves and vines for what seemed to be hours. He couldn't be sure of the time as it passed or even the distance he traveled in the featureless stream cave.

Something alive moved in the dark water beside him, sliding slick and wet for an instant against the skin of his leg. He flinched away, and it was gone, but his skin crawled with the thought of the contact, what it was he might have touched. He forced himself not to think but simply to move.

At one point the stream cascaded down a series of vine-shrouded falls, and he climbed laboriously up the water-slick stone and trudged through a half-kilometer or so of tumbling miniature rapids, bent nearly double but still forced to push his head and shoulders through the tangled mass that overhung the stream.

He slapped fruitlessly at the hard, chitinous biting insects the size of a fingertip that dropped onto his back and arms from the hanging brush as he pushed through.

Eventually the stream began to broaden and become more shallow, the water moving with a constant churned-white quickness, the roof of leaves thinning as the gap between the banks became wider.

He walked, the stream no longer deep enough for him to lie in. With the exertion, the wound in his thigh began a deep and throbbing ache. He dragged it along, using the leg only as much as he had to to keep his balance on the shifting pebble floor of the stream. The bandage at his side was waterlogged and tugged painfully at that wound. He felt feverish and weak, but not so much as before.

He came across a dry streambed that led away from the creek at a slight easterly angle, and he stood at the confluence of the two streams, one dry, dusty gray sand, the other flowing wet and cold around his shins, trying to draw in his mind a sketchy map of the way he had come, which specific direction he still needed to travel.

Despite a natural instinct for orienting himself, he wasn't sure. The spot he wanted was generally northeast, but he could narrow the direction down only to a wedge of some thirty-odd degrees. It was *there*—he gestured with his hand to encompass the wedge—but he wasn't sure enough to choose between staying with the stream he had been following and taking off on the more easterly course that the dry streambed followed.

Either choice seemed equally valid. He tossed a mental coin and struck out up the dry feeder stream.

The forest did not close in so closely around the streambed there, and he made good time. The gray-black sand of the bed was dry enough to send up puffs of dust as he walked, and there was a goodly amount of debris fallen from the surrounding trees strewn in the streambed—enough so that he was sure the stream flowed only occasionally, when the rains were especially heavy in the nearby mountains.

He made another two or three kilometers, limping steadily up the wash. As he walked, the day began to give out, the constant dimness beneath the forest trees deepening by degrees.

He kept walking as the day faded, pushed by a need to make

distance while he still could. As the last of the day's light began to die away, he stopped for breath, the gasps for air wracking his side.

As he leaned against the clay bank, he noticed something glimmer for an instant in the pool of shadow that was the center of the creek bed.

For a long minute he let his exhaustion force him to ignore the minuscule flash of light in the sand: It could have been anything, probably was nothing but some water-polished pebble that had caught some ray of light that had found its way through the canopy.

But the gleam of light preyed on his mind. He could see it now, even with his eyes closed. Grunting at the effort it took, he pushed himself up from the bank and crouched painfully in the sand, brushing his hand back and forth. He tossed away pebbles and sticks, then his fingertips brushed across something metallically cool.

His fingers outlined something small and round, protruding from the sand. He picked it up and felt its small, machined weight in his palm.

He held it up against the darkening sky and squinted to make out its details.

It was one of Rankin's spent carbine shells. With a fingertip, he traced out the ".30 cal." indented into the base of the cartridge.

He thought hard. There was only one place, he was certain, where the shell could have been left, only one dry streambed in which Rankin had had occasion to fire his weapon. He was, he realized, standing in the place at which Rankin had given up the chase for the *yamabushi* on the day Fitzgerald had been killed near the gorge.

He concentrated, listening with every fiber of his being. He thought he could make out, just at the edge of hearing, the distinctive murmur of the river as it roared, churning into rapids deep in the gorge.

He pressed the spent brass cartridge against his cheek. It was as close as he had ever come to weeping with relief.

CHAPTER
TWENTY-FIVE

Clay stretched out against one of the dry stream's clay banks and tried to sleep. There was little sense in trying to climb into the gorge, or even in trying to approach it, until it was again light. It would be too much to fall and break his neck now that he was close.

He slept fitfully, and when dawn broke through the canopy of trees, he was little rested. He felt coltishly weak, his face hot with fever. His leg had stiffened in the night; he tested it and found he could flex it and bend it somewhat at the knee, but only at the price of terrible agony. The flesh around the bandage had turned an angry red with infection.

It would take his weight, though, and that was enough.

A fog rolled down the bed of the dry stream like a new flood from the mountains, curling around him. He pushed up and broke through it, climbing out of the creek.

After a brief search he found the remnants of the trail he, Rankin, and the *yamabushi* had beaten out through the brush and began walking up it, toward the river gorge, pushing the new, damp growth aside.

He remembered the *yamabushi*'s spring trap a half step before he walked into it.

He cursed himself unreasonably for not dismantling it before, when he and Rankin had walked back after having lost the warrior. He had been in a hurry then, with every reason to be. Still, it rankled that his enemy's machine had very nearly killed him long after he had killed his enemy.

He traced out the damp, rotting fiber string and stepped gingerly over it. Then he pulled a branch from a deadfall and tripped the thing, dragging the branch across the string until it caught on the rough jute and pulled free the wedge that kept the bent sapling tied back.

The sapling whipped out across the trail, the sharpened stake tied to it cutting ineffectually through the air at chest height. If he had tripped it, coming the wrong way, from the streambed, it would have driven itself into his back.

Clay smiled wryly to himself. It was one last good try, he thought. I'll give him that.

Clay threw down his stick and continued on.

In another few minutes he was at the gorge.

He found the place where Fitzgerald had bled his life out on the clay of the path and walked out from that point to the cliff's edge. He leaned out over the edge and looked down into the gorge, searching for any sign of the equipment, but anything that might have been visible was lost to him, obscured by the morning fog and the mist from the river.

He studied the cliff face, gauging the climb he would have to make.

The first two meters from the edge were sheer, a vertical, clean face of black rock. Below that was a long, steep slope of a different kind of stone, cracked and splintered, pieces of it broken free and lying precariously suspended against hundreds of small shelves of the same rock that jutted from the slope. The lower layer of rock was lighter colored and no doubt softer, and beyond that there was another perpendicular rock face that Clay guessed to be thirty or forty meters high.

And beyond that, another long slope of lighter colored rubble and broken rock that disappeared into the shroud of river mist.

He stared down at it for a long moment, estimating his chances, planning an attack.

Then he took a deep breath and swung himself over. He hung free against the rock face, gripping the cliff edge with both hands, and poked at the flat stone with the toe of his boot. He found a crack and jammed it in, letting his good leg take his weight.

Then he lowered himself down to the long, steep field of broken stone that led to the next cliff face, pushing at it with the foot of his stiff leg until he was sure of his footing and then giving it his weight.

He stood on a block of stone that jutted from the layer of softer rock below and leaned against the black rock of the cliff, feeling it cool against his face, letting his breathing slow before he tried to move again.

Carefully, making certain of the balance of every rock before settling his weight upon it, he worked his way down the broken slope.

Despite all his caution, twice stones that he trusted with his weight betrayed him, rolling out from under his foot. Both times he caught himself in time with his hands, but once it was a very near thing, the sudden shift wrenching him away from the slope, one hand giving way its grip on the rock above.

He recovered and stood, suspended by one hand and his bad leg, his knee jammed into a shallow depression, over twenty meters of steep, jagged slope that ended in an abrupt drop into the gorge. He swung himself around and pressed desperately against the hard impersonal slant, feeling the whole of his life hang precariously over the abyss.

The pain in his side and leg was a wrenching agony. He groped above for a handhold, found one, and lowered himself down another step.

Bit by painful bit he worked his way down the narrow ledge that preceded the next sheer drop. Once there, he flattened out as much as he was able, a shoulder hanging out over the edge, and rested, his head spinning with the exertion and pain, both hands pressed hard against the spasms of his diaphragm.

The next part of the climb would decide it. He put doubt from his mind, fearing that it would only give it that much of an advantage over him.

When he was able, he began again, easing himself out over the edge of the next cliff, probing with the toe of his boot for a foothold. For as far as he could reach, there seemed to be only smoothness, a sheet of unbroken rock.

With much effort, he pulled himself back up. He pulled off his boots and tied them together with the short lengths of lacing that remained, then hung them around his neck, the boots behind and under his head.

He eased out once again over the cliff face and began to feel with his toes for a hold, a crack or a bulge in the rock that would support him. He hung from the waist and found nothing, then slipped down another few centimeters, holding the edge with his elbows and arms.

His toe ran across a slanting, finger-wide crack in the stone, and he followed it down a few centimeters with his toe until it widened, then jammed his foot into it, the sharp edges cutting painfully at the exposed skin.

He lowered himself, once again giving his weight to the good leg, until he was holding onto the cliff's edge with his fingertips. Then he groped with his right hand for a hold and found one, another small crack in the black rock.

He found another crack with his bad leg, then a tiny ledge, an unevenness in the stone, for his left hand, and crawled slowly, in infinitesimal molasses-slow movements down the cliff. He remembered a fly he had watched once while sitting through some nameless state function; it had been caught in the stasis field that protected the attending functionaries from the bother of insects—it had been a jungled world like Ithavoll—and he had watched as it crawled, dying slowly, down a leaf before dropping into a pool.

He stopped halfway down the cliff face and stood on a narrow ledge half the width of his bare foot, every muscle shaking from the strain.

It flashed across his mind how enormously easy it would be to simply let go and fall, a soaring, easy plunge that would end in the smallest instant of pain and then the soft comfort of darkness.

After a moment the shaking slowed. He hunched down, found a handhold in the rock before his face, and reached his good leg down, probing for another foothold.

He climbed with his eyes closed, concentrating every erg of energy and sensation into finding the cracks and ledges, the imperfections in the smooth black stone that held him to the cliff.

It was with a sense of near shock that he reached a foot down and felt the relative solidity of the next slope. He inched his foot around until he found a stable, flat place in the broken rock and then let himself down. He turned carefully and sat, the stone just wide enough for his buttocks, letting his legs, good and bad, dangle down the slope.

Below, the mist had thinned under the influence of Ithavoll's distant sun, and he could see a stretch of green at the base of the slope. Beyond that was a strip of brush and trees and then the turbid silver-gray of the river, and he could hear a sound that was the compounding of the roiled water and the rushing blood in his ears that seemed to fit the majestic wildness of the scene.

The river was tight between high banks, deep and wide and still so far away, though in reality no more than three or four hundred meters was left between himself and the verge of flowering grass at the base of the cliff.

But it was three hundred meters of tortured, almost vertical, sloping landscape, and he quailed at the thought of it. His arms and legs were already milk-weak and trembling, his breath coming in painful, heaving gasps for air.

He waited, perched on the buttock-wide slab of stone, for what he guessed to be a little more than an hour, letting a measure of strength drain back into his misused muscles. Above, in the still, murky sky over the gorge, one of the carrion birds began to turn in a circling vigil over him.

He watched it soar without lifting his head. Not yet, friend. Wait a little longer, he thought.

He dozed without really being aware of it and snapped suddenly awake a moment before slipping from his perch. He caught himself just as he began to totter off to one side and gripped his seat-rock with both hands for dear life, reeling with vertigo.

"Christ!" The word fell down into the immensity of the gorge and was lost.

He rose cautiously to his knees, keeping his grip on the rock. Slowly he pivoted, facing the slope, and lowered a foot, feeling for a hold. When he found one, he slid away from the rock slab and continued down.

Time disappeared, and he continued to move endlessly, a centimeter at a time, across the unforgiving stone, testing a foothold here, rejecting it, groping around for another, and crawling infinitesimally farther down into the wet heart of Ithavoll.

Another stone rolled and smashed against his already injured knuckles, and he bit into the inside of his cheek, willing the fingers to stay clenched around the knob of stone they held, desperately searching for a hold for his other hand, then giving it the weight and jamming the fist into his mouth, sucking at the bleeding knuckles.

After an eternity he put his foot down and touched the cool roughness of grass.

He sat there for a while, the smell of the river sharp in his nose. Then he unslung his boots from around his neck and pulled them on.

CHAPTER TWENTY-SIX

The grass rose around his bare legs, and he trudged through it, the rough stalks rubbing against him. He spotted the first pack right away, the olive drab showing distinctly against the lighter blue-green of the high grass. Beyond it a rifle butt protruded up from the grass where it leaned against an outcropping of thorny brush.

He squatted beside the pack and pulled at a long tear in the rain-and mist-damp fabric. The material of the pack was tough; it must have struck, with a great deal of force, some protruding jagged stone on the sloping portion of the cliff wall as it tumbled down into the gorge.

Its contents were jumbled, but most of it was still there. It had been Greene's. He pulled out her personal gear and laid it out on the grass, found a sealed-plastic pouch of soya-pudding, and tore it open with his teeth.

He sucked greedily at the warm gelid fluid until the packet was empty, then dug out another and opened it. He ate the sticky-sweet pudding as he walked around the grassy verge before the trees that stood at the river's edge, looking for the other packs.

He found another a dozen steps from Greene's. It was his own. A few steps from that he found the med kit, lying scraped but intact in the grass. He thanked whatever god might be listening that he had had the foresight or pure luck to seal the kit after he had seen to Greene, before the old *bushi* warrior had pitched it over the cliff with the rest of the gear. It was the thing that would save him, heal his wounds, give him strength.

He opened the kit and found a few things broken and out of place, but on the whole it was intact. It had been designed for rough treatment, and all the serum vials were of impact-resistant plastic.

He found the vials of wide-spectrum antibiotics and injected himself above the wound in his leg. Then he resealed the kit and stood.

He would need the river's help to free the foul strips of fatigue pants before he could redress the wounds with the kit's soothing salves and clean bandages. The prospect was in no way a pleasant one.

He hobbled off toward the sound of the river, loud but muted by the trees.

As he reached the trees, a shift in the breeze pushed along by the river brought a familiar smell to him, foul and sickly-sweet.

He walked along the edge of the trees for a few meters upriver and found Fitzgerald, his body in a heap against the base of a tree.

Clay reluctantly left the body as it lay. There was nothing he could do for Fitzgerald that couldn't wait; he would have time to bury the body later. For now, there were more pressing concerns. He turned away from the crumpled form and pressed into the trees.

The river was broad and fast, spilling with a roar over a series of rapids and cataracts fifty meters upriver from where Clay stood.

It was, he had to admit, magnificent. He took a deep lungful of the river-mist-soaked air.

He looked for a moment back up the walls of the gorge and thought about the force with which the old warrior would have had to have thrown Fitzgerald's limp body for it to have carried over the long slopes and into the edge of the wall of trees beside the river. Meters farther than the packs had gone. Much strength there, and much hate. He wondered at it.

He had been a soldier all his adult life—a warrior, if not in the primitive sense that the *yamabushi* had been a warrior—yet he had never been overcome by that kind of passionate rage, had never hated that much, except once, when he had watched helplessly as a boy of no more than ten or eleven had died with his throat crushed by a garrote wielded by a C.F. officer. He had killed that man in a black, blind rage so intense he no longer really remembered the event itself.

But it had happened only that once in an entire career devoted to various forms of violence. The old warrior's rage, at a man he knew nothing of, who had done him or anyone else he could possibly know no harm whatsoever, was something different. It had come from no source that Clay could see. The mindlessness of it awed him. It was unbelievable that anything, even duty or spleen, could command that much raw power over a man.

He climbed down the last clay bank before the narrow beach. The water was slower there, next to the bank, and he found a place where it eddied in a shallow inlet and waded into the cold mountain water.

He sat on a black sandbar and let the water wash familiarly over him, loosening the congealed mass of blood and bandage at his side and on his thigh. The process was considerably less painful than he had anticipated, the water so snowmelt-frigid that it numbed his side almost to the point where there was no sensation at all.

After a few minutes he gritted his teeth and peeled the gory mass back and away, revealing the puckered wounds and the pale, reddened flesh around them. He let the water flow inside him, cleaning out clotted blood and shreds of cloth, the cold pain intense and startling.

Water and new blood flowed out from him as he stood from the water and stumbled up to the bank. He dressed the wounds, painting them with antibiotics and quick-heal salves. Cleaned, the wound in his side seemed less terrible, a bit of red and white rib showing through. It was not truly deep, just ugly and painful.

He wrapped himself in the clean white of bandages and injected himself with painkiller. The throbbing agony in his side and thigh flowed away as the drug found the proper point in his brain and numbed it.

When he had finished, he stood painlessly, amazed at how much of the pain he had actually repressed with only his will, now that it was gone. He felt light-headed and flushed. The wounds began to itch with healing, the quick-heal salves accelerating the cell growth and knitting together the torn flesh.

In two or three days they would be little more than raw scars, somewhat swollen and red but not even especially uncomfortable.

He flexed his hand under its new bandage and judged that enough range of motion had returned to it. He climbed back up the embankment to the trees to bury Fitzgerald.

Before beginning, he injected himself with another drug from the med kit, this one a stimulant powerful enough to make his hands tremble and his legs and arms cramp as it rushed through his system.

The drug made him feel enormously strong, gave him a feeling of endless stamina he knew he would pay for later. Nothing was free, and the stimulant was simply speeding up his metabolism, burning whatever reserves he had left much more quickly than would otherwise have been the case.

Hopefully it would be enough. He hurried to make use of the time and strength it gave him.

He found a collapsible entrenching tool among his gear and dug a shallow grave near where Fitzgerald lay. It was hard going; though the strip of ground between the cliffs and the river was largely rather soft, sandy river silt, it was thoroughly mixed with rocks and debris fallen from the cliffs, and he had to stop every few shovelfuls and pry out some stone too large to lift out with the entrenching tool. After a few minutes the clean fatigues he had retrieved from his pack were drenched in muddy sweat.

When it was about a meter deep, he stopped, not because he judged it deep enough but because he physically could do no more; he could not afford to completely lose the edge the stimulants had given him. He tossed the shovel aside and rolled Fitzgerald's remains into the hole.

He covered Fitzgerald's face with a fatigue shirt salvaged from

Greene's pack and piled stones in atop the body to discourage any digging scavengers, then filled in the hole with shovelfuls of sandy dirt, smoothing the grave over when he was finished.

In a week or so the grass would return, and there would be no sign of Fitzgerald's grave.

But he knew it was better that way; it would keep away the curious and give Fitzgerald the peace he probably hadn't known in life. Clay remembered the weariness that had marked his face. He had been worn, soul-tired; now he rested, anonymously and forever.

Too many soldiers ended that way, Clay thought, buried in unmarked graves and forgotten.

He retrieved the entrenching tool and slung it out into the river. He then searched the area until he had found Fitzgerald's pack and sent it the way of the entrenching tool, out into the river's swift current.

He dumped out the contents of his own pack and refilled it with the plastique that Rankin had carried, the med kit, a few small gadgets that he thought might come in handy, and enough food for two or three days.

Then he threw everything else except one of the assault rifles and two loaded clips of ammunition into the river, though he agonized for a moment at throwing the second rifle, the extra carbine Fitzgerald had carried, away.

But it was a long climb back up the cliff, and he would already be carrying a staggering weight. He heaved it out into the water.

He surveyed the area. Except for the grave and a few flattened spots of grass, the stretch of ground looked undisturbed.

In a week, there would be nothing to tell a casual observer that he had ever been there or that a man was buried in the ground beside the trees.

Clay squinted up at Ithavoll's murky sky and tried to guess what portion of daylight remained. Three hours, he thought, maybe more. No way to be certain. The watch that he had kept in an outside pocket of his pack had been a casualty of the fall into the gorge.

The energy high of the stimulant was already beginning to lose its edge.

He pulled the heavy pack up and settled the straps onto his shoulders. Then he strode through the grass to the sloping cliff face, put his foot on the first crumbling ledge, and pulled himself up.

CHAPTER TWENTY-SEVEN

After the first dozen meters of the climb the artificial ease with which he had initially begun to scale the wall gave way to a straining, automatic pulling upward, his fingers searching out cracks and unevennesses in the rock, his arms flexing and pulling him up almost of their own volition. The stimulant gave him strength and replaced the need to force his battered muscles into action.

He came to the first sheer face and climbed it almost without thought, inching his way spiderlike up the smooth black stone. Then, with painful slowness, he crossed the broken slope up to the last cliff, the two meters of vertical rock, mindlessly pulling and pushing, his abraded fingers finding holds, his arms and legs tugging the mass of his body and equipment forward and up.

When a shelf gave way under one hand, he numbly watched it fall, pieces of gray-brown stone shattering, then shattering again as they bounded down the steep slope.

He groped overhead until he found another hold. Sweat ran across his forehead, stung his eyes. He kept moving.

He finally reached the last stretch of rock and crept crablike sideways until he found a place where he could grasp the cliff's edge. Then he freed the pack and rifle and swung them up with one hand, grunting with the exertion. He pulled himself up, swinging a leg over and rolling onto the flat rock of the cliff top.

He lay there for a long time, his chest heaving, the muscles in his arms and legs jerking from the relief of the strain. His thigh and side throbbed and itched.

It's too much, he thought. Just too damned much.

He drank from a canteen filled with river water and wiped the sweat from his face with his sleeve.

Then he stood and tried to walk. His legs sagged, jellylike.

He sat and pulled the medical kit from the pack and unsealed it.

He pressed the hypo against his arm, feeling a stinging like a thousand tiny needles as the drug sprayed into the muscle of his forearm. He immediately felt better, almost euphoric, though the high wore off a moment later, leaving him feeling strong, but less so than before.

Less effect now, more consequences later. And it was the last time he could use it—a third injection could well kill him. His heart thudded palpably in his chest, and he reflected that in his generally poor condition, perhaps two would be enough to do the job.

After a moment he shrugged the pack up onto his shoulders. He kept the rifle free, balanced across his forearm.

He walked steadily, though at an excruciatingly slow pace. The drug was all that kept him on his feet; the faster his metabolism, the faster the drug in his system would pass through his body and lose effectiveness. He walked as quickly as he was able to walk and still keep his heart rate low.

He came to where the trail forked and followed the western split into the broken country he had left behind three days before.

He had gone only a few hundred meters down the new path before the effect of the drug began to fade despite his best efforts to stretch it out.

After only a few minutes his head swam from the simple exertion of keeping the slow pace he had set, and he slowed, forcing one foot to rise from the ground and setting it down again farther ahead, then giving the whole of his concentration to the next step.

He reeled drunkenly down the trail, the combination of fatigue and the fading of the stimulant hitting him like a powerful barbiturate.

At one point he swayed violently to the side and thought as he did so that he must catch himself before he toppled; then, some black, undeterminable time later, he woke facedown in the sand.

He blew the grit from his mouth and rubbed it from his eyes, then levered himself up, fatigue burdening him down like lead weights. Finally he stood; his injured leg was wobbly, and he was unsure of its stability. He took one staggering step forward, then another, and continued on.

He fell again, and this time had to lie facedown in the dirt of the trail for fifteen or twenty minutes before he could drag enough willpower into play to force his reluctant body to roll over to the side, letting the bulk of the pack support him. He lay there a long while, staring out into the deep blue-green of Ithavoll's forest.

He woke with the sky overhead deepening to purple with the onset of night. His entire body trembled and shook, his stomach surging with nausea. He rolled back onto his stomach and retched.

He tried to stand and found he couldn't. With what seemed a terrible effort, he struggled to raise himself to his hands and knees.

For another hundred meters he crawled, not sure as the night settled in whether the darkness was really Ithavoll's night or was perhaps his vision was leaving him along with his strength.

The darkness was thick and stifling. He reeled with nausea and disorientation. He felt twigs and grass under his hands and was no longer even certain that he was on the trail.

Suddenly there was nothing at all under his hands, and he was rolling headfirst down a steep slope. A stone banged the healing wound on his thigh, and he stifled a scream. Then the world dropped away, and he fell, landing with rib-cracking force on the rocky bottom.

He groaned at the new pain and tried to catch the breath that the tumble down had knocked from him, gasping desperately for air. He was totally disoriented, the darkness velvet-black and absolute.

One of the pack's straps had come loose, and he wormed his arm back through the loop and pulled weakly at it until it was once again snug against his back. The rifle was gone, lost somewhere in the darkness.

He had a torch in the pack, but he hesitated to use it. He felt exposed; the light would make him the center of this dark world. The thought made him tremble. He fought it, knowing that the drug and mental exhaustion were the sources of the paranoia.

He groped blindly around himself for the rifle and found nothing. He found the rocky face of the drop-off and pulled himself up. Then he pushed himself gradually up the slope, feeling ahead, fighting despair.

Suddenly his hand touched not rough stone but smooth off-world plastic. He drew the rifle to himself by its butt and checked it, working the bolt, then pulled its strap around his shoulder.

At that moment the darkness overhead lightened a shade, and suddenly he could see his surroundings. He looked up, startled as a small copter hummed by overhead, a searchlight scanning rapidly over the forest and the trail. Clay hugged himself hard against the dirt.

The machine hesitated over the ravine and hovered, searching, the spotlight playing over the rock-strewn bottom. After a minute it lifted and drifted off over the forest, the single eye of the light shifting, probing into the darkness beneath the trees.

Clay relaxed and released the breath he had been holding with a gasp. With a thumb, he eased the assault rifle's selector back to SAFE.

He doubted the pilot had seen him. The broken terrain and the camouflage of the pack and his fatigues should have made him an impossible target among the shadows.

And in the minute's sight the copter's searchlight had provided, he had found himself. He had fallen into the very ravine he had been looking for, ending up just south of the point where Rankin had been ambushed. The tanque of water was no more than a dozen meters away to his left. Rankin, or Rankin's body, lay to his right, where the ravine rose to the north and narrowed.

He wriggled back down to the bottom of the ravine and rose to his knees, then, with a supreme effort, pulled himself unsteadily up to his feet. He swayed, almost fell, then steadied himself and took a step forward.

Once among the rocks, he used hands and knees to push

himself forward in the darkness. He stopped every few meters, the exhaustion cramping every muscle.

The ravine narrowed until he could touch both sides with his outstretched hands. He stopped and rested against one of the flat walls.

"Rankin?" He spoke barely above a stage whisper.

Then, more loudly, "Rankin!"

There was no answer.

He crawled farther into the crevice and found the remains of the fire. The ashes were burnt out and cold.

He decided to take the chance and dug the torch out of the pack. He cupped his hands around it and directed the beam down, then snapped it on.

The crevice at the end of the ravine was empty. There was no sign of Rankin. He played the torch's beam across the rock floor, and it gleamed dully back from a darker spot on the flat stone.

It was a bloodstain. Rankin was gone.

He sat heavily down on the rock of the crevice floor, his mind whirling in a confused delirium. He touched the bloodstain; it was dry, at least a day old, possibly but not certainly left from the leg wound the *yamabushi* had given Rankin during the ambush in the lower ravine.

He snapped off the light. He forced his mind to clear, tried to order his thoughts.

Had someone found Rankin, killed him, and then dragged away the body? There was a strong possibility that whoever had sent the *yamabushi*, the Emperor Shotoku or his underlings, had grown impatient or had begun to doubt his initial estimation of the team's chances of survival against the old warrior.

If they had sent out patrols or another warrior, the trail would not have been hard to follow.

But Rankin had believed that they had intended the team's deaths to seem the actions of one man, an insane worshiper of pagan gods, a *yamabushi*. An overt military intervention would have defeated the very purpose behind using the old warrior in the first place.

No, they wouldn't do that, not yet, not without solid evidence of the survey team's culpability, and perhaps not even then.

Ithavoll, or rather Shotoku, had too much to lose by irritating the giant that was the United Democracies.

Or possibly the *yamabushi*'s one-man campaign against Clay and the others had had nothing to do with the emperor or his small-world politics but rather had had more to do with that strange weapon force with which Shotoku had wreaked so much havoc in the south. Clay remembered again what he had felt touch him from inside the old warrior. He had no answer and no possible way of finding one, so he dismissed that line of thought and moved on to a possibility that was perhaps more immediate.

Another *yamabushi*—Clay quailed at the idea, felt a deeper lethargic weakness take hold of his muscles. They could have grown just impatient enough with Tind's progress to use the patrol copters to act as spotters for another *yamabushi*. There was a deadly logic to it.

He stiffened at a sound from the darkness behind him.

He felt frozen in place, unable to turn, to move from the relative security of the crevice. He heard it again, a restless scraping sound coming from below.

He gritted his teeth, summoned forth enough willpower to move, and crawled out toward the sound, the rifle held out before him. He felt for the fire selector beside the rifle's grip and flipped it to full automatic. A palpable strength flowed into him from the feel of the rifle in his hands.

He had killed one *yamabushi* already with nothing more than a boot knife and a makeshift spear. With the deadly weight of the assault rifle in his hands, even the specter of another mountain warrior seemed somehow less fearful.

He inched down the ravine, listening.

A rasp of cloth against stone sounded to his immediate right, and he swung the rifle violently toward the noise, fighting against the jerking need to pull his finger on the trigger. His forearm trembled with the sudden exertion.

He held the rifle out with one hand, covering the spot from which the noise had come, letting the strap and his shoulder take the weight. With the other hand, he pointed the torch and snapped it on.

The light flooded out brightly onto the blank face of a great, oblong boulder. Sweat ran into his eyes, and he blinked it back.

What? Where?

An almost inaudible moan came from behind the wide bulk of the rock.

He edged back the way he had come, toward the end of the ravine. The boulder had fallen into the ravine eons ago in such a way that it was flush to the wall of the ravine where it faced down the ravine and angled out to form an overhung hollow where it faced toward Rankin's crevice.

Clay shined his light into the hollow. A withered form lay curled in the narrow space. As he watched, it writhed feverishly and turned toward him. The face was shrunken and distorted with pain, but it was Rankin.

"Rankin!" Clay whispered as loudly as he dared.

The eyes were open, but there was no comprehension in them, only the delirium of pain and fever. Clay opened the pack and rifled through the med kit, finding what he would need. Then he crawled into the cramped confines of the narrow little cave and bent over the ragged, heaving body.

With the tip of his knife he cut away Rankin's pants leg. He held the torch in his teeth and studied the wound. It was purulent and stank of dead flesh.

Clay grimaced. Rankin would probably lose the leg—but perhaps not his life—if the poisons from the festered knife wound had not spread to the point where the medicines couldn't help. A leg was of little consequence in the long run. Modern prosthetics were good enough that Rankin would not be crippled or even seriously inconvenienced by it.

He injected a double dose of wide-spectrum antibiotic near the wound site, gave another drug for the fever, then cleaned and dressed the wound.

Rankin struggled weakly as he poured a solution onto the wound that dissolved away the caked blood and loosened the dirt and bits of cloth matted in the gash; Clay held him down and continued the grim job. After a moment Rankin went completely limp.

Clay placed the bandage and taped it down, then dribbled water from a canteen onto Rankin's cracked lips.

When he had finished, he crawled out of the tight confines of the tiny cave and leaned, kitten-weak, against the cold stone of the boulder, taking deep, gasping breaths of the damp night air.

He sacrificed some of the water from one of the canteens and washed his hands, scrubbing them vigorously with sand and then rinsing away the bloody mix.

He rummaged around in the pack, found a plastic tube of some synthetic meat stew, and pulled the heating tab. He felt the plastic warm instantly in his hand. He twisted off the top and ate quickly without waiting for it to cool. The hot food burnt his tongue, and he relished the unfamiliar sharpness of the sensation.

Afterward, he crawled back into the hollow and pulled the pack in behind him. There was just enough room above where Rankin lay, though the bulky pack jutted out somewhat into the open.

He felt drained of every erg of strength. He settled against the pack, using it as a pillow, and began his mantra, chanting silently until he fell off into sleep.

He slept fitfully, his dreams filled with legions of *bushi* warriors following him through the darkness of Ithavoll's black night.

CHAPTER TWENTY-EIGHT

When he awoke, Rankin was still alive. He checked for a pulse; it was reasonably strong, and the fever seemed to have lessened.

He touched the bandage on the leg, and Rankin's eyes snapped open.

"Damn!" The voice was little more than a harsh croak.

Clay jerked his hand away, surprised.

"You're awake."

Rankin tried to speak and couldn't. Clay retrieved a canteen and dribbled water into the older man's mouth. Rankin drank gratefully and moved a hand up to the canteen.

"A little at a time." Clay pulled the canteen away and closed it. "Too much all at once and you'll either cramp or throw it all back up. You're pretty damned dehydrated. Lost a lot of water through the leg wound."

Rankin nodded wearily. He wet his lips, tried to speak, swallowed, and finally croaked out, "Dead?"

"Yes."

Rankin relaxed back. "Good."

"Maybe. I saw a patrol copter last night. They may have sent out another one, another *yamabushi*."

Rankin gestured for the canteen, and Clay gave in, holding up Rankin's head while he gulped at the water. Finally he pushed it away, then retched weakly, bringing some of it back up.

"You all right?"

"Fine, fine." He cleared his throat. "The patrols are why I moved here. They might have seen me where I was." The small effort of speaking seemed to drain him. He closed his eyes and grew quiet.

Clay spoke. "I've got the plastique. I'll work my way up northward until I find that installation, then I'm going to lay low until dark and get in, set the charges, and get back here. After she blows, we'll get down from here and steal a copter, maybe even have a drink or two of that rank local hooch to celebrate."

Rankin shook his head without opening his eyes. "Hell, we don't even know what it is they've got up there. If it's atomic, we're too close. Even given the explosion is low yield, five or six klicks away is going to be almighty hot."

Clay shrugged. "I don't see as we have a lot of choice. I can set the timer for up to five hours, but you're right, and it'll take me half that long to get back here."

"In five hours, even on foot, you can be well out of a blast radius."

"Ever the noble soldier." Clay grimaced. "I'll take my chances down here with you; these rock walls are plenty thick, and they can treat you for radiation. It's a good bet. We'll weather it out."

Rankin opened his eyes. "Does the thought that they might have sent another of those warriors frighten you?"

"You're goddamn right it does. Scared witless. I'll still be back."

"Your call."

"You're damned right it is."

"Do what has to be done. If you want to be a hero in the bargain, it's no skin off my back."

Clay smiled. "Haven't you heard? There aren't any heroes anymore, just good soldiers."

Rankin made a noise that sounded like a laugh. "That's good enough, son. Damned well good enough."

What they had spent so much time trying to reach, Clay found remarkably quickly. Some two hours north of the ravine one of the devices he had rescued from the equipment packs chirped to tell him he was approaching electronic security devices. He found a comfortable spot in some dense brush and settled in to wait for dark.

For a short time he slept shallowly, alert to any movement around him. As dusk approached, he waited, patiently awake, trying to ignore the pain and fatigue and the insects that appeared as the weak sun waned to drone in his ears and take their small bit of his skin and blood.

When the sky began to darken overhead, he checked his gear and prepared to move. He would have to go as silently as possible, and that meant unloading most of what he carried. He dumped various pieces of small survey gear into a pocket in the tree's roots: grease pencils, a tiny compass—he hesitated over the tiny electronic devices he had brought up from the canyon but finally dropped them, too, into the small pile.

He drew one last object up from the depths of the thigh pocket of his fatigue pants—an identification tag. Greene's. The image of her face came to him with a hard clarity. He held the small plate in his hand for a long moment, relishing its cold reality, then tossed it among the tree roots with the rest. *I got him for you, soldier,* he thought vehemently. *I got him for you.*

He settled for keeping only the rifle and its two clips, a pocket torch, and the satchel of plastique.

He rose from his cover and moved carefully to a spot just outside the perimeter of the surveillance devices the detector had picked up.

Against the trunk of a large, tall tree he packed a tiny charge of the powerful plastique and attached a remote timer to it. Then he set out, skirting the electronic surveillance that encircled what he guessed to be some sort of underground installation.

When he felt he was a sufficient distance away, he blew the charge.

There was a muffled roar in the direction from which he had come, followed by the distant crackle of splintering wood and brush as the tree fell.

Clay waited five seconds, knowing that the falling tree had set off whatever motion detectors or other security devices operated in that part of the perimeter. He wanted to give the security force—soldiers or *yamabushi*—inside time to react in that direction.

Then he turned on a small transmitter that jammed all electronic activity in the immediate area, effectively blinding the surveillance, and buried the device quickly under a windfall of small branches. He advanced cautiously on the area in which he believed his objective lay.

He met no resistance. The security forces were concentrating on the direction from which their electronics had told them their enemy was advancing, firing blindly into the empty forest. From the limited amount of noise they made reacting to his distraction, he could tell they were few and scattered. A few hundred meters beyond the perimeter of the electronic security he found what he was looking for.

One young soldier stood alone among the thinned-out trees of a small compound, standing guard, staring anxiously off into the night beyond the pool of light in which he stood, listening to the few scattered shots that still sounded in the darkness as his comrades fought a stubbornly invisible enemy.

Behind him stood a handful of small two-man field shelters and a plastiform hut of a sort Clay had seen on dozens of worlds. He dismissed the shelters without further thought; they were obviously too small to conceal what he sought. That left the hut.

It was the sort of all-purpose, nearly indestructible utility building used by combat forces for everything from sheltering land vehicles to storing foodstuffs and ammunition. But it was at most ten meters square—not nearly large enough, Clay thought, to house anything capable of generating the sort of

destruction Rankin had claimed had been inflicted upon the nomadic people of the southern continent.

But appearances, as the old saw went, were often deceptive,
and the security given the utility hut indicated an importance
that its outer appearance belied.

Clay moved swiftly through the brush, concentrating on remaining quiet. A renewed flurry of small-arms fire from the
area of his diversion gave him the opportunity he needed, and
he rushed the young soldier head on, bursting, he knew, like an
avenging *kami* spirit from the darkness of a brushy thicket, rushing into the glare of the arc lights that flooded the compound.

The young man's eyes widened in surprise, and he tried to
bring his weapon to bear, but an instant later Clay struck him
hard in the solar plexus. The boy collapsed, dropping his rifle,
and Clay scooped up the fallen weapon and swung it up over
his head like a club.

He began the fatal downswing, intent on crushing the soldier's
skull, and stopped, then cursed himself silently for his squea-
mishness. Hesitating to kill an enemy, young boy or no, was
dangerous and possibly fatal. If the boy recovered, there would
be a dozen or more rifles waiting for him outside the hut's door
in minutes.

He satisfied himself with rapping the boy just hard enough
with the rifle's butt to knock him cold, then rolled the unconscious form into a nearby tangle of brush. It was still chancy,
but an easier conscience seemed suddenly worth the additional
risk.

He quickly examined the utility hut's door. It was securely
bolted and locked; only someone whose thumbprint the locks
would recognize was going to get the bolt drawn. It was the only
door, and the rest of the building was windowless and therefore
impervious.

He had hoped to leave as little evidence of his passage as
possible, but—he shrugged to himself; the whole area was likely
to be blown to kingdom come before much longer. He unlim-
bered his assault rifle and sent a quick burst of three rounds into
the locking mechanism, which disintegrated in a shower of
sparks and plastic shrapnel.

Clay kicked the door open and went in.

Surprisingly, the hut was unimproved—the walls were blank,

open plastic—and seemingly empty. The floor was flat, feature-less stone, gray and unmarked. Clay walked out into the middle of the small room and turned around slowly. There was nothing. Clay's shoulders sagged with a desperate sense of failure. He couldn't have been wrong . . .

He turned again to face the far wall of the hut, his back to the door, and his jaw dropped in shock. Where before there had been featureless stone, there was now a gap in the floor, roughly a meter square.

Clay turned again, scanning the room. It was still empty except for the hole. He knew with absolute certainty that he had not missed seeing the gap when he had entered the hut.

Something, he told himself, was up.

He took the room in two strides and stood over the space in the raw rock. It was a perfect square, the edges straight and smooth, cut, he thought at first, with a laser. On closer inspection he realized that some other energy had cut the stone under his feet. The rock hadn't been lased—there was no fusing at the edges.

Neither was there evidence that the stone had been worked by tools—no chisel marks, no irregularities. It was simply there, as if the matter that had filled the square had simply disappeared.

He touched the edge; it was cool, smooth. The passage was not new, and it *was* a passage. Set in the flat plastic of the ceiling directly above its center was the corrugated disk of a gravity lift. Clay leaned over the dark hole but couldn't lean far enough out without losing his balance to reach the lift's effective field.

If he were to use the lift, he would have to simply leap into its field and pray that it was powered up. He hadn't brought a climbing line; he hadn't anticipated a need for it.

He thought for a few seconds, then shucked a caseless round from the spare rifle clip and let it drop. Almost ten seconds lapsed before he heard it strike stone at the bottom. It would be a very long, very deadly drop if he trusted himself to the lift and it didn't support him.

He pushed another round free from the clip and tossed it through the space under the disk. He thought the round's fall was checked just a bit, just for an instant, as it passed under the concentration of monopoles that made up the heart of the disk. But he couldn't be sure.

He hesitated, frowning, then shrugged, took a step back from the edge, and jumped into the center of the square, where the lift's ambient field should be.

For a gut-wrenching instant he felt himself begin to fall. Then the lift took his weight, and he felt the familiar, fiercely uncomfortable feeling of being held up and slowly lowered by a fist that held him somewhere in his center, a feeling something like being held up by a fishing line tangled in his intestines.

He fell slowly down, about a foot a second, into solid and unbroken darkness. He fumbled around in his pockets until he found his torch and touched its switch, its narrow beam knifing through the dark and revealing below the disk set into the stone floor of the shaft that completed the lift's energy channel. He could see nothing else in the shaft or at its bottom, so he switched off the torch to conserve its charge.

Strangely, the dark in the shaft seemed not quite so absolute as before, the stone of the walls seeming almost to exude a cold and sourceless light of its own. As he reached the bottom, the light had grown to the point where he could see that the wall to the north ceased three meters above the shaft's floor, opening into a passage that led away from the shaft out under the rising bulk of the mountain.

Clay stepped away from the disk, feeling as if he were moving through thin glue, and left the lift's field. The stone under his boots was perfectly smooth and slightly slick. He knelt down to touch it, and it was cool and perfectly dry but so finely finished as to feel almost waxed.

He snapped on his torch and started down the northbound passage.

The torch's beam reached only ten meters or so down the passage and was swallowed. Clay followed, walking steadily down the featureless tunnel for a half hour or more. As he walked, the eerie light that seemed almost to be soaking into the smooth surface of the walls from the living rock behind them grew to the point where, after he had walked about a kilometer, he no longer needed the torch and could see the passage stretching ahead, arrow-straight and seemingly without end. He walked on, and after what he guessed to have been almost an hour, he saw ahead, several hundred meters farther down the wide stone corridor, the blank face of a wall.

Clay quickened his pace to an easy lope. As he drew near, he realized that the passage ended at the wall; there were no side passages, just blank wall on three sides and the long empty passage behind. At the foot of the wall was the disk of a gravity lift. Overhead was a shaft leading up.

He turned slowly around, studying his options. There was only the shaft leading up and the passage leading back the way he had come.

He stepped into the lift's field and felt his weight leave him. The reason for the passage he had traversed was unclear, but the only direction left was up. He squatted preparatory to pushing strongly upward, like a swimmer thrusting away from the side of a pool, so that his inertia would carry him up the gravity shaft to the opposing disk.

He started to push, then stopped himself. Something caught his eye on the blank stone floor of the shaft's bottom. He pushed himself out of the field and picked up the object. It was one of the rounds he had dropped into the shaft earlier.

"What the hell?" he whispered to himself. He searched around and after a moment found the other shell. He inspected the markings on both rounds; they were without question his own, both C.F.-issue and made by the same Terran munitions plant. He looked back down the tunnel. It was as featureless and seemingly endless as before.

"How—" Clay felt suddenly confused and disoriented. Something very strange was happening either around him or to him. He had walked straight, due north, since descending the lift—his own internal sense of guidance insisted that he had— yet there he was, back where he had begun.

He glanced up the shaft again. Though it had been nearly an hour since he had broken through the door of the hut above, no one else, it would seem, had followed him down, and there didn't seem to be any commotion above. That they hadn't discovered the missing guard and the damaged door seemed unlikely, yet there had been no pursuit.

He studied the passage again. There was no change. It was exactly as it had been before.

He knew what waited above; the passage was his only real option. If he could mark the wall as he walked, he thought, he could keep his bearings, and whatever had turned him back to the shaft could be circumvented. He ransacked his pockets before remembering that he had dumped almost everything he had carried with him before assaulting the hidden compound, including the grease pencils he had carried as a detail of his guise as a surveyor ever since arriving on the planet. He ground his teeth in frustration.

He still held in his hand the two rounds he had tossed into the shaft. They were caseless rounds—no metal casings, only a bullet embedded in an oblong sheath of solid explosive propellant about two centimeters on a side. The blue sheath of each of the rounds was chipped and scratched from the fall down the shaft. He rubbed one of the rounds hard against the smooth, glowing stone of a wall, being careful of the explosive primer embedded in its base. It left an opaque, powdery line that blocked the weak light.

He started back down the passage.

Every few meters he drew an arrow on the near wall, pointing forward. When the first round had worn down to the bullet, he dropped it in the center of the passage, where it would be impossible to overlook, and started in again, using the second round.

He soon lost track of time and distance as he walked. There was no differentiation from one stretch of passage to the next; he could have walked one kilometer or ten. Before long, fatigue forced him to stop. He tossed the satchel of plastique down and simply sat on the cold stone floor and leaned back against the glowing wall; he controlled his breathing, pushing the pain and the irritation away from the forefront of his mind.

After a time he opened his eyes and pushed himself up again. On the wall above where he had been seated was an indistinct blue arrow, pointing away, he was sure, from the direction in which he had been moving.

Sometime in the last minutes before he had stopped to rest *something* had without his knowledge turned him physically back around, or—and this was too improbable to consider—the passage itself had been flipped without his being aware.

He shook the half-ground-away rifle round absently in his hand as if shaking a die that could magically tell him what he should do.

He considered that if indeed something was happening *within his mind*, then the trick would be to make it impossible for his mind to be fooled. The arrows he had drawn on the passage wall were only half the answer. He needed something continuous on which he could focus his attention.

He tossed the chalk around in his hand, studying it. It would not last very long the way he intended to use it, and he was particularly loath to waste any more of the rounds still left in the rifle's two clips. Even if he didn't need the firepower down below in the never-ending passageway, above there would doubtless be a considerable welcoming party waiting for him when he returned.

Still, it hadn't been more than three or four minutes before he had stopped to rest that he had drawn his last arrow, and he was certain he hadn't passed any of the earlier arrows before he had come to the one on the wall before him. Which meant that the point at which his confusion—it was the only word he could think of to describe what had happened—began was somewhere between the two arrows.

He touched the round to the wall and began walking, leaving a solid, faint line of blue powder. As he walked, he kept his attention wholly focused on the thin blue line and on the hand that held the steadily diminishing round. After only a few minutes the hand and the line suddenly plunged into darkness. He looked up, startled.

Before him the wall he had been following dropped away at right angles into absolute blackness. He turned. The wall opposite also ended abruptly. From the terminus of one wall around to the next as he slowly turned, staring, there was nothing but the coal black of total dark.

Slowly, almost as if his own will to see had created it out of nothing, light began to rise in the great empty space before him, radiating, as it had in the passage that had brought him there, from the very stone of the ceiling over the city.

For it *was* a city that rose stubbornly from the shadows, spread out before and below him for as far as he could see—at least a kilometer and probably much more—in the dim light. The buildings were low and narrow, some perfect cylinders of only two or three stories, others taller, broad ovals hundreds of meters long, each cut, so far as he could tell, from the living stone itself, as if the cavern in which they stood had been carved out from around them.

Each story in every building, so far as Clay could judge from the nearest, was at least three meters in height. The overall impression was the same Clay had had when seeing holos of the ancient Indian cliff dwellings at Mesa Verde on Terra, an impression of an ancient abandonment, a decay belied by the seeming solidity of the walls.

The silence was immense and absolute. Nothing moved; even the air was stale and still. The city was as lifeless and empty, it seemed, as space itself.

The passageway in which he stood was cut into a sheer wall nearly a hundred meters high. Clay stood about half that height above the abandoned city. Before him a broad, three-sided stair cut from the living stone led down to a wide avenue that disappeared into the heart of the great, dead underground city.

Looking out over the vast cavern that held the dead city, Clay felt an unexplainable, overwhelming despair rise in his heart.

Almost against his will, he stepped down onto the first step and into absolute madness.

CHAPTER TWENTY-NINE

Before his boot touched the first step, Clay was falling, his mind aflame with an indescribable agony, flushed with the twisting shapes of nightmare.

He felt the jolting pain of his body striking the stone of the steps as he fell only as an adjunct to the pain in his mind, a pain that reverberated, growing in intensity as if his mind were a bell being rung so quickly that there was only one long, throbbing tone.

He had no idea how long he lay at the bottom of the steps, his body beaten and bruised and his mind a bonfire of twisting images and searing pain. After an eternity the agony lessened, and Clay took a long, sobbing breath. As his lungs filled with stale air, he realized it could have been only seconds since his mind had been invaded, because he had quite literally forgotten to keep breathing under the intensity of the pain.

The fire that had possessed his mind was not entirely gone, though in comparison to what it had been, it now only smoldered in the recesses of his brain. What Clay was suddenly most aware of was an *other*, the same presence he had felt touch him through the eyes of Tind and the boy he had killed in the city.

Clay focused on the presence that hovered at the edge of his awareness, ignoring the pain in his body and his mind. With all the might he could muster he thrust a question at it. *What are you?*

His mind was again touched by the flames, and he felt he screamed, though he couldn't be sure he had made an actual sound. Images/ideas/near phrases flooded his mind—*Peacemaker, Warmaker, Chaos-God*—but the word that formed clearly in his thoughts was *Hachiman*. He was flooded with gamut of emotions not his own: joy, hate, anger, but more than any other a black despair that pierced to his soul.

Hachiman. The *other* flung the word like a javelin through his being.

"Hachiman." Clay heard the word in his ears and realized that he had said it out loud. The *other* retreated, and there was only the smoldering. Clay groaned and rolled over onto his back, the awareness of physical pain growing nearly as intense as the burning in his mind had been.

He blinked back blood and knew he had some sort of head wound. He searched his scalp with his fingertips and found a gash just above the hairline over his right eye. He tore loose a strip of cloth from his fatigue pants and wrapped it around his head, tying it in the back, binding the wound tightly.

Every muscle seemed sore and abused, though he could find nothing broken. The incompletely healed wound in his side throbbed with pain but had not reopened.

After his survey of his injuries, he took a few minutes and calmed himself. Gingerly, he probed his own consciousness, feeling out the displacement he felt, as if some part of his mind was still not his own.

He tried to stand and found almost to his surprise that he was still in control of his body. For a few moments when the pain had raged in his head, he had felt so wholly possessed that it seemed odd, once the agony had passed, to be able to stand on his own feet, though he did indeed have trouble doing even that as dizziness made him sway and stumble.

When he had steadied himself, he looked around for his rifle and realized with dismay that it was nowhere to be seen on the open stone at the base of the stairway. Nor was it on the stairs as his eyes followed the staircase up to the opening that marked the passageway from which he had fallen.

Which meant that it was still up above, in the passage. Clay took a deep breath and let it hiss out slowly from between his teeth. As beaten and bruised as he felt, he didn't relish the thought of climbing back up the stairway. But he had no choice; he couldn't walk empty-handed into whatever waited for him.

He began to lift his right foot to place it on the first stone stair and found to his shock that he couldn't. It was as if his feet were locked in stone.

He stepped back and found that suddenly he was free again. Experimentally, he tried to walk back to the staircase and found that he could not.

So that's how it is, he thought. Either it doesn't want me to have my weapon or it doesn't want me to leave. Or both. Regardless, he seemed destined to enter the dead city.

"Hachiman." He said the word again, and it sounded loud in his ears, strange but at the same time strangely familiar, as if he had heard it many times before in dreams. *Peacemaker, God of Dreams*—the phrases echoed in his mind like a residue of something he couldn't quite remember.

He shivered at the feeling of dread that overwhelmed him at those words. He steadied himself, trying hard to shake it off.

He slowly turned, surveying his surroundings. At street level the alien buildings around him looked less like ruins, tall and imposing and impossibly perfect, cut from the living stone but polished glass-smooth, even at every cornice and crevice. In lieu of windows, each level of each building was equipped with long diagonal slots about thirty centimeters wide and as tall as a normal man.

But the aliens were obviously not "normal men," not *Homo sapiens* or any other species that had roamed the planet Earth, at least not to Clay's knowledge. Judging from the height of the passage that had led him there and from the heights of the individual floors in the buildings that stretched off in the distance, squatting above the geometrically straight line of the avenue in front of him, Clay guessed their average height to have been around seven feet. As to their size or girth, he had no idea; that was for the anthropologists, if any ever made it this far.

But whatever they had looked like or lived like, they seemed obviously long gone; the slotted windows were empty, the streets lifeless. The air in the city was cave-still and stank of the must of disuse and abandonment. But something here, somewhere close, still lived. A small piece of it still lived inside him, burrowing like a wasp larva in his mind, watching him.

Clay started off, limping, down the broad stone avenue. It was, he thought, an obvious choice: A main street leading from the only—so far as he knew—entrance to a dense concentration of what obviously had once been dwellings should lead to the one place the builders considered most important. And somehow Clay was sure that that place was where he would find what he needed to find.

No longer was his goal simply to destroy a weapon—or a *thing*—that the U.D. wanted destroyed. All that drove him now was the undeniable need to be rid of the thing that insinuated itself, in part, into his head. To do so, he would have to discover where his enemy dwelled.

He hadn't taken more than a dozen steps when he glanced to the side for a moment and the city disappeared.

It reappeared again an instant later. It was if he had blinked his eyes—though he hadn't—and opened them again to a different scene, a different place. He was still in the city, no longer at its edge but somewhere deep in its forgotten heart, the stone ceiling of the cavern fifty meters above his head, the wall with the entrance nowhere in sight.

And he was utterly lost.

* * *

It would seem, Clay thought, that the *other* did not want him closer any more than it wanted him to leave.

He turned slowly around. The buildings around him were virtually identical, all faceless and undecorated except for the narrow slashes of the "windows." The streets themselves were empty and featureless.

Nothing to do but pick a direction.

He closed his eyes and concentrated. In the past his innate sense of direction had occasionally led him out of bad situations with an uncanny accuracy. He hoped it—or his grandmother's nature magic—would serve him as well this time. He wasn't sure, but the narrow street off his left cheek seemed close to "right," though the most direct route was blocked by buildings.

He shrugged mentally and started down it, trying hard to keep his attention from wavering from the path to which he had committed himself. He thought he saw a pattern in what had happened to him moments before and earlier when he had been in the passage. It was when he allowed himself to lose his focus on the path before him, when his mind was distracted from his intention, that the confusion occurred.

Again, as in the passageway, he wondered whether he had literally been displaced or whether it only *seemed* he had been moved.

He walked over to the nearest structure, standing, his internal guidance insisted, between himself and where he intended to go—where an open avenue had been before—and rapped it with a knuckle. It seemed just as solid and real as a spaceliner.

Again he shrugged to himself. He'd play the cards that were dealt him, then.

Soon enough he came upon a gap between the buildings that led in the right direction. He turned into it, and the world seemed to waver as if heat were rising from the stone of the street. He kept his eyes forward, concentrating on the position of the structures before him, the short, perfectly cylindrical building to his left, the odd protrusion that bulged out from the base of the building just beyond. It seemed to work; the waver stopped, and the street before him remained as it was.

I've got your number, he thought toward the *other* who waited in his head. As he did so, the street flickered and was gone.

Again he was somewhere else; a new piece of the alien city

spread out before him. He fought back dizziness, steadied, then ground his teeth in irritation.

He squatted to ease the spinning in his head and asked himself, What now?

Once again he surveyed his surroundings. This time he was in the center of some sort of square. It was crossed by shallow channels that might once have held water, and at its center, where he squatted, was a depression that could have been a pond or a reservoir. But now the pool was dry, the channels empty so long that there wasn't even the stain of the long-gone water on the stone. Radiating out from it like spokes from a wheel were a half dozen new streets.

Again, one, off to his left, felt right. But he hesitated, not quite daring to move across the square to its opening. If he did and once again he was moved, there was the chance that he would find himself in a place from which he could not orient himself, a place that somehow defeated his innate sense of direction. He was tired and so bone-bruised that every movement was torture. It would not be much longer before frustration and exhaustion caused him to simply collapse in whatever new place he suddenly found himself. And once he lay down, he feared he might never rise again.

The cavern was bone-dry; there was no water, no food. He knew he must find what he had to find, and soon, or he would die.

He closed his eyes and rested. The *other*, or at least the piece of it that persisted in his mind, seemed to loom uncomfortably large inside his head without the distraction of the sight of the city.

The distraction of the city. The phrase resonated in Clay's mind.

It couldn't be that simple.

Quickly, afraid somehow that the *other* could know his intention and defeat it, he untied the knot that held the makeshift bandage around his forehead. Gingerly, he touched the gash on his head and found that it had clotted and was no longer bleeding. He refolded the strip of cloth so that the bloodied part was folded in, then retied it around his head, this time with the thick fatigue cloth over his eyes.

Blind, he stood and walked in the direction he knew was right.

He concentrated not on where he walked but on the *other*, on the small spark that still burned in his brain.

Instantly, the spark broke once again in raging flame, and Clay staggered and fell to his knees as the pain flared in his head. Again his mind was a whirl of twisted, churning incomplete images. Nausea struck him, and he retched and tried to lay down against the cool stone, but something took over control of his muscles and jerked him up like a marionette.

He felt himself being walked, like a marionette on strings, along the flat stone street that led away from the empty square and into the alien city.

He struggled against the force that held him and ordered his muscles to act, trying to force the *other* from his mind, but to no avail. He caught himself beginning to panic, to surrender to the chaos that filled his mind. Pushing back the fear, he made a great effort to relinquish himself, to step back from it. He mastered his terror, relaxed, and withdrew, letting the *other* take undisputed control of his physical form, and consolidated his strength, conserving the power of his will. He knew with ominous certainty that the real challenge to the integrity of his self was yet to come, wherever it was the *other* was taking him.

He kept just enough awareness of what was outside his center to note that it was intensely strange, feeling his own body move not against his will but *despite* it.

After a time—Clay made no effort to keep track of how far they had come—he became aware that the glow that permeated the great cavern that held the city had dimmed. He struggled for a second to reassert himself the small amount it took to open his eyes and saw only the cloth of his own blindfold.

In his frustration he almost gave way, almost exposed the small, hard core of himself to the *other*.

He forced himself to calm, then concentrated on forcing one hand up, making the muscles in his upper arm contract, the smaller muscles of wrist and hand move to grasp. The hand came up like something dead, moving with excruciating slowness. It was, he thought, like operating one of the feedback-waldos used in space—the mechanical hands that did as your hands did but were not your hands—but the waldo was damaged in some way and answered to commands imperfectly and without speed.

Eventually he felt his fingers tangle in the cloth and pull it up, and he suddenly looked out upon a vast room half a kilometer or more in circumference.

Like most of the buildings in the underground city, this one was perfectly round. Tiered steps circled the room, making it look like a coliseum or some vast operating theater. He stood at the top of twenty or more concentric rings that focused down to a small open space in the center.

He tried to step down, but the *other* would not allow it, not yet.

As he watched, something rose—or was exuded—from the stone circle at the center. It was misty and distorted, like a damaged hologram, but clearly alive, clearly a living form. It seemed at the same time human and not human, thin and tall and the blue-white color of milk; the distortion, he realized, was not simply perspective.

The figure was, he realized, misshapen and lopsided, one shoulder held low as if crippled, one arm withered and held against a painfully thin, elongated rib cage. And suddenly he realized that he could see completely through it to the stone on the far side, as if it were not wholly there.

Spirit, he thought, hearing in his mind the voice of his grandmother.

God, the *other* answered, filling his mind with the word as if filling a bowl with water.

The figure turned, and Clay had the impression of eyes upon him, staring into his soul.

Come.

Something forced his foot to lift and then drop onto the first step below. As he moved slowly down, the figure began to break up, as though a breeze had passed through mist. Then it began to coalesce again, spinning slowly in a double helix of growing light.

He remembered the image, the destructive column of light, from the satellite's black box that had been replayed on Fitzgerald's machine, and he knew suddenly that before him was its source and that he was walking directly to it, unarmed and controlled.

CHAPTER
THIRTY

The thing below him—the essence of the other *that resided in* Clay's mind—was what he had seen before on Fitzgerald's monitor, now condensed and a thousand times smaller. As he watched, the column of light expanded, no longer the size of the figure Clay had seen, roughly two meters tall and man-shaped, but fully filling the center circle from floor to ceiling, fifty meters or more tall.

It drew him down toward the center of the great building, forcing his muscles to move him jerkily forward, and he could feel a sense of pure evil wash over him from the energies that played from floor to ceiling like a twisting tornado of light and color below.

No, he thought to himself, not evil but *malevolence*, simple and pure, the kind of lingering enmity his grandmother would have told him dwelt in certain places that were taboo to his ancestors back on Terra, a lasting malice that lived in places polluted by angry and agonized souls.

The *other* brought him to within three meters of the column of light and stopped him, leaving him standing, waiting for what would come next.

I am your God.

The words appeared as if written in his mind, accompanied by the punishing whiplash of a jet of pure pain. The center that was still *John Clay* flinched away, and he almost lost consciousness.

Slowly he drew himself back from the darkness. He concen-

223

trated the entirety of his will into projecting one word out at his tormentor.

No.

Once again a jet of raw flame tore through his mind. A strange, violent anger flooded him, strange because it was not his own.

Clay felt his hands cramp as if with age. He looked down at them and realized with dull apprehension that they were no longer his hands; they were rough and gnarled, and in one there suddenly appeared a long stone-polished blade. He stared at it, realizing with a flush of fear that it was the *yamabushi*'s long-knife, the same blade he had left to mark the old warrior's grave.

You will see.

And suddenly he was no longer standing paralyzed before the *other* in the alien coliseum. He squatted on a tree limb above a forest trail, waiting for an enemy to pass under, an enemy he must slaughter without compassion, without mercy.

He was *yamabushi*, and his god had given him the onus of killing Terrans.

Clay cringed back from the hate that flowed like a torrent through him, flowed through *Tind*. He *was* Tind; he felt what Tind had felt, saw what Tind had seen. He knew the intention in Tind's mind, knew what he—what Tind—would do in the next few moments.

But he was powerless. Helpless, he watched as a figure walked underneath the limb, felt the muscles in Tind's legs tense.

Clay recognized the U.D. survey uniform, the loping gait of Fitzgerald. And though he knew that Fitzgerald was dead and that he himself had buried the soldier's battered body beside an Ithavollan river, he applied every fiber of his being to try to force control over the *yamabushi*, stay the leap down onto Fitzgerald's shoulders, even as he felt Tind/himself lean forward and spring.

And then he was on top of Fitzgerald, riding him down. His hand came into his field of vision, bringing the long-knife to Fitzgerald's throat. Blood spurted as he cut, and then he whirled to face a new threat.

Clay's heart leapt in pain. Greene—*Greene*, alive, healthy, whole—charged the old warrior, her face a mask of avenging fury. Clay could feel the muscles in Tind's arm tense to begin the blow, and he screamed, the word never making it to the *yamabushi*'s lips.

He saw the knife's blade slash upward, pulling Greene's vest up and away as it cut through her fatigue blouse and into her abdomen. He watched as the fury in her strong face changed to surprise and pain. He watched as she fell, trying to hold herself in with both hands.

And then Tind was diving into the forest cover, gunfire ripping like mad hornets through the brush behind him, and Clay was back in his own possessed body, standing stiff before the twisting column that was the *other*.

He sobbed once, wracked with pain and remorse. And with hate: Tind's hate and his own, both for what the *yamabushi* had been compelled to do and for the *other*, the alien sadist who had compelled him to do it.

Then the hate was only Tind's hate again, and he again held the long-knife in his hand, his mind reeling with the sickness of the sudden transition. Before him was a hill covered with blowing grass; ahead was a tall, dark stone jutting up from the slope, one of the old relics of the hated *Ainu*, the enemy of *Hachiman* who had lived *before*, and against it stood the dark-haired Terran.

Clay felt the concentration of the *yamabushi*'s hate on the figure as they approached. He watched as the figure stepped forward, swinging a rough club in its hands, and realized with a sickening surety that he was looking out upon *himself*, awaiting the *yamabushi*'s charge.

He felt himself, Tind, break into a heedless run. He heard the battle roar that reverberated in his lungs as he raised the long-knife high and charged the hated enemy of his god, of *Hachiman*.

As he closed on the waiting figure, his mind burned with the blood lust of his god—Clay resisted this, screaming silently, *Not god but alien.* Suddenly the Terran dropped his weapon, and the thought glimmered in Tind's flooded consciousness that his enemy was accepting an easy death, cowering like a dog. Then pain lanced through his entire being as he ran hard upon the suddenly upheld lance.

Clay's consciousness flickered at the shock and pain, and he thought for an instant that he had left the mind of the doomed warrior. But an instant later his vision focused again, and he watched Tind's hand—his *own* hand—reach forward and slowly draw the searing agony of the lance through his body. He saw the long-knife slash futilely at the Terran—at *himself*—and felt the unbearable wrenching through his torn chest as the Terran jerked from side to side the shaft that pierced him through.

He fell, hating the Terran and hating the bitterness of his own defeat. Then he felt the blade of his own knife at his throat. He felt the pressure, the sharp edge cutting into his flesh, and then he died.

Clay's head swam with the doubleness of being Tind and being himself, of fighting himself and feeling himself kill himself. A wave of nausea rose in his throat, and he tried to retch and couldn't.

His body was not his own; the *other*, *Hachiman*, kept his entire body rigid and unmoving. His throat was clenched against the spasm.

Then he was released. He fell upon the cold stone before *Hachiman* and wept uncontrollably, gagging and retching his horror.

No, he thought vehemently. Not for you, you sadistic bastard.

He controlled himself and struggled, gasping with the effort, to his knees. His head swayed, his mind filled with the flickering images of nightmare, but he managed to focus on the being before him.

The idea of even so much as trying to communicate with that being filled him with loathing, but he controlled his distaste and anger and forced a question to form in his mind.

Why? he asked, and in that one word was projected what had been done to Greene and Fitzgerald, to Tind, to the people of the southern continent, and to Clay himself.

There was no answer, only the empty silence of the dead city and the soundless flickering light from the apparition that twisted and flashed before him.

Why? he demanded, screaming the word silently in his head. *What gives you the right?*

I am Hachiman, the reply came. *I am God.*

To hell with you, god or not, Clay threw back.

You will see. Clay felt himself wrenched free from his own form and moved again from his own body into the memory of another.

His mind writhed with horror. In a flash of chaotic terror he had been bound with the ageless, twisted soul that was his tormenter.

He was *Hachiman*. Peacemaker. Warmaker. God—He Who Would Destroy All.

CHAPTER THIRTY-ONE

There was pain in Clay's body, but it was ancient pain, dulled and weathered with time; the deeper hurt was not the physical pain that came from his twisted body but the pain of his humiliation.

Gan-pao wept. He was alone, so terribly alone. He had always been so.

Nothing was more essential to the *people* than the ideal: grace, perfection, the unmarred symmetry of body and line. Gan-pao had been neither graceful nor perfect. His slender body had not been straight, had not been slim and aquiline but buckled and warped, and abnormalities such as his were very rare among the *people*. He was pitied and shunned; every member of his race, who saw in him the embodiment of a fear too terrible to face, avoided so much as the sight of him. He was alone, and he hated them for it.

Clay felt that hate and shared in it. Gan-pao—*Hachiman*, Clay understood, was a name Gan-pao had taken from the memories of the new Ithavollans, Tind's people—nurtured his hate and waited, knowing he would be given somehow, sometime, the

opportunity for retribution. He was a martyr and knew he would
be redeemed.

Clay remembered with Gan-pao the underground city of Irin-
ri, a city glorious and rich with beauty, carved like a jewel from
the heart of the mountain. Clay walked the bright streets, slowly
and painfully moving through a city filled with grace and harmony and light—not the harsh light of the surface but the diffused and comforting light the *people* created, through their
learning, from the stone itself.

And as he walked, his hate grew, for the beauty, for the life
and grace that was denied him, especially for the toleration and
the pity.

For a hundred years he bore his humiliation. And then his
chance came, from above, from the jungle.

Clay felt the exultation that came with the memory, the abiding
satisfaction of what he had done, what Gan-pao had done. It was
a feeling the long centuries alone had done nothing to temper.

It was glory. It was power.

The people who lived in the jungles above were primitives, a
race only nominally rooted in the same original stock as Gan-
pao's own. The *Ainu*—again Clay understood that the word was
chosen by *Hachiman* from the colonists' language—were de-
spised by the *people*; even were interbreeding possible, it would
be so objectionable to the *people* as to be obscene.

The *Ainu* were backward in culture and learning but not in
cunning. The *people* feared them for their growing numbers.
The *people* had become few in the centuries since they had set
themselves apart and had gone below. There were only a few
thousand of them left—and they feared the *Ainu* for their primitive violence.

The greatest fear of the *people* was that the *Ainu* would become bold enough to descend into the caverns—Clay discovered
then, as the image occurred in his/Gan-pao's mind, that the way
he had come was only one of many into the great cavern of the
city—and the *people*, with all their learning, had forgotten how
to make war.

They needed a weapon. Gan-pao, the crippled, the untouch-
able, became that weapon.

Clay found himself alone in a small empty room, his strange
alien body nude and lying flat on a platform. He had been given

time to prepare himself for the ordeal, but he needed no preparation.

What they were about to do to him they considered an atrocity—a necessary atrocity but horrible enough to offend even those who would do what had to be done. Their bodies were precious to them; they delighted in the outer forms in which they lived.

Gan-pao had no such sentiments. His outer form was an obscenity. The chance to be free of it was the first real possibility for true joy in the torment that had been his existence.

He waited in that tiny, sterile room and planned his victory.

Then they came for him. Clay found himself in a pool of achingly bright light, strapped to a wide, flat dais while machines hovered over him, machines built with such skill and grace that even they in their sterile utilitarian purposefulness were beautiful, machines that mapped and coded the even finer machine that was his brain.

Then they descended and quickly cut away his anesthetized, twisted body. Awake, aware because that was what was required by the process being performed, he relished what was happening, and Clay shared his joy.

And then he was God.

And God looked out upon his world and decreed death.

Clay stared out at the rippling shaft of coherent energy that was Gan-pao, was *Hachiman*, and was wracked with horror and pity. *What had been done to him—to them both?*

For an interminable time he had been wholly isolated in the terror of himself, cut off from all sensory ties to the world—no sight, no sound, no feeling. Then slowly, piece by piece, he was made whole once again; but more than just whole, he was made immortal.

The *people* had used the knowledge gained from a thousand centuries of peace and isolation to make of the mind and brain of Gan-pao a weapon. The synapses that had driven the muscles of his pitiful warped body controlled energies that could turn mountains to dust, pulling them apart molecule by molecule. What had been his medulla oblongata controlled now not involuntary muscles but a mass of indestructible living machinery, regulating the forces that composed his new body the way it had once kept his heart in rhythm.

Clay remembered the moment when they had finally finished with the transition. The pain was gone. He was perfect and whole and free.

He rose from the living machine that held him through the stone of the city's floor and up into the *above*.

With a thought he turned the jungle for a hundred kilometers around to dust and vapor simply by thinking away the bonds that held the matter together, absorbing into himself the incredible energies released, growing even stronger. He gloried in the power, exulted in the destruction.

He rose high above the dim cavern of his birth and moved across the verdant surface of his world.

Somewhere not very far beyond the blasted jungle he found a village of the *Ainu*. He descended on the stone huts like the vengeful god he now was and reduced every being there to essential dust. He rose again, bloodied and powerful, and searched out another village, and after that another, until the *Ainu* were no more.

And then he returned.

He stood, his body pure rippling energy, in the center of the Hall of Harmony, beneath which the essence of his brain lay buried, nestled in its framework of force fields and spun silicon glass.

He remembered the fine streets beyond, the grace and the light and the *people*, and with a simple thought he obliterated all but the stone itself. He saved the city to function as his temple.

And then the great cavern of the *people* was silent.

For five thousand years he had lived there, wrapped in silence.

Clay remembered the terrible isolation, the centuries of regret. Not remorse, never remorse, but regret for himself; without others to *feel* for him, he could not feel. Without intelligent beings to worship him, he was not a god, for what is a god without worshipers?

Then the Terrans came. Five thousand years had made him insane; it had also made him patient. For a hundred years more he slowly, carefully insinuated himself into the minds of the newcomers, discovering what their powers were, what learning they possessed.

And now he would be their god, and through them god of all the universe. And every creature would live to serve him, to give him through their pain the sensory stimulation he had lost five thousand weary years before. He could live in their minds the vicarious violence he needed like a drug for his sick and twisted soul.

Clay faced the twisting wraith of light that was Gan-pao, filled with the insanity of blood lust and filled with self-loathing because that insanity stained his soul like a dye on whole, clean cloth. He no longer was Gan-pao, but Gan-pao lived inside him, the *other* still a part of his mind, waiting.

Will you serve me?

Clay's mind was filled with coiling images of battle and slaughter, of destruction and pain. *Hachiman* wanted a soldier who would kill for him, while the wraith that had been Gan-pao of the *people* felt the death through him, a voyeur watching through his own eyes, feeling through his hands, perched in his head like a homunculus.

No.

He was no longer in the hall. Clay sat with his legs crossed, his back erect. He was in a dim room where the plastisteel walls were covered with prints of landscapes and with carefully drawn calligraphy.

The room was quiet and still. It was night, and the darkness was broken only by candles and the smoldering ends of thin sticks of incense.

Before him stood an altar that held the familiar idols brought with his family from the isle of Japan a century before, idols that represented not gods but states of perfection. The altar also held a small, shapeless twisted metal figure, the representation of the form of something that had no form, of *Hachiman*, who was God.

Qianzhi cleared his mind, preparing himself. Both as the emperor's *shikken* and as a servant of *Hachiman*, what he was to do was his necessary duty, a task to be carried out with joy and without fear.

He drew the *wakasashi*, the long-knife, from its sheath. He then folded a sheet of thin rice paper over the blade and held the covered blade in his left hand, the knotted cord of the hilt in his right. Clay could feel the cool smoothness of the steel through the thin paper, could smell the sharp scent of incense and a strange odor that he guessed to be a burning drug of some kind.

His left hand placed the tip of the blade gently against his bare abdomen. Without further thought or hesitation, he thrust it in. Both Clay and Qianzhi gasped at the sudden pain. Qianzhi pulled the blade even deeper, then drew it across, through his entrails, then up and out, spilling himself forth.

Qianzhi died slowly, his life draining out through the wound in his belly. He bit through his tongue to keep himself from screaming.

And as his sight dimmed, he gloried in the final waves of cramping agony. The pain of *seppuku* was his last and greatest offering to the Peacemaker, to *Hachiman*; he would dwell forever in the heaven of his ancestors.

Then, convulsing, his life drained out onto the mat that covered the plastic floor. He died, and Clay returned.

Again Clay tried to retch and couldn't. Awareness returned, and he felt a difference in the position of his own body.

He was sitting, legs crossed, before the pillar of light that was *Hachiman*, the god incarnate Qianzhi had worshiped. In his hands he held the chill hard steel of the *yamabushi*'s long-knife.

He watched as his own hands opened his vest, fumbling clumsily with the simple fastenings, and placed the tip of the blade against his abdomen. For a fleeting instant he wondered if the knife he held was real or only an apparition, something again placed in his mind by the *other*.

Then he felt the prick of the long-knife's sharp tip on his skin and knew with an awful certainty that it did not matter. When his hands thrust the long blade into his belly, he would die, slowly and in agony, without even so much as the comfort of Qianzhi's faith.

His hands hesitated, and he knew that Gan-pao was exulting in the power he held over him, relishing his fear.

Clay drew together his waning strength and willed his hands to move. For an instant they did, and the knife's blade wavered away. Then it snapped back into place, and he felt the steel bite into his flesh.

Fool.

His mind burned like a wound rubbed with salt as *Hachiman* crushed his will and conquered him wholly, forcing his trembling hands to draw the knife inward.

Then, like a gush of cool water, something entered him and drowned out the flames that were consuming his mind.

* * *

Something beautiful and cold soothed his tortured soul, smothering out the pain like a blanket of numbing snow.

For the first time since he had entered the cavern the *other*—Gan-pao, *Hachiman*—left him. Another took his place, or rather, something—not one but many—entered Clay's mind and let his straining muscles relax, pushed his hands easily, gently away, drawing the blade's tip out the centimeter or so it had entered into the muscle of his gut.

Two simple words formed in his mind, drawn not in flame but in mist, as if whispered—*no more*.

The column of light that was *Hachiman* flared into a cylinder of pure flame. He could feel Gan-pao's rage wash over him, but it was no longer inside of him. He could feel Gan-pao struggle to reach him, then fall back, repulsed like surf from a cliff face. Clay watched the raging pillar of fire for a long moment after he was free, fascinated despite himself with the physical manifestation of the crippled and suffering being whose mind he had shared.

He fully expected to see Gan-pao rise from the hall's floor and fall upon him with the same destructive wrath with which he had wiped out the *Ainu* and his own people so long ago, but something seemed to hold the specter in place in the center of the coliseum. The pillar seemed to struggle and flare in frustration against some powerful force or bond that Clay couldn't see.

He realized suddenly that his body as well as his mind had been freed. He crawled away from his tormentor, cringing from the twisting colors and forms that embodied the unbearable hell that had consumed his mind only moments before.

His savior—no, saviors, he corrected himself—withdrew gently from his mind, leaving behind an indescribable feeling of quietude.

A dozen meters from the thing that had been Gan-pao, he stopped and turned back.

He knew with a sudden certainty that he could not leave with what he come to do still undone. He must finish it, not just for Rankin or for Greene and Fitzgerald but because, somehow, it was what he was fated to do.

He was surprised in an almost unthinking way at that thought. Fate, like luck, had always been a thing he believed a soldier made for himself: if he planned well, if he was prepared, what he needed to happen would happen; if it didn't, it wasn't fate, luck, or gods, it was just the way things were, and he accepted it.

But somehow this was different. He knew with a feeling that approached certainty that everything he had done, everything he had become, had been for no other reason than to bring him to this place at this moment.

Were Rankin near to hear him, he would tell him, "I became a soldier, my friend, because it is the one thing that would prepare me for this purpose, to bring me here to do this one right thing."

Clay stood and held the long-knife out before him, but it was no longer the stone-polished steel blade that had killed Greene and Fitzgerald and finally the old *yamabushi* himself but different and heavier, a dagger a half meter long and made of gray stone that was warm and rough in his hand.

Over the length of the stone blade were cut, like names of the dead, Clay thought, hundreds of the same strange runes he had seen cut into the stone before which he had fought and killed the *yamabushi*. It seemed real, heavy and comforting in his hand.

Spirit magic, he thought, remembering the stories his grandmother had told him. *Or insanity.*

His saviors returned, coming back as if they knew that now that he had come to his realization on his own, they were free once again to help him. There was a sensation in his mind of a thousand hands touching, healing, giving him the strength to raise the stone blade over his head. He held it there like an offering, tip in one hand, hilt in the other.

Then he grasped it like a javelin and hurled it into the flame that was *Hachiman*, the point diving at man height into the column of light. He closed his eyes and prayed silently to the gods of his ancestors, to all of them, Occidental, Indian, and Eastern.

A wailing scream shuddered in his mind, and then, suddenly, silence. He opened his eyes, and the great hall was empty and quiet.

And he was free. Wholly, entirely.

Consciousness left him, and he collapsed.

CHAPTER
THIRTY-TWO

Clay dreamed.

In his dream he walked slowly alone across a barren, blasted plain that sloped down before him into the distance.

He knew, without knowing how he knew, that he was in the place that was now thick jungle above the cavern of the *people*, the jungle as it had been five thousand years before, when Gan-pao—or the thing that Gan-pao had become—had burned away everything for a hundred kilometers in every direction down to the bare rock.

The voice of his grandmother whispered in his ear: *This is a spirit place. This is a place for souls, where the dead gather to lament.*

It is empty here, he told her, and his voice echoed in the emptiness. *I am alone.*

No, was the answer, and he realized that he was not alone. For as far as he could see stood brown men, women, and children. The men were his height but very thin.

Their faces were open and expressionless, their mouths wide, their eyes small and wide apart. They were hairless, with small hands and feet, and down to the smallest child they stared at Clay as if waiting for him to speak.

The Ainu, a voice said, and Clay couldn't tell whether it was his grandmother's voice he heard or his own. Maybe his grandmother's voice *and* his own, speaking in harmony.

"Am I dreaming?" This was clearly his own voice, but there was no answer. He shook his head, confused. Too much had happened—so much horror, so much grief and fear and terrible confusion.

The *Ainu* watched him without speaking. His eyes moved across the wide faces. Of their own accord, his eyes settled on one of the slim, dark-skinned people. Spirits, he thought to himself, and shook his head in wonder. The individual Clay now watched was clearly an elder, wrinkled and stooped, his tobacco-colored skin splotched with age. Again without knowing how he knew, he realized that among his grandmother's people this one would have been a shaman, a wise man.

He returned Clay's gaze for a long moment, then spoke.

A debt has been paid. Below this sacred ground the Peace-maker *slumbers. We will never allow him to be awakened. We will never allow this again.* He waved a hand to indicate the multitude that surrounded him.

He is not dead?

No. He cannot die—that is his curse and ours. It is not yours. Warrior, return whence you came. This is no place for you or your kind.

Yes. Clay hesitated, then asked what he needed to ask. *Am I dreaming?*

The old man smiled, and Clay's soul warmed. *Yes.*

Then the blasted plain was empty again. Clay felt the ache of wounds, the deadly weight of his exhaustion in every bone. But he felt at peace. He lay down on the bare smooth stone and slept.

CHAPTER THIRTY-THREE

Sleep. Blackness broken only by the white mist of the spirit voices.

Clay awoke cold and shivering in absolute darkness, not knowing where he was.

Then memory began to return, and he shuddered. It's over, he told himself, fighting back a small, chilling seed of doubt and despair.

He felt around in the pockets on the thigh of his fatigue pants and found his torch. He worked the switch that turned it on and off, and for a heart-stopping instant it would not switch on; a vision of being lost in the absolute darkness, wandering aimlessly through the streets of the dead city, flashed through his mind, making his blood run cold.

Then the torch's beam snapped on, cutting through the darkness. He discovered that he was still in the great hall where he had been brought to stand before the specter of Gan-pao, sitting in the center of the circular dais that had held the apparition.

Below where he sat, if he was to believe his dream—and it seemed much too real to him now, awake, to simply be that—Gan-pao still lived, trapped forever in the indestructible machinery that held his essence, his insanity, like a wasp in a spider's web.

Trapped forever. Clay remembered the dream and wondered how much he could trust that vision.

He pulled himself up as quickly as he was able and stood, swaying, fighting the pain and fatigue in his battered limbs. Then he moved superstitiously off the dais.

He sat for a second to gather his wits on the steps that led up to the hall's entrance. He couldn't shake the feeling that everything that had happened—Gan-Pao/*Hachiman*, the *Ainu*, the dream—was only nightmarish illusion. Only his wounds and the dead city around him stood as testimony to the reality of what had been.

He made the long, slow climb to the top, following the torch's thin beam.

There was still something he had to do, and quickly, before the torch or his own sorely drained reserves of strength gave out.

As he reached the open arch of the hall's entrance, he realized he had no idea how to get back to the passageway that had led him to the underground city. He played the torch's beam around from one side to the other. To either side the light reflected back dully from the stone of walls; ahead it disappeared into an empty landscape of darkness.

That, at least, made choosing easy.

He steeled himself and set out down the broad stone street. He kept his mind from dwelling on the prospect of wandering lost in the maze of the huge city's streets until his torch died, then having to *feel* his way along the walls of the buildings that loomed over him as if they themselves were spirits in the shadows created by the torch's light.

He knew well enough what the chances of his ever leaving the dead city would be then. He would go insane long before hunger and dehydration could kill him.

Then he would spend his own eternity entombed with the madness that was Gan-pao.

The thought made him hurry, ignoring the pain and exhaustion.

Less than a minute later he was at the base of the three-sided staircase that led up and out of the cavern of Irin-ri. He sat on the lowest step to catch his breath and almost wept at the irony.

Gan-pao's "Hall of Harmony" had been only a few hundred meters away all along, a straight and easy—if *Hachiman* had allowed him to do it—walk down the avenue that led away from the staircase.

When he felt somewhat recovered, he climbed the stairs slowly, methodically, forcing his weary legs to lift up his feet and place them down again. The climb was made even harder by the knowledge that he would have to make it again and that even then he would have a considerable journey ahead of him before he could stop and really rest.

At the top he found the assault rifle, intact, lying innocuously in the passageway. Beside it lay what he had climbed back up for—the satchel of plastique.

After he had rested for a time, he started back down into the city.

He took the stairs carefully—it would be too tragic, too ironic to even believe if he let his fatigue cause a misstep and a broken leg—and then walked the short distance to the great hall.

It took almost a half hour, at the slow pace his injuries forced on him, to set the charges. By the time he had finished, the torch's beam had grown frighteningly yellow and weak.

He set the timers for the maximum—five hours—and shuffled away down the street as quickly as he could manage.

Again he dragged himself up the steps. At the top he recovered his rifle, then began the long walk back to the gravity lift.

He knew there was a good chance he was walking to his death; there were probably troops waiting for him either at the lift or above, and they would not be in a frame of mind to discuss the matter. Still, he walked with a certain sense of satisfaction; he had carried through his orders, though it had proved to be a much different mission than Rankin or his C.F. bosses had ever, he was sure, imagined.

He reached the lift without event. The shaft, so far as he could tell, was unchanged from when he'd left it. He passed a hand over the lift disk and felt the lightening sensation that indicated that the device was operational.

Good, he thought. Whatever's up there, it's preferable to being trapped below. One of the details he had learned in his time reliving Gan-pao's troubled existence was that this one opening was the only way left in or out of Irin-ri. Gan-pao had sealed the others centuries before.

Still, he didn't immediately step into the lift's field. First he set his rifle aside and pulled the last two charges of plastique from the satchel. He placed them on opposite sides of the shaft, close against the stone walls, and then set the timers.

He stood from his labors and dusted off his hands. The charges would be enough, he thought with confidence, to seal off this particular entrance to the underground city forever. The thought gave him great satisfaction.

He retrieved the assault rifle and checked that a round waited in the chamber.

Then he stepped into the lift's field, squatted, and thrust himself up the shaft.

As he rose, he prepared himself for battle.

It would be something of a relief, he thought, cradling his weapon, to fight a simple, all-too-human enemy, one armed with nothing more than guns.

He took several deep breaths and tried to steady his shaking hands. Whatever firefight there was would be over in seconds, even if he managed to surprise whoever was waiting for him above. He was wounded and sick, and he had only a few rounds left in the rifle with which to defend himself.

But frankly, he thought, I'm just too tired to give a damn. He just wanted to get it over with.

The end of the shaft above appeared, showing as a dim glow. After another minute the top edge approached, seeming to fall to meet him.

He steeled himself, brought the rifle up to bear.

Then he was inside the utility hut. He swung the rifle in a rapid arc to cover the room, looking for targets.

The room was empty.

He reached over his head to check his ascent. Then, as he stopped, his hand pressing against the lift disk, he rolled and pushed himself away from the field in one practiced movement, landing on his shoulder on the bare rock floor beyond the edge of the shaft and rolling up to his feet, weapon ready.

The door to the hut was open. There seemed to have been no reaction to his arrival whatsoever.

Cautiously, he stepped through the door. It was night on that part of Ithavoll, though the sky to the west was lightening enough to indicate that dawn was not far away. The compound lights were off, but so far as Clay could tell, the area was deserted.

He was almost too exhausted to be surprised.

He looked around in mild wonder. Where, he asked himself, were the security troops that had made such a noisy fuss when he had bluffed his way into the compound?

He could think of no ready answer beyond the fact that the burden of *Hachiman* had been taken from them, and from Shotoku, who had perhaps ordered them away when the god that had lived in his mind had departed.

Or maybe it was just his lucky day. He simply did not care anymore.

Clay made his way carefully into the cover of the nearby brush, then settled in to wait for daylight. When the sun rose, he would work his way back down to Rankin.

Until then he would rest. He closed his eyes and fell into a deep, dreamless slumber.

CHAPTER
THIRTY-FOUR

The dawn rose over Ithavoll like a rose- and green-colored dream. Not since just before the old *yamabushi* had killed Fitzgerald and wounded Greene had Clay been free—or inclined—to notice the beauty of Tind's planet. A bit overgrown and damned dangerous, he thought to himself, but in many ways strikingly beautiful.

He hoped suddenly that her people—her new people, Tind's people—could keep her. Perhaps if Shotoku, now free of the influence of Gan-pao, could create peace between the northern and southern continents, if he could consolidate the scattered colonists without force, if they could make living more bearable for the poor . . . But there was nothing further he could contribute to that possibility. If it was meant to happen, it would.

It was a good feeling, though, to think that some good might come of what he had done.

When he could see well enough to be sure of his footing, he made his way down to the ravine where Rankin waited. He moved carefully but with as much haste as he dared; there was no way to be certain of the time that had passed since he had set the timers on the explosives he had left behind, and he wanted to be well away from the compound and the area over the hidden city before the charges went off.

He didn't fear the radiation that had worried Rankin, but despite what the elder had told him in his dream, he did worry that something else might somehow be released, if only for a moment, by the shock of the explosions. He'd as soon not be near if it happened.

There was still no sign that the charges had detonated by the time he reached the ravine. He found himself hesitating on the trail before the ravine and knew that he still subliminally feared the *yamabushi*, still unconsciously waited for him to spring out from cover to challenge him.

He shook it off and began to work his way up to where Rankin was hidden, then whistled to let him know that he was approaching.

"Come ahead," came the croak from under the ledge.

Clay eased his way up to where Rankin lay.

Rankin looked much as he had when Clay had left him, worn and sick but not defeated. Clay saw a gleam in his eye as he looked him over.

"Son, as my grandaddy'd say, you look like you were rode hard and put up wet."

Clay snorted. "I'll wager we're both ready for the pasture after this. If we make it back."

"Oh, we'll get back, all right. Even if I can't fight, I'll cuss 'em all to death if I have to. Did you do what I sent you up there to do?"

Clay nodded. He didn't bother to remind Rankin that he had gone on his own initiative.

"Any problems?"

"Some." Clay didn't elaborate; there was too much to tell, and too much of it was simply too hard to believe. Even if he himself had not already begun to doubt what had really happened in the dead city.

Rankin respected his silence and didn't push the issue.

"What was it? Atomics? A new weapon?"

"No."

Rankin raised an eyebrow. "Something else? What?"

"I don't know. I really don't know."

"Alien?"

Clay nodded. "Yes. Alien. A spirit, I think . . ." His voice trailed off as he realized how ridiculous that statement must sound to Rankin. All that had happened—Gan-pao, the hidden city, the blasted field of his dream where a people fifty centuries dead appeared to explain to him why he had been saved from an alien who was both dead and alive and thought he was God . . . It was all too much.

An uncomfortable silence fell between them, then Rankin coughed, intentionally, Clay thought, to break it. To Clay's relief, he asked no more questions about what Clay had found on his foray.

"How long before the thing blows?" Rankin's voice was dry and harsh but seemed stronger than it had when Clay had found him the day before.

Clay shook his head. "I don't know. Maybe another ten, twenty minutes. Maybe in the next second."

Thinking of Gan-pao, he almost added, *"Maybe never."*

"Anticipation is nine-tenths of the fun. Gets the adrenals going."

Clay imagined Rankin smiling in the dark. Tough old bird, he thought.

Then he heard it, the solid thump-roar of the plastique charges exploding. He saw the sky turn red for an instant, lighted by the powerful explosives he had left in the shaft. He involuntarily clenched his teeth, more than half expecting something like the unimaginable force of the atomic explosion Rankin had feared.

He waited another long second, then allowed himself to breathe. He heard Rankin chuckle in the darkness. "Scratch whatever the hell it was."

Clay nodded to himself and settled back.

Now, maybe, he could really sleep. The rumble from the north died away, and the night was dark again. Clay stared up into the sky and thought he could see, barely shining through Ithavoll's misty, clouded skies, the pinprick promise of the stars.

Clay slept through the rest of the day and through most of the following night. The rest was deep and healing, and, again, dreamless.

After the sun had risen, he built another travois, scouting out saplings of enough length and heft to support Rankin's emaciated weight, then dragging them back up the ravine. He used Rankin's bootlaces to tie them together.

He anesthetized Rankin's injured leg with what little painkiller was left in the kit, then arranged the travois beside where Rankin lay.

He squatted down beside the older man and shielded his eyes so that he could see into the dimness of Rankin's tiny den.

"Colonel, this is not going to be easy or comfortable, but I've got to get you down out of here."

Rankin eyed the travois. "Hell, I don't care if it's comfortable so long as you get me there without dropping me. This old carcass can take a little discomfort, but these old bones are brittle."

Clay grinned. "Sure, Colonel, I'll do my best."

As carefully as he could, he rolled Rankin onto the travois. Rankin was silent, taking the unavoidably rough handling without a word, but Clay could see the pain in the sudden pallor of his face.

Once he was on, Clay bound him with strips torn from Rankin's own fatigues. Then he crouched down at the travois's head and lifted the ends onto his shoulders.

It took five hours of careful maneuvering to get down the ravine and back to the trail.

It took another five days to get back to the village from which they had begun their odyssey into the jungle. When Clay walked up the path into the village, Rankin was feverish and dehydrated but still alive.

They had missed their pickup flight, but Clay spent a few minutes on the local chieftain's transmitter, and soon enough a copter was on the way from the survey headquarters where Rankin's friend from the Lunar wars waited.

The locals, to Clay's surprise, were friendly and helpful; the local medicine man—using modern enough equipment—patched their wounds and made them comfortable.

Two hours after they arrived Rankin was awake and swearing at the backwoods doctor.

Clay waited until Rankin's ire had played itself out, then sat down in a rickety wooden chair beside the bed where Rankin lay.

"They'll be here soon for us, I think. I called your friend, the major."

"Good. Couldn't be soon enough."

"You're not anxious to leave this fair village, are you, Colonel?"

"Hell, no, son. What I'd really like is about six more weeks in this hole, molesting the local women. Tell you the truth, I'm really starting to like it here."

Clay could see that despite his bravado, Rankin was still nervous.

Clay could understand why. They were still deep in the wilderness on a planet whose authorities might well consider them at the least saboteurs and at the worst spies to be burned down on sight.

It was anyone's guess what the effect of losing his god—though the idea seemed somehow ludicrous—might do for the emperor's fear of offending the United Democracies.

But either Shotoku's reluctance kept them free of harassment or, and Clay thought this more likely, the sudden absence of the influence of *Hachiman* had dampened the martial instincts of the emperor and the many levels of military and government henchmen under him.

A new and lasting peace, Clay guessed, might well come now to Ithavoll.

The copter arrived the next morning without incident. Rankin's friend, the major, arrived with it. Clay saw his anxious face in the Plexi as the copter descended into the field beside the hut they had been given to use—the same foul little hut, Clay had realized with wry irony when they had been led to it from the medicine man's shop, that had been given to them before they had left, far enough from the village to give the impression that they had been quarantined by the locals.

The major descended from the flier as it touched down and breezed past Clay, going to Rankin's side where he lay in his hammock, another of his strange brown cocktails balanced on his ample stomach.

"Colonel?"

"I'm fine, Ben." He winked at the major over his drink. "Mission accomplished."

The major looked relieved. "You lost two?"

Rankin nodded, sobering. "Yes, two. Two damn fine troopers. It's a goddamn shame, but they died brave, as soldiers."

For some reason that statement grated at Clay. They *were* soldiers, true enough, and he had lost comrades all his life in battle. He had, he thought, grown inured to the pain. But those losses were of more than just soldiers; they were men and women, friends.

Grieving again for a moment, he remembered how Greene had died, in pain, with none of the glory of battle about her death. But he said nothing. Loss was part of the job.

"What happened out there?"

Rankin shrugged—quite a feat, Clay thought, for a man lying flat on his back with a glass balanced on his chest. "Hard to say, Ben. I'm not sure I know myself. The lieutenant here seems to think we managed to kill a god."

The major looked at Rankin as if he thought the jungle had addled him a bit. He glanced at Clay, but Clay held his tongue and let the major wonder.

"Listen, Colonel," he continued after a moment. "There's something strange going on in the city. I don't know what happened or if you had something to do with it, but things have sure as hell changed. There's a truce on now with the southern continent; they've been talking peace for almost a week now. The whole damned planet's gone a little insane. Even the U.D.'s people don't know what to make of it all."

Rankin looked queerly at Clay for a long moment, then turned back to the major. "Who knows, Ben. Had a change of heart, maybe. Why don't you get a couple of those strapping young fellows—," he gestured at the survey personnel who waited by the copter for orders, "—over here so they can give me a hand into that bloody machine. Seems I managed to get a little banged up out here . . ."

Clay hobbled over to help as well as he could. Rankin let the two survey men take most of his weight as they struggled over to the copter. Then, once they were there, Clay helped drag him up into its cockpit.

As they settled in, Rankin grunted and sat up.

"No dignity in lying flat on your back," he grumbled. He shielded a cigar the major had given him with his hands and lit it, ignoring the consternation of the rest of the passengers.

Clay heard a bark of laughter from up front and saw the major draw another cigar from a vest pocket. "What the hell," he said, and lit it. "That's what regulations are for."

"Son," Rankin said, looking thoughtfully at Clay through the smoke, "you're a damned fine soldier and a damned fine man. Those don't always amount to the same thing. I've got a daughter I think I'd like you to meet."

Clay laughed, surprised. "A daughter?"

Rankin nodded. "A daughter. And she's the marrying kind,

like her folks. A hell of a girl. Reliable. Damned pretty, too. I think you all just might get along . . .''

Clay relaxed back in his seat, chuckling. He was going home.

EPILOGUE

John Sebastian Clay sat back in his chair on his porch and watched the sunset blaze blue and orange, then fade to purple over the Smoky Mountains.

There was a breeze, freshening from the east, and it made the old house behind him creak faintly. The familiar sound gave him great comfort. He could smell the water from the creek below, and faintly, from inside the house, he could hear his wife singing to herself in the kitchen.

After a time he stood and walked down the front steps and across his lawn of good Terran grass and looked down off his Tennessee mountaintop across the mist-bound valleys.

When the day was gone and night rested solidly on the world, he watched the stars as they appeared, pinholes in the dark landscape that was the sky. For a moment he felt the old ache, the regret for what he had left behind among those stars, the friends, the battles.

But that passed quickly. There were better things in the wide, coldly bright universe that shone down now in a wash of light, a glittering backdrop for the single blind eye of the moon.

He had found a place to stop. He no longer needed to fight other men's battles.

Clay took a deep breath and walked slowly back up the path to his home and his wife and his children.

Life was good.

ABOUT
THE AUTHOR

JOHN M. BLAIR was born in St. Petersburg, Florida, in 1961. He received a Ph.D. in English from Tulane University in 1989 and now teaches at Southwest Texas State University in San Marcos, Texas. He has published articles and poetry in various literary journals and magazines and has been an avid reader of science fiction for over twenty years. *A Landscape of Darkness* is his first novel.